The Busconductor Hines

James Kelman has written and contributed to several collections of short stories, the most recent being *Not Not While the Giro and Other Stories* (1983). He has also had a play and a short story broadcast on radio, and is one of three Scottish writers (including Alasdair Gray and Agnes Owens) who have contributed to a collection of stories entitled *Lean Tales* (1985). He has spent much of his life in Glasgow and now lives in Scotland.

Praise for *Not Not While the Giro*

'The writing has the vitality which can only come from economy, and a grim Glaswegian humour that surmounts helplessness and dereliction'

London Review of Books

'It is the achievement of a unique voice.'

Times Educational Supplement

'A toughness and diversity that is utterly compulsive'

New Musical Express

EF.

JAMES KELMAN

The Busconductor Hines

J. M. Dent & Sons Ltd
London Melbourne

First published in Great Britain by Polygon Books 1984
This paperback edition first published by J. M. Dent & Sons Ltd 1985
© James Kelman 1984

Printed in Great Britain by
The Guernsey Press Co. Ltd, Guernsey, C.I. for
J. M. Dent & Sons Ltd
Aldine House, 33 Welbeck Street, London W1M 8LX

British Library Cataloguing in Publication Data

Kelman, James
    The busconductor Hines.——(Everyman fiction)
    I. Title
    823'.914[F]   PR6061.E5/

    ISBN 0–460–02292–x

For
Marie
and
Laura and Emma

1

Hines jumped up from the armchair, she was about to lift the huge soup-pot of boiling water. She nodded when he said, I'll get it. Taking the dishtowel from her he wrapped it round his left hand before gripping the metal support-ring; he held the handle of the pot in his right hand. He raised it slightly above the oven and paused, adjusting to its weight. Sandra had moved to shift a wooden chair out of his path.

The plastic babybath was positioned a yard from the fire with several sheets of newspaper spread beneath and around it. She had already emptied in a basinful of cold water. After each step across he was pausing to let the water settle. When he reached it he tilted the soup-pot a little at a time, until about a quarter of the water remained, then he emptied that straight in. What a weight, he said.

I put in too much . . . She had returned to the oven for a smaller pot of water which was also boiling. And once this had been poured in she got another basin of cold water; she poured in half of it before testing the temperature then she left the other half of cold water in the basin, and placed it within arm's reach of the babybath. She murmured, almost inaudibly.

What?

She glanced at him.

Sorry; I thought you were eh . . . He prised the lid off his tobacco tin and began rolling a cigarette. Before putting the empty pots back into their place in the kitchen-cabinet she wiped them dry with the dishtowel. Then she undressed. She stopped, and walked to draw the venetian blind at the window above the sink. Hines smiled. Passing helicopters eh!

She shrugged.

It's pitchblack outside!

That only makes it easier to see in.

He nodded in reply and she continued to undress, her back to him, as though she was watching the television, but it was not on. Aside from her bra she took off all her clothes; she stepped into the bath, eventually sitting down with her knees raised almost to her chin. The water had risen to within an inch of the rim. Hines grinned. A moment later he said, Want me to do your back?

No.

You sure?

I want to relax a minute.

Will I turn the fire up a bit?

She shook her head.

Naw, seeing you're still wearing the bra and that I thought you might've been cold.

I'm fine.

He put the cigarette in his mouth and lifted a book which had been lying on the floor next to his chair. Without opening it he laid it on his lap, and he stretched and yawned. Aye, he said, that was a good buy. He chuckled briefly. Heh, what about the time my knees got stuck? Eh! thought you were going to have to send for the Fire Brigade or something.

Manoeuvring the armchair forwards he leaned to place his hands on her shoulders. Fancy a massage? And he began at once, her head lolling a bit to the rhythm. He smiled: Watch you don't bang your chin! He continued for a time, until he sat back to adjust the crotch of his uniform trousers. Then he made to resume.

It's alright, she said.

Naw, I was just getting comfortable.

Honestly Rab, it's okay.

I'm fine but, no bother.

I'm going to start washing though.

O. He sniffed. He manoeuvred the chair back again. He lifted the book and relit the half-smoked cigarette. She had taken off her bra now and the side of her right breast was visible. She got herself onto her knees without too much difficulty and washed quickly. Hines stretched to the mantelpiece and he switched on the transistor radio; settling back on his chair he opened the book.

What we need's a roof over the head, said Reilly when he came into the close. There were four of them sheltering there out the rain. Reilly was Hines' regular driver and with them were McCulloch and Colin Brown, driver and conductor. They were waiting for another driver by the name of Barry McBride who had gone to the gents before leaving the pub.

I'm suggesting the snooker-room, said McCulloch.

Aye but nobody's allowed in now because of that last performance.

Colin Brown had spoken and McCulloch glared at him: You trying to say something?

I'm no trying to say fuck all — but some cunt pished into the corner; and it wasnt me.

Aye well it wasnt fucking me either.

It was me, cried Hines. Please sir I own up. I did it, in protest.

Against the impoverished condition of the buses, grinned Reilly.

Exactly. Hines licked the gummed edge of the rice-paper and stuck the rolled cigarette in his mouth, and lighted it. Anyway, he went on, it doesnt really concern me about roofs over the head, I've got to pick up the wean from the nursery shortly.

They'll no let you in, grunted McCulloch.

Too drunk, added Reilly.

Too drunk fuck all.

Aye you are.

Naw I'm no. Wish to christ I was but. That's the trouble with nowadays, you cant even get fucking drunk.

Aw at last, at last . . . McCulloch had peered out the close.

Barry was staggering; he was being supported by a conductor who had been with them in the pub. He burped then said, Where we going?

Your house, replied Reilly. The others laughed.

Well we cant stay here, said McCulloch, that's for fucking definite. Heh Rab, what about your place?

Ha ha! Reilly snorted.

Hines looked at him. To McCulloch he said, Sorry, out of bounds — even for me by christ! Then he chuckled suddenly and lifted the carrier bag of beer from the floor. We're going to the park, he said, come on.

What you on about ya cunt? McCulloch was shaking his head.

I'm on about the auld men's club, the pensioners' place — roaring fires and cups of hot toddy, games of dominoes. Dry roofs over the head.

Brilliant, laughed Reilly. My conductor! Brilliant fucking suggestion.

They'll never let us in, said Colin Brown.

Shut up, said McCulloch. And he glanced at Barry who was leaning against the wall, eyelids shut. The park's won it, he said.

See that? said Hines. It's his decision.

Reilly nodded.

Barry staggered suddenly away from the wall. The other conductor got a hold of him but he pushed himself clear and said, I'm going to the betting shop.

Naw you're no, the conductor told him.

Betting shop's shut, said Reilly.

Barry looked at him.

That's right, said Colin Brown.

Fucking rubbish, muttered Barry and he made to leave the close but staggered and almost fell.

It's a bevy we're going for, said Hines. Come on ya cunt ye! He took Barry by one shoulder and the other conductor did the same with the second shoulder.

A slash, mumbled Barry.

Jesus Christ, said McCulloch.

The pensioners' club was down by the river, near to the iron footbridge. Barry and the conductor assisting him had fallen someway behind the other four who were trotting along the path, through the heavy rain. Reilly arrived first. He pushed his way inside to be followed by Hines. Silence when the four of them had entered. On a very large wooden table in the centre of the room two games of dominoes were in progress; four players were involved in each and quite a few spectators watched. Other old men sat on the long benches set at the walls.

It's the buses, called somebody. What's up? yous all on strike!

12

Colin said, Is it okay if we come in? It's bucketing down.

We've brought our own refreshments . . . Reilly grinned, indicating the carrier bag. The pensioners glanced at the carrier bag, and some muttering started.

Hines said, We'll challenge yous to a game of dominoes! Alright?

Naw it's no alright, cried a man seated next to the open fireplace. He gazed at Barry who was now slumped on a bench not too far from him, and he spat into the fire. Naw, it's no alright at all.

No business to come barging in here, muttered someone else.

Who's barging? replied McCulloch.

Another silence. Then one of the players looked round from side to side: No harm in letting them in out of the rain surely!

Aye fair enough but they're wanting a blooming game and we've got the tourny on!

A few grunts greeted this.

If they do come in they've got to be quiet, said somebody.

Aye.

We're no wanting any funny business, called the man next to the fire.

Can we no even have a sing-song? grinned the conductor.

Shut up you, said Colin.

McCulloch had taken a can of beer from the carrier bag, he pulled off the stopper. The man at the fire cried, Alcohol's verboten. Heh you Ramsay! you seeing what's going on here?

Ramsay was one of the domino players. He nodded. Alcohol's taboo in here son; it's the one thing no allowed.

Muttered assent from other pensioners. Hines tapped McCulloch on the arm. Heh George, there's somebody talking to you — but dont answer . . . He took a can from the bag, unstopped it and swallowed a mouthful immediately.

That's it, cried the man at the fire. Drinking the howsyourfather plain as you like!

Colin stared at Hines who winked back at him.

That's right out of order, said someone at the table.

A number of voices were chattering quite angrily. Ramsay was being spoken to by three or four people at once, and he was nodding silently. Colin shook his head and he walked across to where Barry was slumped, and he gestured at the conductor as though wanting him to help him get the other to his feet.

13

Reilly glanced at Hines, and grinned; he took the can from Hines and said: Cheers Rab, and he drank from it.

I'm chapping the table, said Hines. Fancy a game Mr Reilly? Eh George?

McCulloch laughed.

Hines went to the table and chapped it. Me and the muckers fancy a game, he said. We'll pick two and challenge two of yous. And you better pick your best cause we're fucking hot stuff.

What's he yabbering about, shouted one of the old men. Bloody tourny day and he's jumping in trying to chap the bloody table!

Nobody's jumping, called McCulloch.

There's no question of yous chapping the table, said Ramsay. I mean God sake if

The table's chapped and it stays chapped, said Hines.

Quite right pardner. Reilly spoke while walking to join him: Me and you'll play the winners of this here tourny.

Ach away and drive your fucking buses, muttered a voice from the back of the room.

Aye, said somebody else, bloody scandal — no wonder you can never get a bloody hold of one when you want it. All off their work drunk so they are. The likes of them shouldnt bloody have a job in the first place.

Come on, said Ramsay to Hines and the others. Yous better just be going now.

The conductor had come over for a can of beer; he knocked the carrier bag as he did so and a few cans rolled. He knelt to retrieve them. He glanced up and said: What is it with they auld yins at all? just in out the rain and what do we get, abuse, a lot of fucking abuse. No wonder they're going to start bumping them all off.

What was that? cried somebody.

Nice weather for ducks, said Reilly.

Your patter's rubbish, grinned Hines. He winked at the conductor: Give us a can.

He took the can and walked to the bench where Barry was and fixed his uniform hat more squarely on his head, then balanced the can of beer on it. Barry snored. Hines stepped back three paces as though checking its position. He returned to the others and aimed with the can he had been drinking from.

McCulloch laughed loudly.

I'll give ten to one he misses by a mile! called Reilly.

Done, said the conductor. Thirty quid; wait till I get my wages.

Lot of blooming weans, muttered an old man.

Ramsay sighed: Come on lads, enough's enough.

Enough isnt enough, replied McCulloch.

And Hines lowered the can of beer at once. He turned to Reilly: Did you hear that Willie? Driver McCulloch there, did you hear him? Did you know he knew that? I mean I never fucking . . . christ sake!

Reilly was smiling.

Colin had returned; his face was red. This is definitely out of order, he said quietly; come on, let's move.

Somebody whispering in the company, said Reilly.

That's barred, said Hines.

I'm no fucking whispering.

Naw, said McCulloch, you never whisper. On and on you go, the voice of doom.

The voice of doom! laughed Reilly.

Even fighting amongst themselves now, said one of the men at the table.

Ach away yous go, shouted another.

Here, what about this bet! The conductor had called; he walked to stand not too far from Barry.

Hines nodded; he raised the can.

Fuck you Rab: cried Colin, and he turned and strode to the door, and pulled it open and strode out, letting it bang behind him. The impact caused it to bounce open again, and rain blew inside.

A moment later McCulloch was muttering, I'm having it out with that bastard; right now, me and him, right fucking now. He left the room. The door was shut immediately by one of the pensioners who then sat down on the bench nearby; he sniffed and drew a half-smoked cigarette from behind his ear which he lighted from a match he had struck along the floor. Reilly had gone to help the conductor with Barry.

Hines began fixing the beer cans in the carrier bag. The man at the fire snorted and started talking to those nearest him. Hines walked to the door and held it open for the other three. Life is difficult, he said to Reilly.

Reilly nodded.

Outside they could see Colin Brown; he was quite a distance away, not running but walking quickly, heading towards the footbridge. McCulloch trotted after him.

Eh . . . you better manage Barry, said Hines to the conductor.

Aw you kidding?

Hines shrugged. Reilly had already begun running after the other two.

When McCulloch reached Colin he pushed him in the back. Their voices were audible above the noise from the rain and the river. Now they faced each other, Colin stepping backwards while the other was attempting to shove him on the chest. Reilly arrived and he put his hand onto McCulloch's arm but got it knocked aside. No fight here, he was saying, you've been muckers too long.

Out my road.

You'll murder him man.

Will he fuck murder me, muttered Colin.

You ya bastard. McCulloch glared at him: You've been giving me a pain in the neck for months with your fucking moaning, on and on and on ya bastard.

Aye well you know what you can do about it.

McCulloch moved forwards and Reilly attempted to restrain him.

Handers! cried Hines. Who wants handers? He put the carrier bag down and held out his fists.

Fuck off Rab, said McCulloch.

Naw.

Nothing to do with yous two.

Aye it is.

I dont need your fucking help, said Colin.

Help ya cunt! what d'you mean help? we're wanting a fucking boot at you.

Just fuck off, said McCulloch.

Naw, me and my driver are wanting a go as well. Eh Willie, if we grab an arm each or something . . . toss him into the foaming briny: what d'you think?

A point for discussion. Reilly nodded. He had taken a crushed cigarette packet from his pocket . . . Let's have a smoke.

See that George! First time he's offered us a fag in 38 fucking year!

McCulloch looked at him.

Hines clapped his hands and sang, Singing aye aye yippee yippee aye, singing aye aye yippee yippee aye

McCulloch moved, he grabbed Colin by the lapels of the uniform jacket and seemed to raise him from the ground, he cracked him on the bridge of the nose with the brow of his forehead, and let him go. Colin was on the ground and clutching at his face with both hands. For a moment McCulloch watched him, then he was off towards the footbridge, not looking back. Reilly bent to tug Colin's hands away. And Hines laid his hand on his shoulder and said, You're a silly bastard Colin.

He might need stitches, muttered Reilly.

Aye . . . The other conductor had arrived, by himself. Maybe we should take him to hospital.

I'm no going to any fucking hospital. Colin held his hands away now; the blood streaked down his face and onto his chin, and was staining his shirt.

You better, said Reilly.

Colin wiped his hands on the grass and the other two helped him to his feet. He said, Any of yous got a hankie?

Use your shirt, said Hines.

Shut up ya cunt, muttered Reilly.

Well no wonder I mean, christ, you seen the state of his uniform trousers? looks like he's fucking pished them. Company property too; tut tut right enough.

Think we should take him to the hospital? said the conductor.

Colin shook his head; he was holding his right hand beneath his nose, covering his mouth.

What d'you reckon Rab?

Hines shrugged. He took out his tin and withdrew a cigarette paper but it became saturated. He closed the tin and returned it to his pocket, then lifted the carrier bag of beer. Come on, let's go, no point getting soaked. Where's that cunt Barry? he said to the conductor.

The conductor pointed back at the pensioners' club.

Maybe he should go for a check up, said Reilly, just in case.

Hines glanced at Colin but Colin shook his head and he began to walk in the direction of the footbridge. After a moment the conductor said, What do we do now?

Hines shrugged.

No think we should take him to the hospital?

Probably be best to, replied Reilly, he might need stitches.

I doubt it. But suit yourself, I've got to go to the nursery . . . Hines

17

smiled. What about that fag ya cunt?

Reilly took out the packet.

ooo

Sandra. She was touching him on the arm and whispering that he should listen. A faint scratching noise. They lay still. Eventually he moved onto his side and stared out from the recess in the direction of the sink. It's been going on for ages, she murmured.

He nodded. He lifted the blankets, pushing his legs out and lowering himself feet first to the floor. The scratching stopped. Hines grinned. He said quietly, You should've banged the wall and got auld Donnelly to come through. He's the fucking expert!

Ssh.

They stayed silent for a while, until the scratching resumed. It came from the rubbish bin next to the sink. Padding across to there he lifted a flat-soled shoe from beneath the tallboy. The scratching had stopped. A time passed till it restarted. Now, said Hines and when Sandra switched on the bedlamp he sprang to the bin with the shoe poised. The mouse was jumping and going straight at him and he smashed the shoe down but missed. The bastard, where'd it go?

The cabinet or the tallboy Rab I'm not sure, my eyes werent right with the light.

Definitely thought I had it . . . He was kneeling to peer beneath the cabinet. Pointless. He glanced at her. Cant see a thing in the shadows. Jesus! He stood upright and lifting his left foot he flicked off a few crumbs. That bloody wean, everywhere he goes he's dropping stuff. I keep telling him as well. He shook his head and wiped his right foot. We've got to keep this place clean Sandra, hoovering and that, it's the only way to ward off these fuckers.

It isnt the only way at all. If you shored up all the cracks in the skirting board then they'd have no way to get in.

Christ sake Sandra he's going about with food in his hands all the time I mean he hardly ever eats at the fucking table; I'm always telling him.

18

The mouse was in the bin, not the floor.

Hines had knelt to see beneath the tallboy. When he rose he said, He's actually planking grub now; did I tell you? Dods of liver I found in below his fucking cot, I mean christ sake.

You told me.

Aye, well I mean where does he learn that kind of thing? the fucking nursery!

Come back to bed.

We'll need to stop him doing it.

Sandra was smiling.

Seriously but.

I know.

Aye, well . . . Hines grinned. Shut up. Before returning to bed he went to the lavatory.

She switched off the bedlamp.

Aw christ. I forgot to check the clock.

You're best not to.

Aye . . . he lay down, tugging up the blankets. What chance have I got of sleeping now anyway; I'll be listening for that bloody mouse all night. Morning I should say.

Sandra chuckled. Then she said, You're freezing.

No fucking wonder.

Give me your feet.

You hungry?

They laughed for several moments. Hines was lying on his back; he shifted his arm so that she could rest her head on his chest; he kissed her forehead. Sometimes you're better off no sleeping, just so's you can appreciate the rest. It's the same with being dead: I wouldnt mind it so much if you could wake up now and again just to savour it.

Rab! She rapped her knuckles against his shoulder.

Naw . . . he chuckled. I'll definitely see to that skirting board the morrow but. I'll buy a packet of polyfilla and borrow a trowel from auld Donnelly. Heh know what I think — if he stopped filling that crack in his front room wall the whole fucking building'd collapse and we'd wind up getting a semi-detached out in Knightswood.

Sandra snorted.

Moments later he said: I'm sorry.

It's okay.

Naw . . . I dont know what's up with me sometimes.

Her hand gripped and squeezed his arm. He made to say more but a movement from her and he said nothing. He sighed, and he kissed her forehead again. She moved closer in to him. He kissed her on the mouth, then broke away.

What's up.

Nothing. Hh; naw, I've went hard.

She raised herself to kiss him, moving her left leg between his. Dont be daft, she said.

He turned in to her, bringing both arms round her, and they continued kissing until he broke away again. Honest I mean . . . it's okay Sandra, if you dont fancy it I mean I . . .

Ssh.

ooo

He clattered out from the close and along the pavement. Two street-cleaners were leaning on their brushes chatting. When he paused at the corner one of them called: A bus is just away there a minute ago.

Hines nodded. He started walking, then striding; soon he was trotting, the cashbag strap wrapped round his fist and the uniform hat wedged under his elbow. It took him twenty minutes to reach the garage. And the bus he was scheduled for duty on was pulling out from the exit as he entered the street. It halted. Reilly opened the side window and shook his head.

I was in the middle of this dream Willie; fucking great so it was; I didnt have the heart to wake myself up.

Reilly struck a match to light a tipped cigarette. Then he nodded towards the garage office. Away and give it a bash.

Hines snorted.

You never know.

It's Campbell that's on.

Reilly shrugged. No harm fucking trying.

Right enough, they can only cut my balls off. Hines turned to go but he stopped: What bus we got?

183.

183 for fuck sake I might've known; the heaters've been blowing cold air for the last ten years.

Come on man, I'll wait a couple of minutes.

Right right, okay, very sorry sir.

In the garage Office the Deskclerk was gazing at a notice pinned to a board on the wall. He continued to gaze at it when Hines arrived at the counter. Eh . . . can I sign for my shift?

After a moment the Deskclerk turned to him. What was that?

My shift.

Your shift?

Aye, 6 duty.

6 duty; 6 duty's away.

Hines gestured in the direction of the street. My driver, he's waiting for me. Okay if I sign for it?

It's away. The spare man's got it.

Aye. Hines sniffed. I could tell him to come back.

Too late.

He's still there but, Reilly.

Then he's timewasting, muttered the Deskclerk. If Reilly's still there then he's bloody timewasting. He returned his attention to the notice.

Can I sign for my shift?

You're too late I'm telling you.

Hines had prised the lid off his tobacco tin. Once he had rolled the cigarette he altered his stance at the counter and inhaled deeply when he had lighted it. The Deskclerk left the notice and walked to sit on a high stool towards the far end of the counter. The large sign-on book lay there. He began to study its contents, his fingers drumming on the counter. Hines inhaled again and he blew a smoke ring. What will I do? he said. Want me to sign spare or what?

The Deskclerk didnt reply. Hines rubbed his eyes. He had placed his uniform hat on the table. He slung the cashbag off his shoulder. No, said the Deskclerk, I dont think so.

Have I just to go home then?

What d'you say?

Hines looked at him.

I've got a spare conductor sitting upstairs doing nothing as it is. The Deskclerk continued to study the sign-on book for a few moments. He raised his head abruptly: You were supposed to report for work at 5. What the hell use are you coming in at this bloody time?

Christ sake I missed the staffbus. I had to run the whole way here. What's that got to do with it?

Hines looked at him. The boy, he said eventually, he's got the flu. I was up half the night cause of it.

What d'you think I'm stupid or something? You slept in the other morning as well and got away with it I mean what the hell d'you think it is at all! d'you think we're just here for your beck and call?

Hines sniffed.

The Deskclerk shook his head; he had resumed his study of the sign-on book. Then he reached into a side pocket of his dustcoat and got himself a cigarette. When he had it burning he inhaled and exhaled, and muttered, 6 o'clock spare. And he turned and walked away from the counter; but then he paused to add: Just dont bother showing your face next time it happens.

Hines coughed. He signed his name in the book. He went quickly outside onto the street and waved off Reilly. Back in the garage he walked upstairs to the bothy.

ooo

The boy fumbled on the door handle. Hines had pushed his fingers through the letter-box flap and was making groaning noises. It was Sandra who opened. He kissed her and stuck the uniform hat on the boy's head. Once into the kitchen he slumped on the armchair. Bad? she said.

O wh . . . Murder, these spreadovers. Heh . . . he got up from the chair: Want a hand with the spuds? When Sandra made a face at him he sat back down, and bent to untie his bootlaces. People go years on the sick and here's me, always beat, even for one miserable week, one lousy bastarn week. See Reilly too! he's just got to walk in the doctor's surgery and they're throwing lines at him.

Paul had come to him with a painting. Hines looked at it and

22

nodded. I mean if I could just get on the sick now and again I could go conducting buses till the fucking cows come home. Heh . . . he glanced at Paul. This is a brilliant piece of work wee man.

Paul leaned to look at it.

Aye. Hines indicated the shapes: There you've got the wavy sea and that, the big sun shining — it's good, exact son, well done. Naw, really I mean it's a piece of nonsense the way some doctors are okay and others — him we've got, baldy bastard, I'm beginning to think he's a C.I.A. plant or some fucking thing.

Paul was watching him; he grinned and Hines ruffled his hair and gave him back the painting. Sandra mouthed something. Eventually she said, It's your language Rab, that's why he's laughing. I'm always expecting to be told he's swearing at the women in the nursery.

Serve them right.

I'm being serious. Sandra washed the peeled potatoes and dumped them into a pot, sprinkled the salt. How was work?

How was yours?

She smiled slightly.

Naw, mine was ebsilutely mervillous; a continual round of tactillian surprises, one minute I'm getting battered by shopping bags then barked at by mangy mongrels, attacked at by sexy office girls.

Away and steep your feet.

I dont have the energy; people have been standing on them all day. They're battered and bruised and sore. I keep explaining that to the doctor but he wont listen sir please sir they're battered and bruised and sore sir. Naw, I'm definitely looking for another job.

O that's a good idea.

I love sarcastic women.

She poked her tongue out at him.

How long till the grub's on the plate?

Twenty minutes at the latest.

What! Merciful heavens, think I'll go to bed to kill the time.

You dare. Anyway, you should be thankful you're getting it cooked for you. If I remember rightly it's my week off.

Hines had closed his eyelids. I cant last it out. Dear god up there in the nether regions please make me unconscious; I'll be yours forever and ever sir, honest.

Turn on the telly.

I refuse.

23

O by the way Rab, they were talking in the office this afternoon, that part-timer from the agency, she never turned up again.

Brainy lassie.

It's hopeless though. It just means we're having to do her work as well as our own. We're managing right enough but it's a push.

Hh; typical capitalist strategy, next thing you know auld Bufuckingcanan'll turn round and tell you the part-timer's services are no longer required.

Seriously though Rab, I was wondering, whether to think about going full-time.

Were you.

Yes.

Hh.

We could manage it.

Aye.

We could.

Smashing, when you thinking of starting? got time to wait for the spuds to boil?

O God.

I'm joking Sandra, sorry, honest I mean I was just . . . He shrugged.

After a pause she got up; taking a cloth from the draining board she wiped the pull-down section of the kitchen-cabinet. Are you really against the idea?

Course not.

If we had Paul in a full-time nursery we'd manage quite easy. And it'd only be till the summer, till he starts school.

Hines raised his right foot to take off the boot; the tobacco tin toppled off the arm of the chair, the lid had been lying off. He picked up the tobacco and put it back inside. Sandra was looking at him. Naw, he said, of course I dont mind you going full-time — the wages I'm earning you'd have to sooner or later. Be better off on the bloody broo so I would. At least till the O.T. picks up again. I heard a whisper right enough, a couple of conductors're supposed to have got working their days-off this week.

Sandra nodded.

Big deal eh!

We could do with the extra money Rab.

I know . . . aye. Heh, he smiled, maybe save a few quid for a holiday or something.

Sandra had her arms folded; she stepped to his chair. We could though. I was thinking if we managed to live on your wages then we'd be able to put most of mine into the bank. God it'd be great. And instead of a holiday . . . we could maybe start thinking about saving for a house. She unfolded her arms and bent to put her hand on his arm. We could, there's no reason why not.

Hines snorted. And she rose away from him, avoiding his gaze. Naw, he said, that's a good idea I mean . . . He sniffed and reached for the tobacco tin.

ooo

A long queue had formed at the stop. The newdriver was gazing into the display window of a nearby jeweller's shop. Their bus was late. When it finally arrived a great many folk got off but all of the queue climbed aboard. Hines waited until the other driver and conductor had stepped down, opening his case and preparing his ticket-machine. The driver was muttering. Fucking murder out there so it is . . . His forehead glistened with sweat.

While Hines adjusted the strap of his cashbag the newdriver settled onto his seat in the cabin, and arranged his rearview mirror. The doors were still open. A few latecomers came rushing up and jumped on. Hines looked at them.

Eh can you fix that mirror for me . . .?

What?

The newdriver was pointing to the wing mirror just outside the doors. Hines leaned to fix it for him.

A wee bit more to the left.

Hines adjusted it and returned inside immediately, and stood with his back to the cabin. At least 10 people were standing along the aisle. He gazed at them; then climbed to the topdeck and found some seats to be empty. Back down the stairs he said: 5 only inside now and the rest of yous up the stair.

As the first of them moved to the staircase the newdriver released the handbrake while depressing the accelerator and the bus jerked into motion; a woman fell against Hines. The man she was with stared at him, and grasping her arm he said: You okay love?

She nodded. She frowned at Hines before going upstairs, followed by the man. Once the correct number had gone up he called: Fares please, and set off down the aisle.

At the terminus the bus stopped and the engine was switched off. The queue waiting there had filed aboard. Hines scribbled the numbers into his waybill and returned it to the holder in the luggage-compartment beneath the staircase. He glanced round the partition into the cabin: What's up?

How d'you mean?

What're we waiting here for?

The newdriver reached for the timeboard and indicated the times: According to this we're allowed 8 minutes here.

What?

The terminus, when we get here it's 8 minutes till we leave.

For fuck's sake man that only applies when you arrive on time. Come on, let's go, we're half an hour late.

The newdriver turned away and switched on the engine. As the bus pulled out from the terminus two more buses arrived in, and came out immediately behind it. Hines shook his head and strode down to the rear, and gazed through the window at the driver of the one following.

Queues had formed at almost every stop and it was standing room only. A fair proportion of people were heading out to the match at Parkhead but many others travelled short distances only and Hines had to move quickly to collect their fares. By the time he reached the rear of the upper deck he turned to find about 8 people standing. He looked at them. Right, he said, down the stair.

Heh wait a minute, began a man wearing a clubscarf and carrying an open can of lager. It was the driver told us to come up.

Aye right enough jimmy, said another.

A few others nodded.

Out my road . . . He squeezed between them and clumped down the stairs. The lower deck was mobbed. A large alsatian dog wagged its tail at the spot next to the luggage-compartment. Hines scratched his head and moved to the cabin but the newdriver was gripping the steering wheel with one hand while reaching to switch on the indicator with the other. Hines stepped back and turned to manoeuvre past the alsatian but the footbrake was applied and he staggered forwards and grabbed for the wrist of the animal's owner. The man took the pressure and pushed to aid Hines' recovery.

The bus stopped, the doors opened, the queue crushed up onto the platform. He dashed forwards. Full up we're full up come on, down, off the fucking bus. He waved his arms till the platform was clear and turned to the newdriver. Come on, get moving.

The newdriver gestured at the doors and Hines glanced round. A middle-aged woman was now aboard and holding onto the safety rail at the front window.

Sorry mrs you'll have to get off.

Dont give me that, I've been standing since half-past one waiting on you.

Come on, off the bloody bus.

The woman snorted.

Fuck sake.

I beg your pardon — dont you dare use that kind of language with me.

Hines sighed. From upstairs feet were stamping, voices rising; a song: Why Are We Waiting. The newdriver was looking at him. Hines nodded and took out his tobacco tin, and began rolling a cigarette.

Will I shut the door?

Naw.

Eh.

Just sit where you are. He struck a match and lit the cigarette, inhaled deeply. The rest of the people on the pavement were now rushing to get onto the bus behind. He looked at the woman. And she turned to the standing passengers; she said: They think they can do what they like.

Hines left the cigarette in his mouth and put his hands in his trouser pockets.

Eh . . . the traffic, said the newdriver, it's piling up.

Aye.

Will I go or what?

A sudden thumping from upstairs and a youth appeared: Heh you — is the fucking bus broke down?

27

That driver's a Rangers' supporter, roared a voice. Then the singing resumed amid a crowd of catcalls.

You better get off mrs, said Hines.

Is this all because of that auld swine? called a female voice from the lowerdeck and immediately an outbreak of angry muttering.

Why dont you get off when he tells you? shouted somebody.

Ya auld ratbag, said the youth from the staircase.

The middle-aged woman's eyelids parted more widely and she glared at Hines: I'm reporting you.

It wasnt me called you a ratbag.

Just you wait, she said but she moved to descend. Once she was on the pavement he peered out and to the rear, at the buses lined up behind; then he stepped back to the cabin, reached inside and pressed the doors shut.

Dont stop till I tell you, he told the newdriver. He nipped off the burning end of the cigarette and trod it out, stuck the still-to-be-smoked bit behind his ear and moved to pass the alsatian.

ooo

Paul was off and racing down the rutted path, his arms stuck stiffly out because of the heavy clothes he was wearing. It looked like he would have to topple over but the momentum of the run carried him straight into the middle of quite a large puddle and he slowed and stopped there. Hines strode down and dragged him out. Paul was off in the direction of the river. A few strides and Hines had caught him by the arm, fairly close to the bank. The boy was fighting to free himself, his face reddening with the effort but Hines maintained his grip on him till reaching the path, just at the spot where it veered behind the renovated foundations of the old flint mill.

A distance in front approached a man and a dog, the dog off its leash and trotting a little way ahead. Paul stayed close by Hines. And when it came near he sidled round him then dashed on to the small dam.

Here the river swelled, spilling over and through a wedge of tangled weeds and debris which two council workers in thigh-length waders were attempting to unblock with long pitchforks. Hines walked to the iron railing and leaned his elbows on it, standing beside Paul, watching the men work.

The water's going in their wellies.

Naw it's no; it's just the spray. He took out the tobacco tin, began to roll a smoke. When he had finished he lighted it and said: Come on.

Paul made no reply.

We better be going.

I dont want to daddy.

Come on, I'll race you to the echo-bridge.

Paul didnt move.

Hines stepped back from the railing and stood for a moment; he made to step back again but the boy turned. Hines took him by the hand.

ooo

He went from the mantelpiece to the cabinet, then to the sink, across to the bed and back to his armchair; he felt down its sides. The door opened. My tin . . . you seen it at all?

Sandra took it off the top of the television set and handed it to him. He yawned. A bit early yet I suppose — the time; a bit early yet, to go to bed.

She smiled.

Naw, half ten, too early.

If you're really tired you should go.

He nodded. He reached for his matches and took one out and laid it on the box; he prised the lid off the tin and rolled the cigarette. He studied it before lighting it. When he was smoking he stared into the gasfire. Then he yawned and started rubbing and rotating his shoulders.

You okay . . . Sandra was looking at him; she had laid her book face down on her lap.

Fine, aye.

Are you sure? She frowned.

Aye.

You just seem as if . . . she shrugged. You've hardly said a word since tea-time.

Just tired.

You could turn on the telly.

Nothing on.

Have you looked?

What?

The paper, to see if there's anything on.

Aw aye; naw — well aye, I did earlier on but there was nothing. He yawned again; he placed the cigarette on an ashtray and stretched his arms. Think I will go to bed.

I feel like another cup of tea.

Hines grinned: Good idea. He stood up.

I wasnt meaning you to do it. She also stood up.

No bother, sit down.

When she remained standing he walked to her and patted her arm. Immediately she laid her hand on his. You're not okay.

What d'you mean?

Rab . . .

I'm fine Sandra.

You are not fine: what's wrong?

Nothing; nothing at all.

You never tell me anything. She shook her head. How can I do anything if you never tell me?

He turned away, briefly, to glance at the clock. But she leaned to kiss him on the lips and they had their arms round each other. O christ, he muttered.

She moved to look at his eyes. I hate to see you like this.

He shrugged then smiled.

Come on I'll give you a massage.

Right then . . . And when she sat down on her armchair she put a cushion on the floor at her feet, and parted her legs so that he could sit down between them. He held each of her ankles.

You should've gone to bed earlier, she was saying, her fingers working in across the tops of his shoulders; he had closed his eyelids . . . just as well I managed to get the legoset for him when I did

30

you know Rab. Mary was telling me a friend of hers had to go to
three shops before she could get one — three shops, gets to this time
of year and everybody seems to go daft. Her hands had moved onto
his back, palms end to end on his spine; her fingers were moving
again.

Hines sighed and she chuckled. What happened to the music? he
said.

I turned it off when you started snoring.

He laughed. Reaching behind he took hold of her wrists, then
lowered his hands to her thighs. For a time she continued to massage
his back. When she stopped she said: I cant do it unless you relax
properly.

He twisted to face her, placed his arms round her waist, his head
on her lap . . . Aye — bed sounds perfect.

Yes. She chuckled. As long as you remember what time of the
month it is.

Hines nodded.

When he sat round again she resumed the massage. You know
Carol — I've mentioned her to you — she was saying she was on the
pill for 7 years, and see when she came off it — the heaviest periods
she'd ever had; and fresh, the blood, that pinky kind — the thing is
though Rab her headaches, disappeared; she never gets them at all
nowadays — when she was taking it though, all the time, all the time
she was getting them; it was when she was talking, I was beginning to
wonder — but she thinks it was different to mine; she tried umpteen
of them right enough — she's just not sure about whether she was
given the one I'm on — she thinks she might've been but she's not
certain.

Hh.

It was just that it made me wonder . . . She breathed out deeply and
paused.

Ah thanks, that was great . . . He stood up: Still fancy a cup of tea?

Sandra yawned.

What about a slice of toast?

Are you having one?

Two. In fact I might even have three — any cheese in the house?

O God!

What's up with you woman!

That stew you made!

I beg your pardon, that stew was a remarkable affair.

It would've fed the close for a week.

Exactly what I've been thinking. Heh what d'you reckon if I stuck a menu up on the landing wall and started cooking carry-out meals? I'm being serious. I think it'd take a trick. Imagine the cash I could make! probably end up chucking the buses and going full-time at it. You and the wee man could help out with the dishes and that. Christ, before you know it I'd be a captain of industry — me and auld Bufuckingcanan, knights of the regalled empire, by appointment to the majestic imperials. Fuck sake Sandra!

ooo

I always wanted to be a barber but, this is the fucking point.

Reilly hooted.

Naw, seriously. D'you never go to the barber's on a Saturday morning? Christ sake man, transistor radios playing, drinking bottles of ginger, the place stowed out with folk chatting about football and everything. Great. Relaxed, everybody relaxed. Used to go there a few of us, then we'd shoot down for a game of snooker and that.

Aye well the fucking barber wasnt shooting down to play snooker; he was stuck in the shop cutting cunts' hair.

Naw, it was good but, honest. That was the thing about living in the Drum; it meant when you went up the town you really went up the town I mean you had to get a blue bus or a train. Took you a while so it did. And you always dressed up for the occasion.

Shite.

Is it fuck shite.

You trying to tell me you got a haircut once a month!

Suavity; aye. A smooth team so we were. The Drum's a debonair district.

Keech.

Is it fuck keech; there was always somebody needing a haircut; the rest of us just sloped along for the outing.

Reilly snorted.

No point in snorting ya cunt ye. Eh! imagine missing out on the barber experience! well well well; a man of the world too, sitting for his fucking Highers and he hasnt even done that! I dont know right enough. Heh . . . Hines bent to lift a $\frac{1}{2}$ pence coin from the floor.

Lovely, you can buy the grub.

That'll be fucking right.

Aye and by the way ya orange bastard; I'll tell you something for nothing: this conductor I was on with the other day, first terminus and off he jumps straight into a wee dairy — two jamrolls and two pints of milk. Eh? fuck sake! Ya cunt ye you've never done anything like that in all the time I've known you.

Hh!

Conductors are supposed to look after their drivers; it's a tradition.

I know, invented by drivers. To think of all these poor clippies down through the aeons all falling for it left right and centre, buying their drivers all kinds of grub while the dirty cunts're earning one and a half times their wages. What a miserable fucking con!

One and a half times their wages. Ha ha.

More or less.

Come off it ya cunt.

Come off it fuck all. Take the O.T. into consideration as well I mean how in the name of christ d'you carry on expecting solidarity with that sort of stupid discrepancy? typical nazi ploy: maintain the differentials.

Reilly laughed.

Aye, on you go. And I'll tell you something else: you'll never catch me driving a bus till it's equal wages all round.

Reilly continued laughing.

Aye and dont think you'll catch my vote for Shop Steward either!

You'll no be here by that time.

What time?

The elections. According to what I heard you were jacking the job.

Hines shook his head. I've never met a cunt like you for the poking the nose in where it doesnt belong. I'm no kidding you Reilly you're a disgrace to the Vatican.

Here we go, evasion of the issue; typical Masonic trick.

I'd rather be a Mason than a Pope.

And who told you I was definitely standing for it anyhow? Reilly had risen from the seat; he paused before strolling along to the cabin.

My lips are sealed.

Did you believe whoever it was?

Course I fucking believed it. My whole picture of you became a hundred percent. A flash of inspiration. That's the true Reilly I pondered, at long last being declared in his actual primaries, enhancing the life fulfilment, setting his sights on the ladder.

Reilly hooted.

An Inspectorship; that's what you're really after. Everything's fitting the gether by christ. Once I jack the job you'll be applying for the one-man fucking bus training then after that you'll be grabbing the Shop Stewardship while sneakily entering the Inspector's exam. O for fuck sake and then it'll be the Deskclerkship! Too much! You and Campbell. The plot's out. Imagine it too; the cunt's too embarrassed to confide in me. Me! His one genuine mucker in the entire garage spectrum. Well well well. What's up? did you think I'd scoff? Aye well you're fucking right I will ya hypocritical cunt ye.

I'm taking the fifth. Reilly switched on the engine and revved it loudly.

Hines waited for a lull and roared: A ladderclimber ya cunt! I always knew it: typical fenian marxist fucking glory seeker.

Up your arse. Reilly released the handbrake, the bus moved out from the terminus.

ooo

Upstairs in the bothy Hines covered his mouth while he yawned. Very pardon, I'm no hinting about my state of utter boredom.

A driver nearby had been recounting an incident from the morning. Someone told him to ignore the interruption but he shrugged. Ach, I was more or less finished anyhow. He also yawned; he drank a mouthful of tea. 2 duty I was on — it gets to you.

So does 92.

Well why dont you go back on the broo ya bastard!

Wish to christ I could George, that's the trouble with nowadays, you thingwy and then the thingwy thingwys. Fucking murder so it is.

He's a three-time loser into the bargain, said Reilly. If he jacks it now he's doomed to a life without buses.

Ah the job's just fucking getting to him.

It's always getting to him.

Aye but it's Reilly's fault, laughed Colin Brown, for jumping on the sick so fucking much.

Nothing to do with me. My life's my own. Reilly shifted his chair to allow someone to squeeze another chair into the company; he munched on his roll and sausage. A different conversation began.

Hines stared at the ceiling. He exhaled a smoke-ring in the direction of the strip-lighting. Can I canoe you up the river. That's what I want to know.

No wonder I jump on the sick, grinned Reilly: It's the only way to stay sane with the cunt.

Shut up ya renegade! Hines glanced round at the faces. This bastard was offered a bit of O.T. yesterday afternoon. Thought it went unnoticed so he did — creeping up to the counter when I was paying in the dough and all that. No kidding you man there's no cunt trustable nowadays.

Reilly snorted.

These fucking drivers're all the same, cried a conductor.

Aye, said Colin Brown. And he'll be sticking his name down for the one-man operating games when your back's fucking turned.

McCulloch laughed: Aw listen to this cunt! As soon as he passes his licence it'll be the first thing he does himself; no danger.

You kidding? Colin Brown looked at him. Fucking last thing you'll catch me doing, eh Rab?

Hines indicated Reilly: He's already done it the snidey bastard.

A few turned to glance at Reilly and he laughed: Heh wait a minute, he's joking; he's joking.

Who's joking! You've joined the arselickers Reilly and you cant deny it.

Shut up you, you'll have them fucking believing it.

Hines grinned and drank tea.

Pay no heed to the cunt, said somebody to Reilly. Hines is just upset because auld McGilvaray gave him a day suspension.

Heh by the way . . . said Colin Brown. I heard some cunt got sent

35

home the other day for no wearing a hat. Eh! fuck sake; imagine losing a day's wages for that.

There's many a slip twixt cup and lip.

Naw, went on McCulloch, it definitely is getting worse but. No doubt about it. Couple of nights ago we gets to the Cross — on the bingo run — I'm no more than 4 maybe $4\frac{1}{2}$ minutes sharp; out jumps Mackie — cunt's been hiding up a close as usual. Over he comes to the window. Heh you he says. What I says you talking to me Inspector Mackie. McCulloch grinned: Cunt hates it when you call him that. You're far too early he says. I'm no too early at all I says I'm only 4. 4 my arse he says you're 7. And if you think you can come charging through here at this time then you've

Well well well.

Shut up ya cunt, muttered Colin.

If you think you can come through here 7 sharp he says and get away with it then you've another fucking think coming. Wait a minute I says. Wait no minute says Mackie take out your watch. So I takes it out and that and

Amazing kettle of cabbage.

McCulloch glanced at him.

O sorry, sorry — I thought you'd finished there George.

Sarcastic bastard Rab, so you are.

Naw George honest; I genuinely thought you'd shot the bolt.

McCulloch looked away.

Hines is right, said somebody. Here we're in for a fucking break out the road and what happens? Christ, you're feart to leave a cup on the table in case it gets knocked down by a wee bus.

Aye change the subject change the subject! Who's got a fucking joke?

McCulloch folded his arms and sat back on his seat.

Ach that's no fair, said a driver.

Course it's no, cried Hines. Come on yous mob, a bit of order for Mr McCulloch here; let him finish the story — I'm really involved in the outcome. What was it again? O aye, along comes Mackie with a $4\frac{1}{2}$ minute cross for a watch and he jumps out a window shouting — what? what was it again?

Bingo! laughed a conductor.

A few others laughed. And Reilly leaned forwards, elbows on the table, glancing about him: Heh; any of yous heard the one about the

36

three-legged priest in Ballymurphy?

Aw Christ naw, no one of his! Quick: get the dominoes!

Good idea, shouted McCulloch; if I cant get talking then neither's any other cunt. And you can blame your mate for that Willie.

I know, he's always hated my jokes the bastard.

Aye and no wonder ya cunt ye I've been hearing them for 43 fucking year!

No this yin you've no. Reilly laughed, and glanced round again. There's this young priest — 3 legs he's got — right, straight out of college and they send him into Ballymurphy, the

aye aye yippee, aye aye yippee yippee aye; she'll be coming round the mountains when she comes, she'll be coming round the mountains when she comes; she'll be coming round the mountains, coming round the mountains; coming round the mountains when she comes; singing aye aye yippee yippee aye, singing aye

The company were laughing. Hines took his fingers out his ears. Reilly was also laughing. Hines prised the lid off his tin: Sorry I missed the punchline, sounds as if it was good too.

Reilly glanced at him. No sense of humour ya cunt that's always been your problem.

Hines nodded. I want to be a cowboy when I grow up.

Get the dominoes! roared McCulloch.

ooo

At the last terminus Reilly had switched off the engine and applied the handbrake. After a pause he left the driver's cabin and came slowly down the aisle, peering in below the seats. Other drivers, he was muttering, they're always supposed to be finding 50 pence pieces and pound notes and the rest of it but no me, naw; I'm no even asking for that much. 10 pence just, a lowly 10 pence; that would do, that would do me lovely.

Hines lay outstretched on the rear seat, his boots resting on the frame of the seat in front; his eyelids were shut.

Other conductors I've been on with, buying their drivers drink and grub and smokes but no you, naw, no him, not Mr Hines; a man could die of malnufuckingtrition with him for a conductor. An apology! Was that an apology?

Time?

Time! No good asking a fucking driver that ya mug ye. Reilly had swung the pocket-watch out from its pocket and was reading its face. 27 past I think and 10 seconds maybe 11, 12, 13 maybe 14.

What?

Reilly nodded.

You kidding?

Nope

22 more minutes to go you mean? Hines had sat up and was staring at him. I dont fucking believe this! Take your time — I told you to take your bastarn time: jesus god another 22 minutes, I'll no make it.

No my fault if the punters dont want the bus . . . Reilly opened a side window and spat out, then closed it.

I cant take it; I just cant take it any more. Hines was lying along the seat again with his eyelids shut. Please doctor, I cant, honest sir I just cant take it sir please sir a couple of weeks on the sick sir.

Reilly groaned.

Listen ya cunt, said Hines twisting to sit upright: I saw you sitting tailing that bus on Paisley Road West. You cant fucking deny it now come on I mean what in the name of god were you playing at? How come you never dived right in and stole his punters? ya miserable imbecilic looking bastard ye, eh? Tell me that?

Cause he was fucking due to be in front ya clown ye that's fucking how. We were 10 fucking sharp as it was ya fucking idiot ye. Anyhow, that red-headed fucking Inspector's always creeping about there at this time of the fucking night as well ye fucking know, so dont give us any of your patter. I was taking a big enough chance as it was.

Hines gaped at the roof.

Reilly opened the window and spat out again.

What a yarn. What a fucking yarn! O christ man the buses really have fucked him up good and proper. I mean what d'you think I'm new at the fucking game?

Sometimes you act like it ya fucking idiot.

Ho; listen to the patter. Look Reilly I mind fine when you were first out the stupid bastarn driving school: couldnt do enough for

38

your conductors. No matter what by christ — a day like this man when here I am in a state of utter desolation, you'd have been out there dragging them in off the street just so's my head could stay as an entire entity, an entire fucking entity ya cunt, but naw, no now; those days of the halcyon era have gone forever.

Shite.

It's nowhere near shite. Another thing: you must think I'm a right fucking bampot! I mean you honestly trying to tell me you'd be running 10 minutes sharp if there was an Inspector creeping about! Ho; that is a good yin. 10 sharp! You! ya cowardly cunt ye . . . Hines closed his eyelids.

I must be off my head coming back off the panel to this.

You've never been on your fucking head.

Get the tin out, I've no fags left.

Fuck off. He took out the tin and tossed it to him. Roll it yourself — if you've got the ability . . . He picked a soiled newspaper sheet from the floor and glanced at it.

Eventually Reilly returned him the tin. You definitely no going to the game next week?

Naw.

The ticket's there if you want it.

Nah; seriously man I need the dough. You'll get rid of the thing no bother.

Aye I know.

Hines grinned after a moment. I just cant take that excitement any longer. Scottish football I mean it really gets you going, my heart, the angina and that.

Fuck off.

Time?

39.

39! merciful heavens.

Ah it's only 10 more minutes.

O jesus sir please sir I'm sick of this eternal busconducting sir; please make them take me up the school for drivers and I promise to be a good boy sir I wont let you down, honest.

Reilly snorted. A solid 2 months good timekeeping would see you there.

3, according to accredited sources.

Okay then 3 — just so long as they see you're making an effort.

Fuck you and your efforts: time?

About 10.

10! What d'you mean 10? it was 10 a half a bastarn hour ago.

It only took me 6 weeks to get there.

Aye I know ya crawling cunt ye — a couple of Masonic handshakes and all that. A good genuine atheist's got no fucking chance in this grey but gold bundle of shite of a fucking city. And anyway man things have changed as well you know. They were overloaded with conductors in those days.

Reilly hooted.

Hines looked at him.

They're still overloaded with them ya cunt.

Aye okay, right, fine. Hines nodded. Then tell me this ya imbecilic bastard: how come all these days-off are getting worked by the nicely nicely brigade?

You talking about conductors?

Course I'm talking about confuckingductors.

There's no conductors getting working their days-off.

Dont kid yourself man it's going on; it's going on alright — they're just doing it under cover.

Shite.

Is it fuck shite.

Well it's the first I've heard.

Hh! so it cant be the genuine article! Well well well.

I'll believe it when I see it.

Hines grunted, he shook his head and his eyelids shut; he inserted his forefingers into each ear and began chanting unintelligibly.

ooo

Hup two three hup two three hup two three, come on there ya young whippersnapper let's be having you. They stopped outside the entrance to the nursery then up and into the lobby. He helped him with his coat, hung it on a peg in the cloakroom but Paul grinned and lifted it back down, and he carried it to one with his name written below a picture of a submarine. Hines examined it. Did you stick this item up here? I mean d'you realise it's a case of the imperial twitters?

Paul grinned. Just then a woman came in, with a very wee girl who stared at Hines while her coat and mittens were being taken off.

Cold yin the day, he said, real winter stuff.

The woman smiled.

He followed Paul into the main play-area and on to the library cupboard at the far side, away from any of the other kids. Picking a book he looked at the opening pages. Dont tell me you read this kind of childish rubbish!

Paul grinned, nodding. His attention was caught by a long table nearby; on it were a stack of games and puzzles. He walked off.

Right then, cheerio . . . Hines returned to the lobby, passing the Supervisor in the corridor.

Mr Hines. Oh . . . your wife — is she in the play-area?

What? No.

O.

He had the cashbag strap knotted round his fist, the hat tucked beneath his right elbow. Is there something wrong?

No — well . . . she frowned. I was sure it was Mrs Hines' turn for rota-duty this afternoon. Eh, could you just wait a minute please . . .

Hines looked at her.

It'll only be a minute.

He nodded. While she had gone he rolled a smoke, strolling up and down the corridor, looking at the paintings on the wall. She carried a file on her return.

Yes, she said, indicating a list of names. Your wife actually should be here this afternoon.

She's working.

O.

She works part-time in an office.

Mm. The Supervisor nodded. She did say she would be able to arrange things if and when her turn arose. You see Mr Hines we really do require parents to play their part occasionally — even if it is only once in a while. We feel it's important.

Hines nodded.

She glanced at the listed names, holding the file in such a way that he too could read them. She cleared her throat. Did she forget d'you think?

41

I'm not sure — probably, I mean I suppose so.

Mm.

He said nothing. He glanced at the names again and sniffed.

You see the names . . . She was pointing to them. Mrs Semple there, she's in this afternoon next to Mrs Hines and there tomorrow morning, Mrs Bryce — in fact Mrs Bryce'll most likely stay the whole day; actually she enjoys it — a lot of parents do.

He nodded.

And really, we do feel the children benefit to quite a large extent from having their own parents involved. Actually it can relax them, particularly during the early settling-in period. Of course children are wary of new things Mr Hines. And they do like to know they arent simply being dumped.

Hines inhaled on the cigarette. He's been here a good few months now.

O yes I know that. I wasnt referring to Paul especially, not at all — it's just that some parents do seem to look on a nursery as a sort of child-minding organisation. And it isnt you know, it's much more than that.

Hines looked at her.

She nodded, her head bowed over the file.

Can I do it? I mean d'you want me to do it? I can do it if you like.

O.

If you like.

Can you? it really would be a help.

I'll have to use your phone but — have you got one?

Yes . . . if you're sure it's alright.

Aye, I'm supposed to be starting in an hour but as long as I tell them in advance it'll be okay.

If you really are sure . . .

Hines smiled. He followed her along to the office. She waited outside in the corridor while he was making the call and when she came in he said: Is it okay if I leave the hat and bag here?

Of course. She chuckled. To be honest though Mr Hines, I have an idea the children would enjoy seeing them — the boys in particular. Paul mentions you quite a bit you know. I'm sure they'd be interested if you were to show them how to wear the bag. And your hat, your hat especially — you know how they are at that age!

He had poured hot water from the kettle into the basin in the sink and was dabbing at the soap with his shaving brush. Then he stopped and glanced round at Sandra. These eyes of mine, he said, they're like slits so they are . . . He began lathering his face and neck but paused to squint into the mirror again. A grey face. Two slits in a grey face. Even my hair by christ! I'll need to get to that fucking barber.

Mmhh.

Terrible . . . He started shaving. When he had finished and was drying himself he continued, It's good to know that in a short while from now I'll be getting transported from point A to point B and charging a price for the privilege. I wonder if the fucking world'll be standing still for a change. Tell you something Sandra: I'm definitely thinking of looking for another job.

She made no response.

Naw but seriously; one is occasionally required to consider the future.

He felt the teapot and poured himself a cupful, added the milk and sugar. Just got time, he said, and he sat down on the armchair. Heh you wee man! no about time you finished that beautiful dinner your mummy made?

He's okay . . .

Hines glanced at her and winked. He got up and walked to the table and bent over the boy's shoulder. If you dont eat it I'm going to take it to work with me!

Paul shifted on the chair.

Hines pulled a face at Sandra. As he returned to his chair he glanced at the book she was reading. Good story that; quite influential in the formative years . . . He grinned and sat down, then he reached to the mantelpiece for his tin; he sipped at the tea. It was lukewarm; he set the cup onto the mantelpiece and rolled a cigarette. He glanced at the clock. Well . . . I suppose I suppose. He looked to Sandra but she didnt acknowledge him. He lit the cigarette.

Five to three I thought you reported? Her gaze had remained on the book.

What? aye. 1457 to be precise. I suppose I can hang on another 10 minutes. A quick coffee maybe.

Sandra was still gazing at the book but it was now lying on her lap; and her left hand came to the side of her face, shielding most of it from him. He stared at the fire-surround for a time, then gradually moved his head so that he could see Paul — he was still attending to the food on his plate.

Her shoulders quivered and she had brought both hands to her face. Hines cleared his throat quietly and left his chair. And he stood between her and Paul; when he touched her shoulder the quivering halted but then continued.

He bent to her and put his arms round her and cuddled her very tightly, and made as if to speak but didnt; he cleared his throat again. At last her body stiffened; she allowed her head to rest against his shoulder. Then she moved from him and taking a paper tissue from her sleeve she dabbed at her eyes. O God, she whispered.

Hines was still holding her; his hands to the tops of her arms; he knelt between her legs.

I hate Sundays.

I know.

She blew her nose.

He kissed her on the mouth.

Daddy! Paul twisting on his seat and showing an almost empty plate.

Right fine okay okay, you can leave it, you can leave it.

I've nearly ate it all.

Aye, you're doing fine.

Paul was already down off his seat and coming towards them; but he switched on the television and got himself into his usual position a couple of yards from the screen.

You better go.

I dont better go at all.

Of course you do.

He paused. I can come home during the break.

Dont be daft.

I can.

There's never enough time on lateshift — you just get here and you've got to be leaving again.

Hines looked at her.

It's alright.

Jesus. He shook his head and rose a little, so that he could lean in more closely to her and they kissed. Paul tugged at him and called: See this!

He winked at Sandra and turned to see the screen. O aye, christ! He turned back and kissed her again, and when they broke he said: How come I always get kissed like that when I've got to walk out the fucking front door!

She grinned. So you'll come back.

Hines laughed. Heh, why dont the two of you go over to your mother's?

She shook her head.

Go to the Drum then; my maw and da'd be delighted.

They prefer it when you come.

He shrugged.

I might do.

It'd be good if you did actually — a while since we've seen them.

Sandra nodded. You better be going.

Aye . . . He leaned to kiss her again.

2

Holding Sandra by the elbow he pushed a way through the crowded lounge bar, passing directly in front of the raised platform upon which the entertainment would take place. In a sort of alcove to the far side Reilly was sitting with McCulloch and Colin, and two other men; at a table adjacent to theirs sat Isobel with McCulloch's wife and Colin's fiancée, and two other women. Sandra noticed and he whispered, Sorry . . . she didnt reply. I'll try and get it sorted out, he muttered. He watched her go to the empty seat at the women's table and then sat down on the one the men had kept for him. The other two men were introduced as Stewart and Donnie; both were drivers, operating out of a garage on the south side of the city.

McCulloch was in charge of the kitty; when the waitress eventually appeared Hines passed him the £5 and called to Sandra: Brandy and champagne Mrs Hines?

She smiled. The other women were involved in conversation.

Naw, he said to the waitress, a martini and lemonade — dry. And a pint of heavy. The others had just ordered a round. Hines winked at Sandra then he brought out the tin.

Eh Rab? McCulloch was attracting his attention, the other four glancing at him. A guy called Farquar, a driver? You must mind him surely! smashed two buses on his first day out on the road?

First week, added Reilly. Conductors used to sign off sick when they knew they were on with him.

Aw aye, aye. Hines yawned. He grinned suddenly at Colin. Great being on with him man, a shift went by in a matter of moments; no kidding you . . . He stopped, looked from Colin to Reilly.

Naw, said one of the two other men, I was just saying there, he's dead — a head-on out near Rutherglen.

Taxi, said McCulloch.

Private-hire, went on the man. Cortina I think he was driving — he wasnt carrying any punters at the time.

Hines shook his head.

How long since he chucked the buses? said Reilly.

Och a good while, the other man replied.

Terrible, muttered Hines.

Aye, never knew what hit him.

Killed instantly.

Aye, we've all got to go. The man raised his beer and sipped at it. I could think of better ways right enough.

Well at least he never knew. Reilly said: Imagine lingering on a vegetable or something?

Hh; at least it's better than being dead.

Come off it Rab!

Naw I mean, what happens if they come up with a new wonder drug? the day after they've cremated you? Fuck sake.

Aye, said one of the men.

Where there's life etcetera. Hines drank a mouthful of beer. He gave a vague toast: It's alright for you christians but what about the rest of us man? no after-life or fuck all.

True, said Colin Brown. End of story.

Reilly shrugged.

But a vegetable . . . added one of the men; his nose wrinkled; he reached for his drink.

See yous mob! McCulloch smiled and leaned back on his seat. What a conversation! To the two other men he said: That's what happens when you go for a night out with the cunts in this garage!

Ach I dont know though George, I like a good discussion.

Makes you thirsty but, added his mate with a grin.

Aye. Come on George, you're supposed to be organising the bevy.

I'm getting put off with yous mob . . . He stretched over to the next table to get the women's order.

On the platform the two entertainers in red trousers, tartan waistcoats and red bowties, singing a song and accompanying themselves on accordion and rhythm guitar. At the next table Sandra was smiling at something being said by McCulloch's wife; and she smiled at Hines when she noticed him watching. He prised the lid off the tin. The waitress had arrived again, her face perspired; quickly she transferred the drinks from tray to table and collected the empties. Why dont you join the Foreign Legion, he grinned. Either she failed to hear or she ignored him. He reached for the water jug and added a measure to his whisky.

Reilly was talking. He was saying, No chance, they'll never give in without a fight. Look at that last bother we had over the rise; I mean after the autumn agreement it was supposed to be a formality, but was it? was it fuck!

Aye and we're still waiting for the backpay, said Colin.

What they'll do is toss it into us at Christmas week then every cunt'll think they've had a fucking bonus!

Hines laughed with the others.

McCulloch shook his head at Stewart. You're just encouraging them.

Ah you cant escape politics.

Dead right Stewart, but it's no good telling this yin.

What you want to do is get a transfer down to our garage, said Hines, then you'll find out: bunch of fucking houdinis so they are.

They laughed again. Rab's right but, continued Reilly. It's murder polis. You've just got to mention the word strike and no cunt'll speak to you for six months.

No wonder. Union union union, muttered McCulloch.

See what I mean!

Aye well fuck sake if I started talking about the job yous mob'd soon be shooting me down in flames.

Hines frowned. That's actually true.

I know it's fucking true!

And this big forward we had . . . the driver named Donnie was saying: Eight goals in three games before he does a vanishing trick. Fuck knows what happened to him. One day he's there the next nobody's seen him. Same thing with another yin we had, a full-back — just a young cunt but he was big as well, a rare header of a ball; it was like having an extra striker at corner kicks. Caught by a plain clothes.

Aye, went on Stewart, the bastard jumped onto his bus a couple of stops from George Square and told him to keep the ticket. The daft cunt did and that was that; a 10 o'clock line waiting for him when he paid in his money. Bumped out the door right away, no messing.

Heh wait a minute, began Colin Brown.

Agent provocateur, said Reilly. You trying to tell us the plain-clothes told him to keep the ticket and then done him for fiddling? I mean what was your Shop Steward doing?

Fuck all he could do. The boy never told any cunt. And his driver was a Paki — one of them that never speaks to a white face.

Aye but surely there was a case for reinstatement?

Stewart shrugged. One of the lads went up to the place he stayed but the landlord told him he'd fucked off down south or something.

Rare player too. Donnie shook his head: So all in we lost half a team in about three weeks. Next thing you know we're losing five games on the trot. Then the shield: knocked out in the first fucking round.

Aye, said Reilly, when something like that happens you've got to act fast.

Colin muttered, Your branch sounds as bad as ours.

Salt of the earth. Our branch is the salt of the earth; especially during the long hot summers . . . Hines lighted his cigarette, reached for a drink.

I thought you were asleep, said McCulloch.

Wish to christ I was man, that's the trouble with nowadays, you yawn and then you yawn and what fucking happens?

Dont worry, grinned Colin to the other two drivers, he's always like this.

Handy to know, replied Donnie.

Reilly was calling to Sandra: Did you and him have a drink before you got here!

She smiled. Hines winked. One of the women said something to her and she smiled again, and then was involved in a conversation there.

The men had laughed at something.

Donnie was saying: I'm telling you — and when I ask for a fucking omelette I get a hard-boiled egg!

I heard that! called his wife. To the others at her table she added: Just because they're sitting over there they think they can say what they like.

Away and give us peace! grinned Donnie.

Stewart winked: I knew it was a mistake to bring them. We should've dumped them out the road somewhere.

Aye, said McCulloch, and we could've nicked into the bar and had a game of dominoes.

Colin snorted. Chauvinist bastards.

Just wait till you're married, said Reilly with a grin. Then you can start telling us!

Heh that reminds me . . . Stewart leaned forwards. I'm on backshift last week, second run of the day — picking up the workers and that

Hines had risen. Sorry I've got to miss this. Take notes Willie, I'll get the punchline when I get back.

Something up with the way I talk? Stewart smiled.

Naw, said McCulloch, just ignore the cunt — he'll go away.

Hines grinned, he moved his chair back to leave.

Approaching 10.30 p.m. the waitress cleared the table of the empties while the round was being taken by McCulloch; and he was advising everybody to order doubles in case they couldnt get one later. For the past half hour members of the audience had been singing along with the duo. Hines unbuttoned the top of his shirt and stuffed the tie into his inside jacket pocket. Reilly was pointing to him. Aye, he said, I'm no kidding you!

What's he fucking on about? said Hines.

You ya cunt ye — turning it on at the football; when we used to have a team. Aye George, you want to have been in the garage then.

The driver named Donnie was looking at Hines then he cried: Now I fucking know you! I've been sitting here all night wondering where it was — I forgot yous used to have a team. Aye! He snorted. About six years ago, we beat yous 5-0. You were playing.

Me! What a load of keech.

Queen's Park it was, said Donnie to the others. Right in the middle of a fucking snowstorm.

You've got the wrong man. I was injured in those days.

McCulloch and Colin were hooting along with Reilly.

You're a liar, said Donnie. You were playing in the forward line.

51

Rubbish.

Eh? roared Colin. To think of all the patter we've had to take off the cunt!

Galloping down the wing. That's it, I knew I knew you, cried Donnie.

I cant mind of galloping down any wings! Anyhow Reilly, if I was there you must've been there.

Not guilty. No six years ago I wasnt.

Aye, laughed Donnie, no wonder your garage chucked it!

The laughter was cut short by urgings from the next table. A general hush throughout the lounge while the entertainers announced names and dedications for those in the audience with particular cause for celebration. After a bout of applause for one the accordionist held up his arm then continued: And I want to say a special good evening to a couple spending their . . . he paused to glance at the bit of paper in his hand; to a couple spending their 20th wedding anniversary with us. It's no very often you come upon that these days! He glanced at the paper again. Mr and Mrs Reilly— Willie and Isobel. On your feet and give us a wave now; dont be shy!

The guitarist was strumming Happy Anniversary and several in the audience were humming the melody with him. Suddenly McCulloch nudged Reilly: It's you man. Heh! Here's one of them here! he shouted.

Cheers and scattered applause.

20 years married by christ you wouldnt credit it! Hines shook his head.

Reilly stared at him. Then he glanced to the other table where Colin's fiancée was laughing while attempting to hoist Isobel's hand above her head. Isobel resisted; her face was bright red. Sandra was studying the table. From the raised platform the accordionist was announcing something more in connection with this coming song, that it was especially for all those whose name had been mentioned. The song began. One of the women was speaking to Isobel now and Sandra was sitting there listening though she was still looking at the table.

Reilly's face was red; he sipped at his beer; he glanced at Hines and shook his head.

Convinced it was me eh!

Course it was you: laughed McCulloch.

Aw that's no fair man; how come I'm always the guilty party: fuck sake. Hines smiled. He got the lid off the tin to roll a smoke; he swallowed some whisky. Sandra was pulling her coat across her shoulders. Hines swallowed the rest of the whisky. He finished rolling the cigarette and lighted it. Anyway, he said, that's us . . . He had stood up.

What?

You're joking? said Colin.

Fucking babysitter man, couldnt get an allnighter.

But I've bought in the carry-out, said McCulloch. Christ sake Rab, and she's got all the sandwiches done I mean . . . all waiting.

Hines shook his head. Naw, the woman we were supposed to be getting let us down at the last minute; had to make do with a neighbour, and she'll no stay later than 11.

I know the feeling, said Donnie.

Ah that's a bastard, said McCulloch.

Sandra was standing, pausing to say something to Isobel; and when she started walking Hines said, Right, see yous later. He followed her out from the lounge. On the pavement he waved to halt a taxi, held the door open for her and before getting in beside her he gave the driver the address.

They gazed out opposite windows.

He walked up the stairs behind her, passed her just prior to reaching the second-storey landing, and unlocked the door. In the kitchen he fixed a kettle of water for tea. She had gone straight into the front room. He switched on the gas-fire and used the light to get his cigarette burning. When she came in he went ben the front room to take off his suit.

He was standing at the sink, whistling quietly, gazing through the slats in the blind; in the backcourt opposite the rear of the tenement building which was not yet demolished, the sky with that reddish glow, light reflecting on the ripples of the enormous puddle that stretched from the middens to the mouth of the back close; a smell of smouldering rubbish from somewhere, but vague.

The television had been switched on by Sandra; a late film was scheduled.

When the tea had infused he poured the two cupfuls; he carried

53

hers over, laying it on the floor next to her armchair. Back at the cabinet he lifted his own to his lips but once the steam met his lips he lowered the cup then emptied it into the sink and ran the tap to clear the tea down the drain. I'm just going to bed, he muttered.

ooo

His hands and head came out of the blankets. And he was breathing in gasps, his eyelids parted quite widely. At first he gaped in the direction of the sink then resting his head on the pillow he stared at the ceiling. Sandra was on her side, facing into the recess wall, her breathing scarcely audible. He turned and moved to press the front of his body against her; and he laid his forehead at her hair, his right forearm across her hip. But an instant later he had reverted to the old position; then he shifted even further from her, to the edge of the bed, from where he began to study the rubbish bin and its surrounding area. Eventually he was on his back and staring at the ceiling again, his left arm outside the blankets and his right arm beneath them. He remained still. Then his left leg was moving towards Sandra. When it touched he brought it back. And then he slid out of bed altogether, he had an erection, he went to the lavatory. On his return he noted the time on the alarm clock. Across at the sink he gulped water straight from the tap, he went back to bed afterwards.

ooo

Along the footbridge he stopped to chip the dowp of the cigarette over into the river. He peered down. Not too far off was a bend in the river, the driftwood flowing towards him, passing below; he went to the other side to watch it reappear. Pools of rainwater on the flat rail where his forearms rested, the wind rustled the higher branches of the

54

trees. On the opposite bank the grass also being rustled on the steep slope up to the street, a kind of shimmer. He struck a match but the flame didnt burn for long. The sound of wheels needing to be oiled. A high-pram, being pushed by a girl maybe as old as Sandra but probably younger a couple of years. She was wearing a thick anorak and jeans, and thick boots. He cleared his throat; then he moved to allow the pram to pass more easily. She had long hair. The pram bumped down the short flight of steps: and along the path, behind its canopy, the girl's head and shoulders could be seen above the big weeds.

ooo

For a while he tidied the house, before making a slice of toast and cheese, and coffee. Carrying it ben the front room he laid it on the floor beside the settee. He put an L.P. record on the music-centre, setting the arm so that it played continuously. He closed the curtains. When he sat down he bit a mouthful of the food and shut his mouth on it. But within moments he emptied it onto the plate, then stretched along the settee, resting his heels on its arm. He got up and switched off the light. He lifted the cup but put it down without tasting the coffee. He made a cigarette. When it burned he laid it on the ashtray on the floor.

The wallpaper peeled at the corner of the room nearest the front of the building, on the same side as the boy's cot. Beneath the peeling section were several air-pockets. He was reaching to press his right indexfinger into one of the larger ones, to make contact with the wall; he continued to press when the contact was made.

Back on the settee he raised the cup to his lips and allowed the coffee to enter his mouth; but he was restricting the gap so that it could only trickle through. He pushed a finger against the skin beneath his bottom lip, to the point where the coffee would have been parallel on the other side. Fuck sake. He drank most of the rest at once.

Toys and books were among the fankled blankets on Paul's cot.

Hines hadnt tidied there. He got up from the settee but he went ben the kitchen and got the quilt from the bed and back on the settee he stretched along it, drawing the quilt over himself, right over his face, and turning in to face the rear of the settee. He closed his eyelids, he stuck his indexfingers into each ear.

ooo

Paul — bouncing on the edge of the settee and grinning at him. Hines sat up, shielding the light from his eyes. The music was no longer being played. Paul was laughing . . . Granpa gave me 50 pence and we got trifle and crisps.

Good.

Sandra came in, her coat off; she walked to the cot and straightened out the bedclothes. Your record was blaring, she said, I dont know how you can sleep with it like that. I'm surprised nobody was in complaining.

He nodded; he lifted the unsmoked cigarette from the ashtray on the floor and lit it. Sandra was now tugging on the sleeves of Paul's coat and she got it off then knelt to help him with the rest of his clothes but he twisted about and she told him to stand at peace. He continued to twist, not letting her get ahead with it all.

How was your mum and dad? okay?

For God sake Paul. Yes. She pulled the jumper over his head and shoulders then he jerked out of her grasp and she smacked him on the wrist. Just stand still this minute!

I dont want to go to bed.

O for heaven sake.

I dont want to!

Hines reached over and whacked him on the bottom and his knees caved in; and he fell so that his chin could have landed with some force on the floor but it was avoided, his hands arriving first and taking the impact. A moment's shock before the greeting fit. Hines got off the settee then Sandra sat down on it. She murmured, He's dead beat, he's been on the go all evening; dad had him out in the garden after tea.

56

Hines had knelt on the floor, one knee raised, and he sat the boy there and continued undressing him, then helped him on with his pyjamas. He told him to go to the lavatory and began folding the clothes onto a chair next to his cot. Paul was no longer crying when he returned. Hines put him into the cot and he pulled the blankets up to his chin. Good night son . . . He gazed at him; he leaned to kiss him on the forehead. See you the morrow eh!

He turned and smiled at Sandra and went to the kitchen, switching on the television and the gas-fire.

More than quarter of an hour passed. He was glancing at the situations vacant column in the *Evening Times* when she came ben; and he nodded at the television. I think there's something coming on.

She didnt reply. He made as though to speak but said nothing. She was sitting poised on the edge of her chair, her hands gripping the edge of each of its arms. Without looking at him she said: It's no good Rab.

She looked at him for a moment. He flushed. What d'you mean Sandra?

But she only shrugged and then he gazed round the interior of the kitchen, breathing steadily. Soon the flush had gone from his face and he repeated the question. Again she shrugged. He shook his head slowly, then more quickly, the flush back on his face. I honestly dont know . . . he was saying, really — I dont know what you mean Sandra honest; is it the house? I mean if it's the house you're talking about then christ I mean, we'll get one. He cleared his throat: In Knightswood too if we bide our time.

Mmhh.

His eyelids closed and opened. He looked for his tobacco tin. We could get a place just now if we wanted . . .

There's no sense in resurrecting this argument.

It's no an argument. He sniffed. Anyway, there's a lot of good bits in Drumchapel.

I'm not saying there isnt.

And we wouldnt have to take their first offer. Something else you seem to forget: if they do slap a dangerous-building notice onto us then they're going to have to give us somewhere good I mean cause if they dont we can just sit it out till they do.

You're dreaming.

Hines looked at her.

It's a place of our own we should've got. At the very beginning. You've been listening to your dad.

She turned to face him. I have not been listening to my dad. It's just so bloody obvious. We should just never have come here. We could've used the money as a deposit.

No we couldnt have — not unless we'd bought a dump.

But we would've moved onto another. Look at the way prices have risen? if we'd bought five years ago we'd have sold for a lot more than we paid and then we could've afforded something better. God, when I think of what we paid just to get the key to this bloody place, bloody dump.

It wasnt a dump then.

Well it is now for God sake when did you last look out the window! I knew it was too much to pay. I told you so at the time but no, you let that woman talk you into it.

Evelyn Donaldson, she was trying to help.

O Rab I know she was trying to help, I'm not saying she wasnt— but that doesnt mean we had to take it.

We got the furniture as well.

Furniture!

Aye furniture. What we had was absolutely fuck all if I mind right. And another thing; you seem to forget the big repayments we'd have been making — interest as well; probably 5 or 6 times what we've been paying rent and rates.

Rab, we would've managed.

Hh.

We would've. She was looking at him and she spoke quietly: I mean how could we be worse off than we are just now?

What?

Rab; she gazed at him. We've got nothing — sorry, £83.

He returned the gaze; then he glanced at the gas-fire, his hands clasped. I should never have started back on the buses that last time, it was a mistake, no a 3rd time, daft, it was daft; I should've known better — even the broo, I should've stayed on the broo, christ . . . He stretched his fingers and reclasped them; he looked up to the mantelpiece then to the floor round the foot of his chair.

Your tobacco's in the room.

Aye. He turned his head slightly, away from her. She was up from her chair and coming to him. He grunted unintelligibly. She knelt;

she cupped her chin in both hands and smiled at him. Shaking his head he said: Stop looking at me as if I'm cracking up.

Rab.

Fancy a cup of tea?

I've made some already.

I didnt see you.

When I came in, it's probably cold by now.

Aw aye, christ.

Rab!

I'm fine.

You're not fine at all, if you would talk. If you would just bloody talk! She held each of his wrists now. I hate it when you act as if I cant understand you.

What?

You know what I mean.

I dont.

You do, you bloody do . . . She let go his wrists. Sometimes you're really arrogant. You are you know. Then you half mumble things and expect me to catch on right away and I cant — how can I? how can I if you never tell me?

After a pause he said, There's nothing to tell.

. . .

Sorry; I didnt mean it like that.

Yes you did. I'm going to bed.

Dont.

Yes, let go my hand.

Dont go yet Sandra, please.

God Rab I'm sick of it, I really am, the way you get at me.

What?

Yes, get at me, all the bloody time. That stupid joke in the pub; it was me you were getting at; dont think I didnt notice because I did, I bloody did!

What?

Why did we go there in the first place! I hate that kind of situation. The first time we'd been out in ages and look what bloody happens. O God, bloody dump bloody dump, I hate this place. Sandra's hands were covering her eyes and she had been standing for a while. She withdrew her hands: Do you know what happened 2 nights ago? — you were asleep in front of the bloody television — do you know

59

what happened? I was propositioned; I was propositioned. I was with Paul, coming back from the dairy. An old man in a red car.

Jesus christ.

I was coming back from the dairy, a shopping bag in one hand and him in the other.

Christ Sandra. What d'you no get me for?

Because it wouldnt have done any good, she said after a moment.

What?

He was just an old guy; it wouldnt have done any good. Anyway, he would've been away by the time you went down. She shook her head. And I didnt want you to.

How no?

I just didnt want you to.

Hh; christ. He glanced to the mantelpiece and to the side of his chair. He got up. He stood by her then put his hands on her shoulders.

Rab, I just want to get away from this place.

I know, I know.

ooo

Across the yard Reilly had appeared from between the row of parked buses; he carried a watering-can which he used to top up the radiator in the engine section at the rear. Hines stepped round the blind side from him, to the front of the bus and he sat on the first seat there. 5 more minutes till they were due out the garage. And Reilly waited until then before boarding and getting into the cabin; he switched on the engine at once and when they reached the 1st terminus he left it to idle, periodically depressing the accelerator pedal. It was dark outside and his reflection could be seen in the front window; he was reading a newspaper. Hines was on the rear seat, only moving when it was required by a passenger. Both this and the next journey were busy but the one following less so and Reilly switched off the engine at the terminus.

Fuck off: called Hines as he opened the tin. On his first drag on the cigarette he exhaled a large cloud of smoke and shouted: Good King Wenceslas is a daft bastard.

Reilly peered round the partition, then returned; the newspaper rustled.

Although I'm sorry I'm no really sorry. And I dont mean that I dont mean it cause I do, I do mean it. I apologise and do not apologise. The apologising takes precedence.

What I mean is I apologise because I've had to speak first since under normal circumstances you would've been yapping like fuck for the past 43 years; instead of that here you are finding yourself in the unnatural position of keeping the gub shut at all costs because of certain events of an unhappy nature which took place at a recent friendly gathering in the local hostelry ya bastard ye I'm sorry, honest. Honest. Hines sat upright on the seat, glanced out the back window. Hail was blowing across the street. Fuck it. He stood up and sat down. Look ya fucking bastard, if it makes it any better, the whole world's crumbling about my ears, the wife and the 38 weans are leaving, the building wherein I dwell is falling to fucking bits and I never emigrated to Australia when I should have; and that fucking doctor of mine, baldy cunt that he is, he's an unabashed card-carrying member of the C.B. bastarn I. I mean what fucking more d'you want?

The newspaper rustled.

Hines swivelled on the seat, to stretch along it, his boots resting on top of the framework of the one in front. Then he roared: Fuck off.

What d'you expect? shouted Reilly.

What do I expect! fucking farce: last time I'll ever be caught afuckingpologising.

That was never an apology.

Course it was.

Was it fuck.

It was fuck.

Shite.

Come off it man I mean what're you wanting at all? a hands and knees game! Away and give us peace ya Fenian bastard ye.

Leave politics out of it.

Hines sat upright, grinning: Okay ya cunt come on, read me a titbit on world exploifuckingtation from your bastarn *Star*; I think I can take it.

Reilly shifted on his seat so that the newspaper lay onto the cabin door.

Are matters up or down, that's what I want to know.

Up.

Ah, so questions're being rasied in the House are they!

Right, centre and right of centre.

Christ Reilly your patter's improving right enough; there may yet be hope.

Shut up ya cunt. Heh — did you notice that Inspector at the 2nd terminus there? 8 minutes sharp I left and he didnt bat a fucking eyelid. What d'you make of it? point for discussion?

Could be. A strange kettle of parsnips.

Exactly what I thought.

Maybe he was asleep standing up.

He was puffing a pipe.

Did the witness see the actual smoke?

No your honour.

Then he'd definitely given up the ghost and who can blame him! Imagine having to creep about at ungodly intervals just to check up on drivers leaving termini.

With blobs of snow dripping down your collar. And big fucking buses screeching past every 10 minutes. Eh, what a shitey job that must be!

Hines laughed. He got up to change the destination screen. It's your turn to buy the chips by the way.

Naw it's no.

Aye it is — my memory's no that fucking bad.

It must be.

You kidding?

Naw, fuck, I'm serious.

Serious? what d'you mean serious!

I mean I fucking bought them the last time. No mind? that spread-over we were on?

Hines shook his head. Everything's a fucking blur these days. No kidding you Willie I'm going to write to Any bastarn Questions about it. Outraged of Tunbridge fucking Drumchapel: how in the name of christ is a body to keep track of time when the world's crumbling about his fucking ears.

Reilly laughed as he folded away the newspaper. I'm starving as well, he said, think I'll get a fish-supper.

Aw christ naw, the poor auld cashbag.

Midway through the 2nd part of the shift an Inspector rapped the door. It was a different Inspector and they were at a different terminus. Reilly had left the cabin to go down the aisle checking for dropped coins beneath the seats. He muttered, O fuck, while returning to open the doors. Hello Inspector.

You're no due here for another 11 minutes driver I'll have to book you.

From the rear seat Hines cleared his throat. Glancing at him the Inspector turned to Reilly: Does your conductor always sit with his feet on seats? When Reilly didnt answer he continued: 11 minutes, how did you manage it?

To be honest with you I never knew we were sharp till we got here. We only lifted a half dozen punters since Union Street.

The Inspector snorted. And he brought a pencil out from where it had been wedged behind his ear and beneath his hat; he flicked through the pages of his notebook then looked at Reilly.

Reilly, William, 6214.

Hines coughed. The Inspector stared at him. I told you before son get your bloody feet off that seat — people have got to sit there for your information.

Hines swivelled round; his boots clattered onto the floor.

Come here.

Me you mean?

The Inspector continued to stare at him.

Hines rose, he walked up the aisle with his hands in his trouser pockets, and he stood closeby the Inspector.

Your waybill conductor, I want to see it.

It's in the waybill holder. Hines gestured towards the luggage-compartment. Then he got the waybill when the Inspector nodded at it.

Okay son, read me the numbers from your machine. Better still, let me see them for myself.

Reilly coughed as Hines raised the machine so that the Inspector could check the numbers there were corresponding to the last waybill entry. I'm not cheating the ratepayer if that's what you think.

63

I'm no saying you're doing anything. The Inspector sniffed and nodded before returning him the waybill. I dont see your hat.

Eh.

Where is it?

In fact I've not got it with me this evening; my child's fault: he spilled a tureen of chicken vindaloo all over it. The wife had to leave it to soak. Still no dry when I was coming to report this afternoon. Smell of curry everywhere too; the neighbours were in complaining.

Name and number? The Inspector turned a page in his notebook.

Hines Robert 4729. Am I being booked?

Incomplete uniform. What was your name again?

Hines Robert.

His mates call him Bobby, said Reilly.

Well, some of them call me Rabbie right enough; I blame the auld man, he was a great believer in Burns.

I like comics, said the Inspector.

Glad to hear it.

Look; I've a bloody job to do same as yous pair. If yous were doing it the way yous're supposed to I wouldnt be having to use my book.

Very sorry, muttered Reilly.

The Inspector glanced at him. Dont mention it . . . As he turned to exit he squinted in at the destination screen, and said to Hines: Mind and change it before leaving here now, else I'll be having to book you again.

When the doors were shut behind him Reilly laughed briefly. Fuck them all, that's what I say.

Hines didnt reply. He walked to the rear of the bus, shaking his head and occasionally snorting. He sat down. He sniffed. Naw, christ naw, no now, definitely, definitely not, bastards, the decision's made and that's it final; hh; fuck it; the bastards, them and their fucking promotion, all I wanted to be was a fucking the Busdriver Hines.

So you admit it! Reilly was laughing, having come halfway down the aisle.

Hines covered his face with both hands. Too bad to be true, too fucking bad, no kidding ye man bad, too fucking bad, really fucking bad man I'm no kidding ye.

And the door was being chapped. The Inspector. Reilly saying, It's that cunt back again.

Hines dropped his hands. They lay so that the wrists balanced on the edge of the seat, his head moving to rest against the rearmost panel of the bus.

Heh conductor. I want to see that destination screen changed right now.

I'll do it, said Reilly.

You're no the conductor. Heh. You. I want to see it getting changed, right now. So's I know you arent forgetting.

The doors had shut.

The bus was really swaying. Reilly could drive too fast; other times not fast enough. He was slowing it down now, for a queue of persons, having formed to file upstairs or down. Hines had got off the seat and was marching to the front as the bus moved away from the kerb. Stop again man I'm jacking it. Pull into the side. High fucking time I mean it's getting to the ridiculous stage. Come on for christ sake Willie stop the bus when I'm telling you.

Reilly's frown.

Christ sake man hurry up, I want to jack the bastarn thing, right now.

Fine ya cunt.

It's no fine at all; come on, pull into the fucking side.

Reilly glancing at him.

I want to jack it I'm telling you come on.

Right then you can jack it, I dont have to stop the bus but.

Aye you do, I need to jack it; I want to have jacked it.

Well you've jacked it.

How can I have fucking jacked it if I'm standing here in the scabby bastarn transport green with machine and cashbag for christ sake!

Careful man, dont poke.

O very sorry sir please sir I'm poking. Hines was slinging the machine and cashbag up over his shoulder and off, lowering them to the floor that they lay upright against the bottom panel of the driver's cabin. He took off the uniform jacket and turned to be facing the lower-deck passengers: Any of yous got a spare pair of breeks?

Reilly hooting.

Honest, I cant absolve myself in these greenly yins I'm wearing.

65

Come on now, a spare pair of breeks; who's got a spare pair of breeks? External condition irrelevant. Women's slacks'll do champion. Eh? come on, I've got to be having jacked this kettle of cabbage.

A middle-aged couple rising from their seat; the man first down and holding out money. The fare son.

I'll swop it for your trousers, and throw in a ticket-machine of a money-making nature.

The man smiling while placing the money onto the grooved top of the cabin door, and half turning his back to mutter, Just keep it for yourself — we're no needing any tickets.

And the woman grinning back to the other passengers.

Dear god. Naw, I beg your pardon sir please sir never let it be said sir if truth be old I've no fiddled a coin for nigh on 4 year sir honest, and such an item cannot be contemplated during one's penultimate conducting moments.

So you've no jacked it! Reilly laughing: I might've blooming known!

The bus slowed to a halt. The couple disembarked. Other three people came aboard. The doors shut.

You're a stabintheback cunt Willie did anybody ever tell you that?

Ssh. Reilly smiled. Away upstairs for a smoke.

Hines looked at him.

ooo

The tea was lukewarm; he gulped it down and replaced the cup on top of the television, then stretched out beneath the blankets. Sandra came in from the lobby dressed in her going-to-the-office clothes. She smiled: I thought you'd gone back to sleep.

Naw.

When she noticed him still watching her she said, I'm meeting mum in town remember — to do a bit of shopping. Christmas, she mouthed.

O aye, aye.

Mind and give him something to eat.

Hines nodded, and got out of bed.

I dont mean just now Rab — before he goes to the nursery. She smiled. Stay in bed if you like . . . I better hurry or I'll be late.

He continued dressing, went to the tallboy for a fresh pair of socks and a T-shirt. Then Paul kicked open the door, carrying an armful of toys and stuff. Hines looked at him and made to say something but he shrieked and jerked his shoulders back the way. Sandra: she had come behind him and put her arms round him. Jesus christ.

O Rab I didnt mean it!

The fucking buttons Sandra, freezing.

She grinned.

He shook his head. He laughed, and drew her into him, held her closely. Trying to kill me woman. Heart attacks etcetera — at least wait till I get myself insured!

She chuckled. I better go . . . She hurried to Paul and kissed him on the head.

These feminist career women! no time to kiss their weans properly! Dont worry wee man, just call me mummy from now on.

Paul grinned. Hines winked at him.

Conspiracies as usual, muttered Sandra with a smile.

Aye well we've got to stick the gether, said Hines, following her into the lobby; he gripped her shoulders for the last couple of steps; and at the door he kissed her again — until Paul tugged at his trousers. Jealous wee . . . He stepped back to lift him up.

The front door was open and Sandra on the outside landing. Watch out for these bastarn salesmen, he cried.

Ssh Rab.

Mummy, shouted Paul. Kiss!

O God. She returned quickly. Hines was laughing; he also kissed her. Away and put your socks on, she said, you'll catch pneumonia.

Aye aye sir.

Paul was down onto the floor and off and running ben the front room before Hines had locked the door. He went to join him, by the windows, seeing her appear on the pavement, and crossing the street, going to the corner where she paused to turn, and wave.

The water was on to boil for coffee. But when he opened the tin he saw it to contain only enough for two cigarettes; he rolled a thin one. He studied it. He stuck it behind his ear and shut his eyelids. One should have fucking guessed. No, naw son, naw it's okay, definitely not, no need to panic I mean your auld man's just going to jump out the fucking window but everything's fine, honest I mean ... He leapt out the chair and strode to the tallboy then to the kitchen-cabinet and to the draining board at the sink, the mantelpiece and the top of the television set and to the front room and the places where money may be found, then to the wardrobe in the lobby, the pockets of the clothes inside there.

Back in the kitchen Paul glanced at him when he tugged open the top drawer in the tallboy again.

There's no smokes son and there's no fucking money to buy them. What am I supposed to do? Did your mummy tell you that! Eh?

Paul raised his left arm.

A smoke, I'll be needing a smoke, and there's no fucking cashbag. No good telling me to shut up. What in the name of christ am I going to do? The neighbours — nah, not at all, no chance wee man no chance. The fucking Pawn! Brilliant — christ sake, mature boy for 4 right enough! Well done the wee Paul fellow. Here, get your coat.

Hines had sat down already and was knotting his bootlaces. But Paul was still kneeling amongst his stuff on the floor. He took the cigarette from behind his ear and lighted it, he collected his uniform jacket. Paul!

The boy jumped up and raced ben the front room, Hines right behind him: When I tell you to do something you do it — eh? you listening? Right?

Paul didnt answer, his face red.

Okay?

He nodded, avoiding Hines while getting his coat from the settee. Hines fixed the buttons for him then got the suit from the wardrobe.

Going downstairs he had the boy on his shoulders and was jumping the steps 2 and occasionally 3 at a time. And they were both laughing when they reached the close. On the pavement he lowered him to the ground and took him by the hand across the street. Round the corner and along and Paul kept pausing and rubbing at his ears. Hines told him to stop it, but he began doing it again. I told you to stop that!

Paul stared at the pavement.

After a few strides Hines stopped. Okay; what's up?

They're sore daddy.

What d'you mean sore? d'you mean cold?

Paul didnt reply.

Ah christ, up in the Arctic they'd be falling off. Frostbite, so cold it makes things like ears fall off. And your toes if you're no wearing plenty of socks.

Clearing his throat he spat a mouthful of catarrh into the gutter. The Eskimos son, they wear a lot of fur and that to keep the cold out. Wrap it about their ears and toes. See if they didnt, that'd be them, finished. They have to go about the whole year wearing them as well because of that fucking weather they've been landed with. They eat whales and stuff. Use up every bit of the bodies — oil out the skins; and this oil they make into various items, fuel and that. Short people with stumpy legs though maybe it's the furs makes them look so fucking stumpy I dont know. If they unwrapped all their clothes and that they might be skinny underneath. Skinny by christ. Aye but that's it about the ears son I'm no kidding you, they have to wear stacks and stacks of clothes. Never catch a cold either. I mean imagine somebody from this bloody dump going up to where they live son, they'd be dead in a matter of moments — pneumonia or some fucking thing. Unless they started doing the same as the locals. And vice versa down here I mean they'd probably wind up catching a disease. Really desperate. Poor auld fucking Eskimos son it makes you sick so it does.

ooo

¾lb beef links, 1lb of potatoes, 2 onions medium sized and 1 tin beans baked. And that's you with the sausage, chips and beans plus the juicy onions — and they're good for your blood whether you like it or no. This big pot with this grill type container is for the chips, it lets them drip so the fat goes back into the pot. Simple economics. And even if your mummy's sick to death of chips, what should be said is this: she isnt the fucking cook the day so enough said, let her go to a bastarn cafe. 2 nights on the trot is okay as long as it's not regularly the case. Fine: the items should get dished no more than 4 times per week but attempt to space it so that 1 day can pass without. 7 days in a week. What is that by christ is there an extra day floating about somewhere? Best to ignore fixed things like weeks and months and the rest of it. That's the time thing they set you up. Just think of the days. The minimum to cover all of the things i.e. breakfast, dinner, tea. Right: chips number 1 day, 3 day, 5 day, 7 day; missing 0 day, 2 day, 4 day and 6 day. Alright, 8 times a fortnight. But 7 every 14 days. So there you are you can maybe get left having them twice on the trot but being a chip lover you just ignore it. Let's go then: right; Monday is fish day — rubbish. Monday is mince and potatoes. Simple, get your pot. Item: 1 pot. Item: $3/4$lb mince. Item: 2 onions medium sized, then a $1/2$lb carrots, a tin of peas and also a no—not at all, dont use a frying pan to brown the mince; what you do is fry it lightly in the same pot you're doing the actual cooking in. Saves a utensil for the cleaning up carry on. So: stick mince into pot with drop cooking oil, lard or whatever the fuck—margarine maybe. Have onions peeled and chopped. Break up mince with wooden spoon. Put pot on at slow heat that it doesnt sizzle too much. While breaking up mince all the time in order that it may not become too fucking lumpy. Toss in onions. The pepper and salt to have been sprinkled while doing the breaking up. Next: have your water boiled. Pour a $1/2$ pint measure in which you've already dumped gravy cube viz crumbled into the smallest bits possible. Stir. When mince brownish add mixture. Stir. Place lid on pot. Having already brought to boil. Then get simmering i.e. once boiling you turn gas so's it just bubbles and no more. Pardon. Once you've got $1/2$ pint gravy water poured in you'll probably need extra. Lid on. Handle turned to inside lest accidents to person. Then sit on arse for following hour apart from occasional checks and stirring. 30 minutes before completion you get the spuds peeled and cut into appropriate sections and fill the other pot with boiling water, having already dumped said spuds into pot while empty for fuck sake otherwise you'll splash yourself. Stick on at hot heat. Sit on arse for 15 to 20 minutes. Open tin peas of course. The bastarn fucking carrots. At the frying mince and onion stage you've got them peeled and chopped and you add to same. The peas get placed in wee saucepan and can cook in matter of moments. When time's up you've got mince, potatoes and peas set to serve from trio of pots.

ooo

He stared across the street between the curtains, watching the frost glint on the roof guttering of the tenement. On his way back he paused by the cot. Paul's feet poked out from the blankets. He tucked them under.

Once in bed he lay on his front, on his elbows, the side of his head resting on his knuckles. A slight sigh from Sandra and she moved, her leg touched his. He shifted to kiss her on the tip of the nose. A smile on her face. Her eyelids flickering: What time is it?

Eh, about half two I think . . . He watched her for a spell; she hadnt replied. She was genuinely asleep — as though nothing could disturb her.

After a while he turned onto his back, gazed sideways, to the long line of light on the wall, it entered the space between blind and window-frame. He grinned.

ooo

Honest, he was saying, I just walked in the door and bang, 63 duty — a 2-hour dinner-break. Best shift I've had in years!

She looked at him for a moment, then laughed and kissed him.

Heh — anything in the pot?

O God, just some soup. I could make a quick omelette?

Naw, the soup's fine . . . He followed her into the kitchen. Where's the wee man?

Bed; I put him down half an hour ago.

He'll be asleep then eh?

If he's not he should be.

While she went to the oven he took off his uniform jacket and with a loud sigh he lifted the *Evening Times* from her chair and flopped down onto his own. Then he got up and got his tobacco tin and matches from the jacket, put them on the floor beside the chair.

Jesus, he said, this is wonderful.

Sandra laughed. She was opening the cabinet and getting two slices of bread. I was thinking, she said, just before you came in Rab, you know that wallpaper in the front room?

Aw naw.

I knew I shouldnt've said anything.

Too late! He glanced at her and grinned: Only kidding.

No, I was just thinking

Hang on, before you go any further: if we take down the stuff that's up the fucking building'll collapse!

I thought that was what we wanted!

Another thing: with our fucking luck we'd probably get word of a new house as soon as we'd stuck up the last roll!

She was looking at him.

Naw, on you go.

After a moment she said: Actually I'd be happy to do it myself — these nights you're away on backshift.

Like tonight for instance, aye.

She smiled. To tell you the truth Rab I'm sick to death of seeing that design. I think it'd be worth doing — even if we were only here another six months.

Ah we'll be long gone by then.

Will we?

Course.

You never know though. Even just painting it. Anything to cover it up; it's awful. I'm surprised Paul doesnt get nightmares just from seeing it. Can you imagine having to lie there night after night!

Hines nodded.

And it isnt as if it would cost much ... The soup had reheated. She switched off the gas, ladled the soup into a bowl and quickly spread margarine on the bread. In fact a $2\frac{1}{2}$ litre tin might do it all.

I'll get you one for Christmas.

O thanks!

He grinned, taking the food from her, and he began to eat. Back at the oven she got the kettle; then she laughed suddenly. Rab — God — mind I was telling you about Doreen the cleaner the other day? the one with the three grandchildren? what a scream she is. This afternoon at tea-break — you know how Mr Buchanan's away down in London just now — o God. Sandra laughed. Jean had sent her out for cream doughnuts, for herself and me and Mrs Monaghan . . .

And Sandra continued with this tale about the cleaner coming back from the baker with the 4 cakes and going on about this the cakes, her coming back with the cakes and not the cream doughnuts it was, she was continuing on about this, the Cleaner Being Sent For The Cream Doughnuts And Not The Cakes while Mr the erstwhile fucking Buchanan was off down in London on a Brief Business Trip very strictly speaking in all probability not playing about at all, no, just being forced into it of course, he would much rather be staying at home in the nice Suburbs having by no means any notion of gallivanting about the place, yes, 1 thing about auld Bufuckingcanan, he's the salt of the bastarn Earth. I dont know what it is with you Sandra I really dont I mean . . . He shook his head. He had glanced away from her. And he placed the soup and the bread up on the mantelpiece. Then he turned: I mean something definitely stinks about sending a woman like Doreen out for cream doughnuts. A grandmother for christ sake. Out for cream fucking doughnuts; Jesus christ almighty! He flung the *Evening Times* from his lap and grabbed the tobacco, getting the lid off the tin, seeing the fingers twitch, the fingers twitching away, in their grasp at the lid, of the tin.

DANGER: HM Govt. Health Depts' WARNING
THE MORE YOU SMOKE
THE MORE YOU RISK YOUR HEALTH.

The door closed. The door had been closing. And its bang. He pressed a forefinger against a nostril of his nose and blew through the other. There is a gas-fire such that 3 sections exist, each containing 24 toty rectangles behind which lurk several 100 pointed particles of an unknown nature but that they glow whitely when at hot heat; this gas-fire can be leaking mysteriously. The occasional whiff 1st thing in the morning. It is the gas. The inhalation of such fumes doth annihilate the white corpuscles of one's bloodstream. Hence the cause of death. In you come night after night and slump into your chair — a chair you have been positioning as close to the feedpipe as is surreptitiously possible — and so on till the loss of the white fills your being with total red unto black. Get yourself insured and that's you the bona fide articles for the etceteras, the wife and 38 weans being provided for. All you need is a short note: Dear Sandra, As I've

73

often told you in the past, most people either know they've got to die and wont believe it or believe they've got to die and know they wont, but what I want to say is this — 1 thing and 1 thing only, and you can give us an aye or give us a naw — re. you and the boy, the wee Paul fellow, you and him, aye, just the pair of you, I want to talk to yous a minute, you and him, no other cunt, nobody, nobody else, none, forget the lot of them cause it's just the pair of you, no other cunt at all, they dont matter the bastards, the dirty fucking bastards, not a

no chance, not an iota the bastards

Sandra was standing at the door. Listen, she had said. She was still wearing the pale-coloured blouse, the tan-coloured skirt, the top three buttons of the blouse being undone still. Standing with her arms folded beneath her breasts and the nipples firm against the material there. She was saying how Hines didnt have the right to say what he had said, that he hadnt the right, that he was treating her like somebody that, somebody that. She was not able to make contact in this part of it, not able to say just how she saw herself being treated by him but that this treatment she regarded as totally wrong, as really unjustified. A crucial factor: the cleaner has always finished a certain part of her work in time for tea-break so she can join in the chat with the office-staff, that she likes a cake the same as the next person, that it's never a question of her being sent but that she offers and is usually doing nothing till commencing the next part of her work, that . . . Doreen.

Hines looked away. He stared at the soup and began rolling a cigarette.

He looked at her and shook his head, closed his eyelids; he opened them and replaced the cigarette makings in the tin and shut it. O fuck . . . he rubbed at his eyes and gazed at the fire.

Rab. She had come across, parting his knees and resting her knees on the edge of his chair. She gripped his shoulders, forcing him to meet her gaze.

He laughed; it was derisive and become a low snorting sound. She made him continue facing her. Then she gave him a shake! Jesus. He shook his head. Sorry.

Shut up. She hated him saying that. She leaned to whisper into his ear and he embraced her quite roughly, his face averted; and he sat forwards so her position would be more easy to maintain but it wasnt, and she fell on him and he went against the back of the chair.

Both laughed, and she pretended to nibble the lobe of his ear till he shook her off from it. I wonder why you dont like me doing that? she chuckled.

Too tickly.

Liar.

What d'you mean! He kissed her again, attempting to make it last a while but not able to do so because of a shortage of breath, being unable to breathe properly, and having to stop and try to breathe more regularly before continuing. He tugged the blouse out from the waistband of her skirt, and got the catch unclipped at the back of her bra. Hang on . . . and she got off the chair, arms snug to the sides of her body, stepping to the sink to draw the blind.

These helicopters, everywhere.

She smiled; saucily, it was a saucy smile she was giving him; it was really great to look at. He grinned at her noticing his watching her. She was balancing herself — the right hand on the arm of the chair — to take off her tights — at the last stage of that manoeuvre. She was sticking her tongue out at him; and a smile — but not directly to him — while turning to get into bed. There she shivered. A mime. Come on, she shivered, while getting the blankets to her chin.

When he was in beside her she clung to him, still shivering.

Naw, he laughed, there's plenty of time.

There better be.

They were kissing then and very soon he moved to enter her. Once he had climaxed she told him it felt good. His breathing wasnt right to answer yet. But he kissed her, and eventually rolled onto his back; she laid her head on his chest, then said, What a waste!

He chuckled.

Well, you're still hard.

No I'm not.

Feels like it to me.

Ah you could probably bend it in two the way it is.

Rab!

He laughed. And you're the one that wanted to be a nurse too!

She shuddered: a mime, the way she could shudder in the circumstances. He held her there, on his chest, stroking the side of her arm, her hair on his left cheek.

When have you got to go back?

A while.

Are you sure?

Aye. He sniffed slightly, gazed at the ceiling for a moment, before shutting his eyelids. He opened them again.

ooo

The man on the kerb was sitting so that he seemed to be attempting an actual connection of his feet with the tar and stonework. How to manage it; there are the feet encased in the socks and the boots and there is the street upon which they have settled. Shoes he's wearing, not boots. A man of uncertain age but a dosser of course, and waiting for the garage canteen to open to strangers, strangers not being permitted entry until breakfast has been eaten by the garage employees. He stares at the shoes on the street; a rigorous posture though it could appear relaxed, his elbows fixed or resting on his raised knees. The cigarette Hines has been smoking he chips to land less than a yard from the man's left shoe but the man made no outward movement. He steps in the man's direction, as though preparing to clobber him a hard one on the shoulder but instead of doing that he just continued along the street.

A driver came striding round the corner and nodded to him in passing, then he called something which Hines ignored.

Along the pavement of the main thoroughfare he was swinging his machine-case while walking. Snow started to fall. The bus was at the stop. Beside it stood another driver and a bespectacled Inspector by the name of Mackie. Then out from a shop doorway strode a busconductor exhibiting a mixture of relief and annoyance, the annoyance now taking precedence; and he headed toward Hines. Fuck sake Rab what happened to you?

Slept in, grinned Hines. He drew the cuff of the sleeve of his uniform jacket under his nostrils and sniffed. He smiled at the Inspector. But the deepest form of frown screwed the Inspector's eyebrows and he was wanting to know what bloody time this was to arrive. Hines chuckled. Aboard the bus the faces of the passengers. And the driver already inside his cabin and adjusting his seat and rear-view mirror. As soon as Hines stepped on the automatic doors banged shut and within moments all moved at a fair clip. He blew his nose into a piece of toilet paper before arranging his machine and cashbag. Some passengers watched. He shook his head with a smile and was soon conducting his duties. And his nose dripped again, 1 drop on his wrist while another onto the ticket he was issuing to an aged male passenger. The poor auld latter! What he did was hold the ticket by the skin of its teeth then place it with tremendous aplomb on the spare bit of the seat beside him. Blooming nose, said Hines, been like this for months so it has!

He continued down the aisle, collecting the rest of the outstanding fares.

Soon he was asking the driver to halt at the next convenient general stores. And he got off to buy a packet of paper handkerchiefs as well as the $\frac{1}{2}$ ounce of tobacco, making the payment from the cashbag. When he came out the bespectacled Inspector was there — he would have been on the bus immediately following that of Hines. He gazed sternly, saying: Name and number?

Hines grinned. He replied and yawned, proceeded back onto the bus, to be followed there by the Inspector. Opening the packet he took out a handkerchief and blew noisily into it. The blow was a good one but and he felt the benefit. Am I being booked? he said.

Course you're being bloody booked, whispered the Inspector, glancing over his spectacles at the passengers; then he began to write into his notebook.

Hines nodded. He enclosed the pinkie of his right hand in the handkerchief and stuck it up his right nostril, and he yanked about there. That's how I went into the shop, to buy them, these handkerchiefs. Runny noses! Murder polis so they are.

Get the bus moving, the Inspector told the driver.

Is it no a bona fide excuse?

Under no circumstances is a conductor allowed to leave his bus, as well you know. He lowered his voice. And dont try to take the effing piss out of me Hines, I'm warning you.

Hines sniffed and looked at him.

The bus had been going. Just before the next stop the Inspector nodded at the driver and soon the bus halted, and he got down onto the pavement to stand there with his hands clasped behind his back, and facing away from the bus. Then the bus moving and the driver engrossed in that, the passengers gazing at various objects of interest but not connected to this situation. It was quite peculiar in a sense, and Hines raised his left arm though soon he lowered it. He muttered.

What was that? said the driver, his head twisting to the side then back to the front. What d'you say Rab?

Mackie.

Hh. The driver shook his head. I mind him before he became an Inspector.

So do I. I conducted to him quite a few times.

Did you? the driver glanced round.

Aye. Hines sniffed. I hadnt long started in the job right enough.

The driver nodded, turning his head but then returning it at once and he was hitting the footbrake . . . Knew he was going to do that, stupid fucking . . . He shook his head, and he glanced back to Hines.

Aye, quite a few times.

Hh! The driver now reaching behind his seat for another bottle of milk and he swigged a long one then replaced it and getting a packet of his tipped cigarettes from the panel above the dashboard, and glancing at Hines and also to the front while extracting a cigarette.

Aye; I hadnt long started in the job right enough.

The driver fiddling with the box of matches, eyebrows raised. Hines turned and began to manoeuvre the farestage numbering device on his machine; he shrugged and went up the stairs. It wasnt busy. Towards the rear he sat down and he rolled a cigarette.

ooo

Once she had gone into work he went back to bed and attempted to sleep but this was not to be possible because of the boy who was both playing with toys and watching the television. He got up. He too watched television, drinking tea, smoking cigarettes; then he went to the front room with the quilt, put on a record and lay stretched out on the settee. Paul entered. He got up, he walked to the windows. Aye, he said, real winter stuff the day. He frowned at the sky.

Paul continued to stand near the settee. Hines sniffed and nodded to him then returned to the kitchen. The atmosphere had clouded, the tobacco smoke. He leaned over the sink to force up the window a bit. One of its sides was jammed. He tugged on the other side first then applied pressure with both hands to the jammed side; it appeared stuck fast; he got a small hammer from the toolbox beneath the sink and gave it a few taps until able to move it by hand. Paul was watching him. Hines nodded. It's these auld mineworkings son, causes subsidence. He shrugged, filled a kettle to heat for tea, or possibly coffee. What about you? he said, d'you want some milk or what?

Yes.

Milk you mean?

He nodded.

What about a piece? want a piece on jam or something?

Paul grinned.

Hh; god. Hines shook his head with a smile.

ooo

This rectangle is formed by the backsides of the buildings — in fact it's maybe even a square. A square: 4 sides of equal length and each 2 lines being angled onto each other at 90°. Okay now: this backcourt a square and for each unit of dwellers up each tenement close there exists the $1/3$ midden being equal to 2 dustbins. For every 3 closes you have the 1 midden containing 6 dustbins. But then you've got the prowlers coming round when every cunt's asleep. They go exchanging holey dustbins for nice new yins. Holey dustbins: the bottom only portionally there so the rubbish remains on the ground when said dustbins are being uplifted. What a bastard. Lift a dustbin then aware of how light it feels and then to be finding all the rubbish lying in a heap on the fucking floor — having to rush out to the midden-motor and get your shovel and back again to swipe it all away before the animals get a whiff and come out to get into it. Animals eat everything. No matter what it is they'll fucking eat it.

They're starving right enough. And they are not to be having·
anywhere to live. They keep trying to stay one jump ahead of the
demolition men. You get the building knocked down and then the
equipment gets transferred round the corner, and so on down the
line, getting nearer and nearer to this very window. And all the time
the poor auld fucking animals go running for cover, scrambling
along beneath the floorboards and up and down the stair they go
dropping between walls, in behind all those layers and layers of
fucking wallpaper dating back to christ knows when son it must be
near a hundred bastarn years the dump has been standing, which
throws you a century's rodent shit plus the decayed corpses all lying
wedged here there and everyfuckingwhere no doubt supplying
sustenance by christ to lesser mites so that springing to life the rising
generations and even evolution for fuck sake what next.

The District of D.

There can be long hot summers in the District of D. Dont let
anybody tell you different. And it can be good in the long hot
summers. Even the fucking buses, these early mornings, before the
bastards are up and about and jumping aboard your platform.
Great, the dawns, when the alarm goes off and it's daylight already
and there you are there you are there you fucking are right enough. It
is baffling. It is baffling and yet it is not fucking baffling. Here you've
got a family comprising husband wife and wean whose astounding
circumstances are oddly normal. This trio are as 1. But the husband
is to be no doubt leaving his job of work to take to another. And the
reason is clear: he has failed to make a go of things at this the third
time of asking. It is his considered opinion that the door must soon
be shown him for being a bad busconductor. And in the long run it'll
probably prove possible that just being an actual conductor will be
reason enough because 1-man-buses are the vehicular items of the
not too distant future. He would to have become a busdriver in view
of this, to have been preparing for that. But there is now no hope of
his ever becoming a busdriver. Okay: so, either he leaves of his own
fucking volition or else he gets the boot. Fine. And the broo does
seem the thing to do. Fuck sake but he has been knowing that for a
while. Let it pass, fine, okay, as long as the course is foreseeable past
opinions on the future are irrelevant. Shut all that kind of stuff away,
away. It is a straightforward matter, a simple question of producing
the finishing line. And the actual means of production though

important are nevertheless not too important. Of course you're still left with the fucking house.

What might be worth noting here is the strange kettle of cabbage. It is fucking a strange carry on altogether. Here you have a house — a flat — a flat cum house — up a close in a tenement building. Now: there is a — many in fact — singular bits involved in this problem about the house. Not least is an item of an apparently insurmountable nature. It calls for wide heads. The past and the present have got to be considered. When the immediate past is not only today but also tomorrow. What the fuck. The time things they set you up. 5 years is never to be described as 10 minutes. That would be fucking ridiculous. 5 years is a host of days; then for each 1 you get 3. Even if you only want the 1 you've got another 2 stuck on. You're best paying no attention. You just go along. You can just go along okay. You can be getting along fine, just going along, you can eh — then the house coming on top of the job or maybe beforehand, the flat, it is to be being demolished so the flit out from here to the next place and getting the space, clearing for the space, getting shot of the auld brickwork and concrete, the debris, you get it stacked then wheel it away in your wheelbarrow, right up the ramp and into the skip, the debris. Your head gets thick. You can be watching and waiting. It is fucking a strange carry on because then there you are. And you are not able to look properly.

ooo

She had spoken. He glanced at her, replied, and she nodded. When she got to the oven she switched off the gas and poured the boiling water out of the kettle into the two mugs and added the milk and the sugar, and carried one to him and the other back with her to the chair; sitting down there and resuming reading; about four inches of wrist showing beneath her jumper sleeves; her chin resting on her cupped left hand, hair shielding most of her face. He said that the coffee was good and she asked if he wanted anything to go with it, there being biscuits in the tin. And the movement of the book as she settled into position, the concentration, left leg crossing to the right, the foot to be resting halfway there on it, between the knee and the crotch; she scratched at her ankle. When she had walked to the oven her steps appeared as though measured.

She asked if he wanted the telly on it wouldnt bother her but he said no, only if she did. She looked at him. A moment later he looked away, shrugged; he reached for the tin and got the lid off, the cigarette made.

She was yawning. Closing her book she got up and left the kitchen. The lavatory door creaking; soon the plug being pulled and the crash of the cistern emptying. Then her footsteps from the front room; she was now undressed, and getting into bed, to be facing into the recess wall.

Eventually he turned the gasfire down to its minimum power and settled his heels on the fender, lifted the cigarette from the ashtray, but put it down again and lay back on the chair; he looked at the ceiling and smiled, shaking his head briefly. It seemed as though there was nothing to say. That that which could be said must have been said already. She was in bed and facing the wall, her breathing inaudible but eyes maybe open, attentive — waiting for him to move, even for the match being struck perhaps that a further 10 minutes till the light went out and he in beside her. They had looked at each other. What could be sadder than that. Nothing could be sadder than that. It is terrible. Nothing has ever been more terrible. In 10 minutes she would be asleep. She would be unwilling to sleep so soon but soon she would be. She can sleep like a trooper. Then next day; it will soon be Christmas and the New Year comes next and the house to be tumbling and the layers of wallpaper, the slow thud of snow on the window, the poor auld fucking eskimos right enough. Hines is to get away, away; he is to get away. There is the red and there is the white, the pure and the pure, this is the trouble nowadays, not being 5 years or even 6, not being the 6 but today, this night, her facing the wall from him and their inability to talk, he having nothing to say, and it being that that she is so well aware of, that has stopped her from talking. Here he is and they are here, the unit, the trio. And it is all so fucking long, so long, and yet here he is, still fucking here and not doing, not doing anything, still here, on the buses, back on the third term. And if the connection is now to be severed there can be no return. It is the third term of transport and fourths are not having ever been heard of. Thirds are unlikely and fourths are out of the question. He was fortunate to get reinstated the last time and is to have been being on his best behaviour throughout the term. Nothing further can be said. He should just never have returned. It is bad that here he is. Sandra told him he was daft, that returning was a step to the rear, steps to the rear not being of the present. But if he was daft he was also not daft. The latter stages of the last spell on the broo had blinded him to certain items. These items are not always apparent. Life on the broo had not been good, however, offering as it did, nothing. And so he neglected to consider the certain items.

Now, these items, while of great importance on some occasions, are not too important on others.

ooo

He slithered through the snow for the last few yards up to the corner, and walked along to the stop. Several moments passed before the staffbus came bombing along. A loud screeching as the driver moved down through the gears instead of applying the footbrake normally. Hines was positioned at a spot beyond the stop so that he could jump aboard and grab for the handrail, and as the doors bounced open at that instant beyond the stop he had jumped aboard and was grabbing for the handrail, and the doors had shut, the driver hooting his laughter while ramming the gearstick from 1st to 2nd that Hines was jerked down the aisle but managing to grab onto the safety rail by the luggage-compartment, swinging himself round to be sitting on the seat there. He gazed at the rearview mirror, seeing the driver laughing at him and he frowned.

Heh, called the driver, dont go blaming me now Rab I mean it's a hell of a shoogly bus they've gave me. No my fucking fault; how can it be my fucking fault! Never mind but at least it's waking every cunt up. Eh?

Hines ignored him, got the lid off the tin. The driver was still laughing and glancing into the rearview. Come on down and talk, he called. Heh, I dont even know last night's football results. Eh? Heh you hungry? I've got a couple of chits left from my dinner here you want them? Eh? Heh Rab you wanting them, I'm no feeling like them man you're welcome. Eh?

Hines had a brief coughing fit on the first drag on the smoke and then was rising to push back the small window above the big window, and he spat out the catarrh.

Heh what d'you think! last night, point for discussion, prostitute gets on my bus. I'm stopped at the lights up the top of St. Vincent Street and I opens the door — thought she was just wanting to ask me the time or some fucking thing but naw, on she gets. Yoker she says but I've got no money. Aw aw I thinks. None at all she says. Know what she does? now I'm no kidding you man she must've been near 50 years of age: at least, at fucking least. Know what she does? hooks up the kilt. Hooks up the kilt man I'm no kidding you; I've no money she says. What I says get to fuck, big smelly fanny like that you kidding, and anyhow I says it's a staffbus, staff only. What d'you mean she says. No passengers allowed, that's what I fucking mean. Well what did you stop for in the first place ya stupid looking clown ye. Eh? I mean . . . eh? Fuck sake I mean I wouldnt take that kind of patter off the wife never mind a clatty auld cunt like her man I mean — heh I says down you go before I put one on your chin. Aye just fucking try it she says and I'm no kidding you man she's all set to get the coat off and go to the boxing games. Eh? Heh Rab know what I done! Eh? Heh Rab wait till you hear this yin man: know what I done! drove right into the polis fucking office!

Hines winked at the floor.

Aye, Elliot Street — I drove right fucking in; and then out she jumps soon as I opened the doors, going like the clappers she was man christ, you want to have seen her — the 4 minute mile wasnt fucking in it . . . The driver changed suddenly down from 4th to 3rd gear, Hines' cigarette falling out of his hand and landing in a pool of water on the floor.

Heh Rab you been on your winter-week or what? I've no seen you for ages. Where you been hiding yourself eh! Heh, I heard that cunt Reilly's going to stand for Shop Steward, that right?

Hh. Hines shook his head and replied that he was about to acquire a gun. He had the lid off the tin and was lining the tobacco along the centre of the rice-paper. A gun.

A gun! what d'you mean a fucking shooter?

Aye.

The driver laughed. What're you going to kill some cunt?

That's my business.

The driver roared unintelligibly. Hines was grinning. He stopped this grinning by a prolonged stare at the saturated cigarette on the floor.

After breakfast he set off on one of his occasional rambles round the garage periphery. Then he was at the stop. An Inspector was also here, taking notes on the times of passing buses, but soon he crossed the road to continue his work. Hines leaned against the display window of an adjacent shop. The few people waiting for a bus were standing back from the kerb. Slush was being sprayed onto the pavement by passing vehicles. A young girl came along while he rolled a cigarette. She got sprayed by a big lorry. She stopped and studied herself. The slush on her clothes, dripping. She seemed surprised but not astonished. Her face had flushed. Glancing from side to side she turned and went back the way she had come, neither too slowly nor too quickly although it could be seen that something disturbed her. Hines licked the gummed edge of the rice-paper and dropped the cigarette to the paving; he took out the tin to roll another, pausing to wipe at his nostrils with the cuff of his right uniform sleeve.

He was to go home immediately.

Across the road the Inspector was strolling to a different vantage point, hands clasped behind his back. When next he looked over it was the intention of Hines to fall. If the fall was properly accomplished coins would spill from his cashbag and his uniform breeks would get soaked, and maybe he would graze a knee. All this would be worthwhile if only he could get home. Sandra would be there and would be there for a further 2 hours. It is not that a Hines should not work. A Hines should certainly of course work. Hines has always been in favour of work. He considers it good for the thing.

The fall was rejected.

Signing off sick in order that one may return home immediately is nothing less than a step to the rear, the which step belonging to the

85

past and not the present. And the present should not be said to be yesterday. One of the more fascinating aspects of the lower orders is their peculiar ideas on time and motion. This used to always be being exemplified by the Busconductor Hines. He had assumed the world as a State of Flux. All things aboard the world are constantly on the move. Ding ding. Being an object aboard the world I am indeed on the go. As a method of survival it is marvellous. Hines can marvel. He can look at the faces and cannot look at the faces. They approach the platform individually and in pairs and in groups, talking and not talking. They are hypocrites. The men and the women, the children. It is not that he knows this in particular but that everyone knows this and is also known to know it, by everyone else. Such a thing cannot be concealed. For each individual a guise exists but this guise is shabby, it can be seen through; face upon face, the tired the sullen the crabbit, the timid the cheery and so on. In the windows he could see their reflections, the strange frowns every now and then. That concentration.

Snow was falling. He raised the lapels of the uniform jacket, huddled his shoulders, the uniform hat squarely on his head, hands deep in the uniform trouser pockets; that fine cigarette burning away. Over the road the Inspector stamped from foot to foot, smacking his hands together, his head twisting to right and to left in his continuing search for promptness.

And Reilly had arrived, to go straight into the doorway of the shop without acknowledging his conductor's presence.

The bus was late.

A thin layer of snow now covered Hines' hat and his other exposed regions; he felt his boots, however, to be in good repair. Soon it would be time for another cigarette. At the end of this shift he would retain the price of a further $\frac{1}{2}$ ounce. Too much was being spent on the habit. He had to keep Sandra in ignorance of the extent. But more than $\frac{3}{4}$ of his pocketmoney was required for it and he was not able to cope. He would have to stop. To stop is not simple. As a gesture of some sort he had reduced his own pocketmoney several weeks ago but this was only leaving him short of funds and he was having to take from the housekeeping purse or otherwise reimburse himself — frequently he retained cash from the cashbag but this cash was deducted at source from the following week's wagepacket while providing the file with additional Black Marks. Some conductors earn extra monies by means of positive ploys. Hines used to be such a conductor during his first term of transport. Nowadays circumstances have to be extremely odd before he will even contemplate action of that description. The present situation may well be demanding but the circumstances are not odd. They are baffling. They are baffling and they are not fucking baffling. He can see himself seeing the faces. Maybe he is just timewasting. The matter cannot be considered. But waiting for the bus could drive him crackers. He was standing there; he smoked 3 cigarettes. And Reilly in the doorway made things worse. He brooded about the not talking. He likes talking to Hines who doesnt not like talking to him. But what is the point in such talk. It is that which they have accomplished for years. Years are not minutes. In the garage the talk is endless. To discuss the talk of the garage is pointless. Such discussions do occur among the uniformed employees and are integral to the thing itself. Without such discussions the talk of the garage might even be becoming absent. Hines has endeavoured to reject both the talk and the discussions of the talk while aware of the absurdity of doing even that. Presently he remains silent. He is unsure as to whether the language of death is the language of the unalive. He only hopes a bus will stop soon, that it will be his.

ooo

The final notice on the gasbill had been placed upright against the wall above the mantelpiece. He did not look at it more closely. He went ben the front room to play a record, and he began the tidying. Under the boy's cot he found a neat pile of chewed food beneath a jersey. He hoovered the carpet thoroughly, swept the lobby and toilet floor, checking for other batches of food, going carefully in case he discovered signs of mice. Hines hates mice. They induce a terror in him that could be described as irrational. When Sandra or Paul is present he copes; he acts as though indifferent and can attack them quite the thing. Worrying about mice is pointless because they do not do anything much. Rats, however, can kill infants. It is not their fault.

They are rats. A rat is an entity that will scavenge; and being bigger and stronger than a mouse it can tackle more onerous tasks. It can bite the neck of a wean. The infant lies sleeping in the pram and up climbs the rat softly, padding along the quilt, to pick curiously at the fleshy object. During the long hot summers the women sit downstairs in the backcourt, their chairs lining the foot of the tenement, a sun-trap, their voices carrying, that peaceful part of the afternoon when the older kids are in school. Sandra used to go down when Paul was a toddler. They were all sitting there chatting and this big rat the size of a dog got disturbed out the midden, and yet not so much panic as anger that a few moved to corner it, and a woman by the name of Joanne Hughes banged it dead with a shovel belonging to the demolition workers.

Mrs Montgomery was washing the stair when he went out. He remarked on the weather but she replied only in a monosyllable. Sometimes she would speak to him but generally not. She prefers Sandra. A couple of Hogmanays ago he went down to wish her the best for the coming year but for some reason got involved in an argument over religion. Although he was not sober he should not carry all of the blame. The politics of Mrs Montgomery are well away from the question.

The snow.

He decided against returning for a coat. And did he have an actual coat. Yes. He also had a good suit, plus a few other items he never seemed to have time to wear because of the putrid green. When was he last not wearing it. His last dayoff. He even wore it on some of those. This is why it looked so shabby, the trousers in particular, like a pair of fucking concertinas. And when he came home after a shift he seldom bothered to change clothes unless Sandra mentioned it. And when he was due out on a backshift he usually stuck it on first thing in the morning, to save doing so later.

Paul was already in the cloakroom, his coat on and his balaclava in his hand, eager to be away. This normally meant he was in the bad books with the bosses. He wasnt wearing his mittens; they were inside his coat pockets. While Hines was fixing things he tried to find out what was what but Paul was saying nothing. It could be hard getting him to talk. This amused Sandra, that it was obvious whom he took after; but Hines had been nothing like him as a boy.

They trudged along, with Hines walking so that the boy could be stepping on the untouched snow to the side of the pavement; and he did seem interested in seeing the prints he left, but not for long. Taking off his uniform hat Hines attempted to exchange it for the balaclava, but Paul tensed and he returned it to his own head. He scraped a handful of snow from the bonnet of a parked car and gave it to him but he let it fall quite soon. It was hopeless. What was it to be a real father. He was it, a real father. But other fathers might be finding out what was up, if something really had occurred to upset him. What could have occurred to upset him. Something or nothing.

They went into the butcher's. The man behind the counter made a fuss of weans and could also quip merrily at adults — often Sandra smiled at these quips. Then into the vegetable shop where he added an apple to the purchases, giving it to the boy on the last lap home. It was good that he liked fruit. Fruit is good for kids. Sandra works that such items go more easily. She works parttime but hopes to go fulltime. Her boss' name is Buchanan. Imagine a cunt called Buchanan. Here you have a cunt by the name of Buchanan who is the boss and has always regarded one's wife in a favourable light, as someone he would always reinstate, her work having been exemplary since first she started working for the cunt directly upon leaving Secretarial College. An employee of ideal proportions. Never a day's illness but that such an illness is of a bona fide variety. A credit to all and sundry eh, excuse me madam you by any chance being employed on an informal basis by the Heads of the Monarchic State. A simple question. Give us an aye or give us a naw.

He watched the boy staring at the television from his usual kneeling position, the thumb in the mouth, that incredible concentration. How can weans do wrong. Such a power; just kneeling and staring at the television. Unless somebody had interrupted what he was doing — if he was in the middle of doing a jigsaw or something, painting a picture maybe — then okay, he was entitled to get upset, to go in a huff, to give the Supervisor a mouthful perhaps.

Nor did he seem to have any pals. At first he did have and it was good to see because he was an only child. Maybe he would turn out to be a genius. A lot of geniuses have lonely childhoods. Name one. Jesus. That's cheating. Are football players allowed.

The bacco son, seen my bacco?

Paul rose from the floor with his thumb still in his mouth, his gaze shifting a moment to capture the tin; and he was passing it to Hines without any sign of resentment; just a thing to be done, you pass tobacco tins to the auld man.

Heh wee man what happened in that nursery? did you kick one of the ladies or what?

Paul glanced at him but that was all, he didnt smile and nor did he signify one solitary item — not even that he was at home in a particular situation.

What had to be done was educate him properly. Fill him full of milk and apples. Cram that fucking protein into him, making sure he grew into a different size. And no more getting called Big Yin because you're a magnificent 5 foot fucking 9 and a $^1/_2$. The wee man could become a big man, broad chested, built like a barrel, with an educated brain, a head full of his auld man's teachings. Come with me son and I'll show you the ropes. How d'you fancy a potted history of this grey but gold city, a once mighty bastion of the Imperial Mejisteh son a centre of Worldly Enterprise. The auld man can tell you all about it. Into the libraries you shall go. And he'll dig out the stuff, the real mccoy but son the real mccoy, then the art galleries and museums son the palaces of the people, the subways and the grave-yards and the fucking necropolises, the football parks then the barrows on Sunday morning you'll be digging out the old books and clothes and that and not forgetting the paddy's by christ for a slab of last year's tablet son plus the second-hand pair of false teeth right enough, aye, very useful indeed though it's a pity about the ferries of course cause he would've liked to take you on one before they shut down son and it's too late now though you'd have thought it was good son the carry on backwards and forwards from one shore to the other but never mind never mind you've got your parks with the paddle boats and the swimming baths by christ he keeps meaning to take you there he keeps forgetting son and he's always fucking promising son, it's these bastarn shifts that fuck you up and it's good too, the swimming, hell of a good for you, the shoulders and that it makes you grow big yins and strong as fuck you'll be able to take care of yourself anywhere anytime anyfuckingbody you'll be able to do it son, control, take control, of the situation, standing back, clear sighted, the perspective truly precise and into the nub of things, no tangents, just straight in with an understanding already shaped that

that which transpires shall do so as an effect of the conditions presented; there will be no other course available; you shall know what to do and go and fucking do it, with none of that backsliding shite. The backsliding shite; there can be reasons for it. Things arent always as clear as they sometimes appear. You can have a way of moving which you reckon has to be ahead in a definite sense and then for some reason, for some reason what happens is fuck all really, nothing, nothing at all, nothing at all is happening yet there you are in strangely geometric patterns wherein points are arranged, have been arranged, in a weird display of fuck knows what except it is always vaguely familiar, whatever that means, though this is what it seems like, the carry on backwards and forwards to your work each morning so early it is still nighttime and the streetcleaners just about ³/₄ way through their quota and maybe stopping off for a quiet chat and a smoke when sure the coast is clear that their gaffer isnt in the vicinity to surprise them at it, the smoking, the fly wee puff for christ sake son I mind when your auld man was up at that School for Busconductors on his second time round there was this exIndisputable acting as teacher and he spotted him one morning having a fly wee puff at whatever the fuck age he was the old exIndisputable with the thin moustachio, the short back and sides and his You there Hines Robert 4729 I hope to hell you'll wear a shirt and tie once you leave here to take charge of a blooming bus the poor auld cunt that he was, North fucking Africa with Monty or something son your da'll never ever be like that — you kidding! these fucking books son, papped right into you, he'll show you what's what, the whole A to B that the C is a map of the world, the Beginning of Time son, your ancestors and the rest of it, you had them forging a path along the riverbed way back before Wallace got stuck on the iron gates of old London Town the bastards they were at it even then with each other and long long before it as well you had them fucking every cunt about in the name of the father and the son they were robbing you blind with their kings and their queens and the rest of the shite the chiefs and so on making it to the top in their entrempeneurial mejisteh son they were stealing the bread out your mouth and if they couldnt reach it you were opening the mouth wider son the eyelids shut that you didnt offend son that you didnt see son in case you actually saw son that you had to actually do, because one thing you didnt want was to do son so the eyelids shut you put forward the mouth with head lowered while the

91

slight stoop or curtsey and forefinger to eyebrow the sign of the dross, we do beg ye kindly sir we do beg ye kindly, for a remaindered crust of the bread we baked thank 'ee kindly y'r 'onour an' only 'ope as we might bake 'em more sweetly for 'ee t' nex' time 'appen y'r 'onour as'll do us t' privilege o' robbin' again sir please sir kick us one up the arse sir thanks very much ya bunch of imbecilic fucking bastarn imbeciles.

Heh were you kissing the girls! is that what it was!

Good christ, maybe he was kissing the boys. Hines got up and grabbed him, raising him as high above his head as he could, and laughed. Ya wee mug ye, you and me are going to the fucking swimming baths tomorrow — like it or lump it.

Paul grinned but then was glad to get put back down on the floor, and he was definitely not comfortable as he knelt there. It was the unpredictability. That is how he was uncomfortable. Hines was well aware of this.

After 6 p.m. and the food being ready but still no Sandra so he had to switch off the gasrings. She could have been late. She was late. Sometimes she did come home late, because of the office, having to stay on to work an extra wee bit — which for some reason seems acceptable to office workers though Sandra receives no extra cash as far as Hines is aware. Office workers may believe unpaid hours are an entry fee into the Big Time. Sandra shrugs. She says Mr Buchanan never minds about her showing up a few minutes late and is always ready to let her off or whatever if there's a problem about Paul so why should she mind staying on late if ever there's a rush job needing doing. It is reasonable. And if she is off sick she will get paid as though she is not off sick but simply there at the office instead of not being there at the office. What a fine relationship between boss and worker. Hines is in favour of such keech. It is really good for the thing. And anyway, all this office stuff has been gone over time and time again since from way back even before they got married. But what he still has difficulty in comprehending is the way an office can be in existence when nothing else seems to. There is an office and there is a staff for that office, and they do office work for which they get paid office salaries with the usual office perks. But the money. The actual fucking money. Where does it come from. Private commerce is rumoured the source but can it be likely the Patrons of the People are responsible! That the outfit is a secret body being funded as a sly branch of the M.I.'s! Sandra having been recruited through her carnal knowledge of the Militant Latencies — they have wiretapped his prick, tuning into his fantasies — at the first sexual stroke the line

sorry. Sorry sorry sorry. Really and truly. How could anybody even think such a thing. He definitely doesnt mean it. Not at all, honest to christ he doesnt, he just has a bad tongue, things come out, they do sir sorry sir please sir — although the problem is one a body becomes accustomed to over the years, the past 5 sir, the through thick and thin yins you see sir him and the Sandra lassie and the Paul fellow — that's the wee man — the 3 of them, the trio of persons sir the 1, the unit, that impetus for continued survival viz the bastarn grub in the pot, howsomever it be better known as the loaves and the fishes sir the poor auld starving multitudes you see they are gathering about the plates of meat sir I mean your fucking tootsies and what is to be done what is to be done you see they are to be pulling the house down about his ears sir the poor auld fucking lugs I mean you've got it being shattered all round them sir the falling bricks and mortar, the layers and layers of wallpaper for christ sake right onto their very heads sir, the respectable blooming classes sir I do beg your pardon though it should be said at this stage of the game that, yes, that eh

Although predisposed toward speculative musings the Busconductor Hines cannot be described as a dreamer. Yet certain items do not always register. That itchiness for example: the material of standard issue uniform breeks is thick and reminiscent of wool; it probably isnt wool a 100% but it seems as if this is all it can be, because of the itchiness — the coarseness of the cloth somehow making you think of the fleecy coat of a wee sheep, the straggly bits left on the barbed wire fence you can picture as hell of an itchy if dangled against the skin. Now: towards the latter stages of his last spell on the broo a certain husband and father's marked aversion to nought led him into what can authentically be called a pragmatic assessment of life, the outcome of which was his renewed determination to become a the Busdriver Hines.

Upon fulfilment of particular conditions of a positive nature the Department of Transport will allow the busconductor/busconductress to take up a position within its Training School for Busdrivers. It was the intention of Hines Robert to fulfil those conditions. Besides acquiring a licence to drive he was also expecting to realise a certain sum of money which while of unknown extension was nevertheless fixed inasmuch as he appears to have thought to recognise the sum once it had accrued.

Beyond all of that lay a future. But hazy visions of distant travel did recur. Upon receipt of his twofold objective the wild blue yonder could be vanished into, the sunbaked shores of Australasia perhaps for an open outlook, bright scapes; where one can stand on one's tiptoes and glimpse at a stretch, unlike bloody dumps where one can be lucky to get glimpsing such a thing from the topdeck of an omnibus. Take weans for instance: plant them down under and one can watch them sprout, plenty of milk and apples, vigorous limbs and sturdy bodies; where one can send them out to play and forget about everything else, unlike certain squares wherein one is obliged to think twice in case of dire imaginings one cannot hardly name lest one's head caves in.

It can scarcely be wondered at that some mothers remain so staunchly opposed to allowing their children alone out of doors — although one's upbringing can be a major factor, plenty of grass and the rest of it. The District of D. was bad enough, especially during warmer weather, seeing the green hills faraway in the knowledge one could go a lengthy walk right out to them with maybe an invigorating dip in a brackeny loch to follow. Hines knows the place inside out. During the formative years he resided there with his grey but gold family. It is a district where vacancies readily occur in most sections whereas in other sections they always occur. But Hines would flit to there. He would flit to anyfuckingwhere. Yet he will not advise Sandra of this, at least not outright, for it is of consequence to her where they flit. Her faith in specific vagaries is deeply rooted. Her parents have much to answer for.

It was their expectation she should one day meet her match in the Higher Realms. Their only son, having secured a fine situation within an established group of civil engineers and married an upstanding young lady, has now contrived to appropriate a variety of snug objects. Little wonder they should be so dumbfounded to learn of their only daughter's curious infatuation with a lowly member of the transport experience. Here they had been having a lovely young wench of a golden-haired lass whose space they assumed as a logical second step on a nailed-to-the-floor ladder. Not only was she not now moving forwards, she was falling backwards, into the lusting arms of a uniformed ne'er-do-well.

Arguments there were plenty.

But finally the day was saved by the prospective young suitor himself. And the girl had had faith in this. She knew it would happen! How in the name of christ could her parents fail to pay heed to such a vision! Did he not have a great way with Planets! Was not his perception of the Universe of an expanding and technicoloured Insistence!

If truth be told he was displaying the manifold characteristics of the Imminent Go-gettor. On subjects of a metaphysical nature he provided the family with a few stimulating evenings. Sandra had already informed them of the plethora of books to be found in his rectangle. Little wonder, therefore, that they soon gained an impression of a youth whose sights were fixed on the World of Higher Education. Having shucked off his adolescent excesses he would no doubt be buckling down to serious studies thence picking up on a rung of a not unparallel ladder to that of the Civil Engineer. All would indeed be well. And education was, after all, the Scottish Way. Surely this erstwhile nation had once been the forerunner of the concept of Equal Opportunity at a Spiritual Level. And did this spiritual levelling not include the possibility of Social Transport! Ding ding. Why, throughout the length and the breadth of this grey but gold country toty wee mites were being befriended by the Sons of the Laird and going on to become steely-eyed village dominies or gruff but kindly members of the medical profession, and even preachers of the gospel in far-flung imperial establishments.

Thus did the engagement take effect, the marriage go ahead; and soon a wean was to be born — although signs of advancement were yet to be discerned in the youth. And was he not getting a bit old to be described as a youth. At his age the girl's father (and his own father for that matter) was a serving member of the Majestic Indisputables.

Little wonder, therefore, that tensions were to arise, that Sunday visits for tea became a strain. And to be fair: was a bedsitter the ideal situation in which to rear one's firstborn. Fuck them all. The young couple conceded the point while unable to immediately rectify the problem. But at length it did transpire that through the machinations of a certain middle-aged busconductress (now retired) a dwelling place appropriate to their needs became available. It was, to be sure, as a particular father (his own) laconically remarked "a no-bedroomed flat" but it was fine for the time being. It got them out a hole. And Evelyn didnt have to go to all the bother she did. And nobody else rushed to fucking help. It wasnt a bloody dump then. You could still look out the window and see the kids in the backcourt, playing okay. It wasnt good right enough. It could not be described as good, not really, not in relation to certain grassy areas it couldnt, not at all, be described as good. But at the time. At the time it was fucking great. Shut the door and that was always that. Coming home off a late backshift, the kitchen really warm, and Sandra there with some grub in the pot, and sometimes even a bottle of fucking beer, that beautiful innocence for christ sake the gesture to the two of them, on behalf of them — the three of them for fuck sake, the unit, on behalf of them, the young marrieds and the baby

When the food had reheated he roused Paul and sat him at the table, telling him not to worry too much about finishing every last thing on the plate. His mother's absence was not bothering him too much. Weans can be unperturbed by astounding events while the slightest exaggeration can terrify them. Hines told him she was late and this he accepted as the natural order. And once the meal was over he returned to her armchair and quickly became engrossed in a TV programme relating to Concrete Manifestations of Good and Evil in a Large American City.

The utensils washed he left them drying on the draining board; he lifted Paul onto his knee, sat down on her chair. It was pointless worrying over foolish items. She had merely gone a message and forgotten to advise him beforehand.

She could have phoned Mrs Montgomery. She could have forgotten to phone in her rush to go the message. What message. She could have required to see her parents. Even his parents maybe about the New Year or something. Or just gone to see a friend. Did she have friends. Of course she had friends. She had more than he. Is that right. It is precisely right. As far as friends are concerned his is an unlucky personality.

He rose from the chair, to pour himself another cup of tea, then gazed through the blind; the street parallel to this one was clearly visible between the tenement ends. Until recently 2 dairies and a launderette and a not too bad newsagent shop had been open for business within a couple of minutes walk. Now only the one dairy whose owner no longer appeared to be restocking on anything other than perishable goods. A scandal. What did Hines intend doing about it all. Did he intend doing anything. Of course. He would burst out greeting. Tears are a fine response. They can wipe away the film.

The loss of Sandra is such an extraordinary notion that he is not able to consider it without an accompanying sense of guilt almost as of the pleasure to be had from tackling the extraordinary.

Hear the clock tick.

If she does not return the outlook is entirely bleak. If she does return the outlook is of a bleakness he can handle.

Hines can encounter problems. He can and cannot cope with many but with some the coping takes precedence. You've got the pair of them, the young married couple, the way they are to be going on ahead, into the rest of it. This is fucking a baffling thing in itself. It calls for wide heads. Think of him even, how he

wait a minute. Here you have a Busconductor Hines. How he must have been walking about in a trance and that. What he used to do was. He really didnt do. He had an idea. He conducted himself in a manner such that, his method of being, it accorded to certain factors. Certain factors appear to have governed his movements. What we know is mainly average. His goal was twofold: to obtain a PSV licence, to acquire a sum of money — a sum of money which while of unknown extension was nevertheless taken for granted as settled in some unshadowy region as for example consider the striving to a goal where the goal lies in between the lines while the lines themselves are the striving and can produce the goal seemingly in themselves but not really in themselves for the goal lies in between and though some daft cunts have no knowledge of this they assume its existence in accordance with the existence of the lines. Now this is fucking nonsense of course because there doesnt have to be any in between at all, there can be nothing whatsoever. This is what has happened to Hines. A classic case, striving for the fucking nonexistent goal. It is a strange thing. And Sandra makes it stranger — she was always a brainy bastard; and sensible. What does she do. This is a hard yin right enough.

The problem is the surrounding i.e. the flitting from here to there. Things may not be too bad.

They remain the same as before. What is not the same as before. Important side issues. He just requires help. What Hines actually requires is help.

Now: let us take it slowly, slowly and calmly. One might start off by too late it is too late, too fucking late, it is too fucking late for the shite, for this imbecilic carry on; it is too late. The problem is that it is too late. 5 years is not 10 minutes. This is the problem. Hines really does know it now, at long last, he is in full realisation of it, as he has been before right enough it has to be admitted at this stage of the game that eh he has known it before. He used to know it. He gets jolts. Jolts come along. Hines gets jolted. Certain items transpire. It is just that eh he can touch her hand, the soft bits between the joints on each finger, she has three such bits on each finger, and two on the thumb, the soft bits, and what he does is press gently his fingertips there on the soft bits, seeing the skin dimple out and whiten as flattening. Ah christ; poor auld Hines. He really is a poor soul. There he goes: see him. He's about to take care of things. He is going to get a gun. He has connections with gun-gettors. He can banish the problems. Give him an A and give him a B. Bang.

And yet the prevailing climate is not only unsound it is stabley so. Let us expand:

The position in which he is to be finding himself is no worse than that of countless others whose efforts are no longer negotiable but that that position, that position might yet have become tranquil that they could have multiplied inasmuch, inasmuch as Hines could eventually, he could have become

He was wanting that becoming.

This is what it's about. Now then: just remember the way she jumped aboard the bus. She knew as well as he did that her and the wee man, the pair of them, along with him — although to be honest, it was probably just the two of them, her and Paul, it was probably just them. And yet the presence of such as a Hines Robert could have proved a boon for all that contemporaneous conditions would appear to have rammed home a wedge that he, that he from the pair of them, Paul and herself, Sandra, that eh

A cup of coffee would certainly go down well if she was making it; a nice cup of coffee and a doughnut. Sandra likes doughnuts. So does Hines, especially if they arent snowed under by cream or something cause that can spoil it and nothing should be spoiling, a spoilsport, we dont want their kind, we need to try and get along, to face things out, consider her breasts, how soft they are, that fullness, how his lips can work upon them so well.

Out of hand it's getting. Certain factors must be brought to light. These factors are not to be being neglected. But the manner in which: what is the manner in which a gun acts. A deafening blackness by all accounts a gun goes in 1 ear and out the other. Quickly quickly quickly, the pure on the pure; 1 question and 1 question only. Give us an aye or give us a naw—because in betweens no longer exist in any scheme of the world that Hines, that he might be said to be participating within, in any intentional sense. Now, if he. He has little more to say, to be honest. The final finitos and so on. That's if he's being honest I mean if she really wants a bit of honesty from yours truly Hines, the husband, the father, of the wean by christ if she really does want an answer. And that's an actual answer, a genuine answer, none of the fucking rubbish, just a genuine answer to a genuine question being asked from an entire world. An Entire World. None of the fucking rubbish. Hines has never been Reilly. Sandra hasnt always understood this. Maybe she does. But if so there was never any point in just confining herself to those wee smiling kind of looks in the off chance what lay behind would be comprehended, as well as its contingency. Contingency by fuck — dependence on a possible future event which is not very likely. Hines would be true under certain conditions and is false under others. If certain conditions had come to pass that they were at large then he would have been being true. He would have been true under such conditions. Their recognition — such conditions. Let us consider absent

A gun right enough. It is so blatant — christ he's been playing, he's been playing.

Wait a minute. One wee fucking minute. To get it straight — just to get it straight. Right then, now: here he is in conditions, certain conditions, the astounding circumstances of which is the eh o jesus jesus dont let it be lost dont let it be lost dont he is true, he is true, he is true under certain conditions that can have come to pass, that they would be being at large. He is dependent. He is a thing that comes to life under certain conditions for if they do not obtain then he is to be being false i.e. unalive. He would be an unalive bastard, for whom death is the probable second step.

Well well well, I mean he was fucking knowing that, the Bus-conductor Hines, he has always been knowing that, for years; years are not fucking minutes.

He had been getting himself into a state; and it is daft getting yourself into a state. You sit there getting worse and worse. What is the unnameable. That which is not to be articulated. Some things are not articulately. A horror of rodents is articulately. But the things that are not unable to be not said. What about them. They are not good. They are not good but must also be good.

A taxi entered the street. He heard it while coming out of the lavatory but returned to the kitchen instead of dashing to the front room windows. If it was stopping outside the close it would stop there. He shut the door firmly though gently, Paul being asleep on the chair. And with the volume of the television down to its lowest he knelt on the floor, gazing at the images flash, a programme Concerning Topical Interests within the Halls of Planetary Finance. Often, when alone, he could experience joy from their lips, chin and neck flesh. An issue debating. Each exponent an individual method, the hearty the wry the earnest. It was interesting to see. He moved closer, mouth wide and eyes staring, and ruffling his hair till it was on end, out and in stretching his fingers into fists, clawing manoeuvres. Here you got this yin and here another. The representatives. They could all look as though choking.

His eyelids widened even farther and out poked his tongue. Then he turned up the volume and smoothing his hair down sat on his own armchair. But he got back up at once and went through to the front room, and put on a record to play, before walking to draw back the curtains, and look down at the vehicular tracks in the snow. He rejected the record, unplugged the music-centre, returned to the kitchen. Music could play but the sounds didnt connect. It made no difference burying the head beneath quilts, not even with the volume at full blast. Stronger sounds were not required. The lines had snapped. Lines extend from sound to point. When the points are absent the connection has become a shambles. Now what he really does wish to know is a problem. Upon receipt of a genuine problem he can provide an answer. Books were tried. Books are fucking hopeless. Maybe he was reading the wrong ones. Not at all. He was reading particular books after a particular method. Now this method, this method is relevant, it is relevant to eh o jesus jesus jesus how long to journey now sir is it nearly over now sir or only just beginning sir I mean aye, the younger Hines, the wee man, he keeps fucking sprouting sir he cant be stopped, he keeps on at it, the growing, he was thinking of watering his milk — Hines — he was thinking of a million things but what he will probably do is leave everything to nature, toss him a few items and let him get ahead with it. There you are son that'll sort you out, put you on the vertical path, climb aboard the social transport. Ding ding, fares please, and fuck the eskimos. The eskimos. The poor auld fucking eskimos by christ it makes you sick, the way things happen, 1 minute you've got the ball at your feet and the next you're fucked. Hines is a 3 time loser, if he jacks it this time the present is less than brightly. The broo is not the thing to do. What happened the last time. Nothing. He just couldnt get another fucking job so he had to come fucking back, and he was lucky as fuck to get back. A hands and knees carry on. Hines Robert looking for his job back. *His* job back! What does he mean *his* job back! He means his old job back sir he used to work here before sir before he left that last time, after the one before, when he left the first time, and now here he is reporting back again sir will I tell him to fuck off or what.

Jesus christ.

The point is though sir, if you exist sir, Jesus, he was to have been being on his best behaviour sir for this the third term you see he was needing your assistance sir he just required help, the Deskclerks sir, no longer asking him for overtime and they no longer wished him goodmorning and they no longer spoke unless spoken to and sometimes not even then sir for christ sake he is in dire fucking straits, honest, and he has truly given up all thoughts of getting advanced to the School for Busdrivers, a childish dream, a romantic fancy, one which has long ceased to exist in the land of real items — Real Items sir. Fuck off. Just get to fuck please, please leave.

This is no longer something that Hines is finding; and what is said — all of it — all that is said, of that, of what is going on the fucking shite going through him ear to ear a sickener, he has been sickened. That's it. The lines split and the curves tailed off. A pile of lines left lying about. Each being there for the taking. What you do is choose one — like Hines. Hines has chosen 1 and this 1 leads maybe as far as the sky and that point up there, the point is somewhere up there you see and there is no lurch backwards because the line is always curved, the choice is being made; either you fucking go or do not fucking go. Understand the position. Hines has been having a think. The curve has been perceived. What he is doing is becoming the curve that the way is forwards only, there being no backsliding nor turnoffs nor tangents of any kind; the 1 way forward, and it can even be a charge; and from this charge the 1 fell swoop delivered, the pure on the pure the red on the white; staged in an absent square; one clear stretch for one fell swoop, the sweet implementation of a rightful strategem, ah, good on you Mr Malthuse, the fresh air and the green pastures.

Paul was yawning and staring about the place, amazed to find himself where he was maybe. It was well past his bedtime. Hines helped him undress, conducting a cheery conversation about the joys of snow.

Yet the District of D. can be fine during colder weather. Hines used to live at the top of a hill and his gang held the bottom gang at bay. It was fucking great fun. Snow can be really exciting when you live in a place where it lies. You build your snowmen and that, the good slides etc. Even going to school's a laugh, throwing snowballs at the lassies, big fights in the playground, sneaking piles of it into the classroom to leave melting beneath your seat, kidding on you've pished your trousers to see the look on the teacher's face. Great; and always plenty of other kids to play with, it's good, a good place, Drumchapel's a good place.

Paul resembles either parent, depending on the position looked from. Hines had wanted him circumcised at birth but allowed himself to be dissuaded by a variety of agencies. Why had he wanted it in the first place. He wanted him different. He wanted him to think of things. And it could have been a good reminder. Every time he went to the toilet he might have been remembering what was what from his auld man's teachings. Too late now. That's the trouble with the present. Never mind.

At first sight the position he is in is of an appalling nature. It is not appalling. He is empowered to take care of items. All he desires to add as father is that the world should be admitted at an early age. This can help stop folk careering round the dump like a bunch of imbeciles — the poor auld fucking imbeciles! Sandra should never have needed telling but. She looked for him to do something. Yet if she had worked things out she would have recognised the extent of the choice. She didnt work things out. She stayed with him in the rejections but failed to see the sum as finite.

There is a clock that is ticking.

She gets set about things right enough. A person like Sandra thinks first and only acts after a great deal of thinking. A person like her will do nothing until reckoning out all that appears to matter in that connection. Then she goes and does it, bang, no bother. That's how she went fucking out and got married to him. No cunt forced her. She made up her own mind. Her parents were against it. Quite fucking right.

Hines' head gets thick.

Sandra was not acting correctly. She was going about in an absentminded manner, not really speaking to him properly. What was she speaking about: questions concerning the festive season maybe; Xmas with her parents and Hogmanay with his, the usual — although Reilly and Isobel were wanting them up to their place or something, after the Bells, they could be leaving Paul up in Drumchapel and then trying for a taxi or something, fine, it would be great to

The current situation cannot be said to be good. It is not an irretrievable disaster nor yet absolutely pathetic. Get-outs must certainly exist — although the bastards they have it so well worked you sometimes dont know if you're coming or fucking going man these real early starts where you're out the close and it's still darkly, the fucking streetcleaners man, the slipshod busworker, one whose shoulders ache; he spends his life leaning; he dishes the tickets from the pleasant machine. So what is to be done. The rude ticket dished from the pleasant machine while the replete suit of the colour bottle green on lucid days. He does hanker, however, after primaries. Let the reds also appear, and where are the blues.

It is the subtractives.

The magenta the yellow the cyan. The black. It has to be the black. To fuck with the white it's no good. The items to be being produced.

Take it calmly. Send over a cross. Up go the heads. Bang. It was a windswept wintry forenoon and the bent figure, huddling into the morrow.

Naw son, naw; nah, fucking rubbish. I'm sorry. Hines had an idea. At a certain stage he would — naw, he was not in a state of harbour. He would to have had. He had the things. What it was son, he went round in a series of rigid quicksteps. He was a funny kind of a cunt. He got a hold of facts. He would be getting a grip on such as are regarded as facts, as items not for the challenging. He got a hold of them, and his head was supposed to

Now, his head: it was a pattern producing entity. Unlooked for stuff just shot in; and while in there went dangling about till clamping together with other stuff. And the result: he wanted to be eh, an assortment of things. That's him. An assortment — smelly and not smelly. Your mummy now, your mummy. Things are very black really. There is no question of this any longer. This blackness. You take your 3 colours and stir. They mix, and then the black. This black doesnt have to be not nice. This black can be a clearing away to the transparency. Your head can get filled with the black and what comes out is distinct. Take 3 colours and stick them into your head; they clamp about on each other; and then the pattern's jet black. Onto this black other black is clamping, odd variants of it, clinging together as though merging, until at last out shoots the transparent item. Stuff like eyes are filmy and are set up for this kind of thing.

And once there it is always there. It is the magenta, the yellow, the cyan. Once the line exists they must always come in. Admitted once they can only return. There is no option. At first spasmodically it becomes more regular then constantly for christ sake that everything enters becomes the black.

And similarly the white. A lot of the time what go in are the green, the red, the blue. They go in that white is being produced. This white but is not the transparency. It is coloured that no black is to be seen. That no black can appear to exist. This is it, the whole fucking story really, of how colours come in and come out. This is what Hines is seeing, that strand, the o jesus aye, you see the thing then, happening, that it is happening now, and has always been happening, is having always been being happening. You see this clearly because of the transparency, the items produced transparent that the world has become distinct, the black transforming into the most clear, the pure, it is the purity.

And the white just makes everything opaque. And most cunts go about like this, heads chokablok with the primary rubbish that what they realize from input has been shovelled into them. And being so choking on the rubbish they cannot, they can never, never even hope, to realize the black, that depth, from there into transparency. No chance, not a fucking iota, not a solitary fucking hope.

And then you have got to do something becomes the cause. The things being seen, no longer whitewashed. It can take a while. It can rumble about for ages, in different forms even, but the result will be fine; it will be fine if allowed to come to pass. It rumbles around gathering force, then bubbling up and spewing out in terms of whatever the fuck it doesnt matter, it doesnt matter; it does not matter, fuck them all, just straight in, straight in to clear it all out.

3

She used her own key to open the front door and thereafter a while seemed to pass; she would have been taking her coat off and so on, checking to see Paul was okay in the cot, that he was sleeping. Then she was in the lobby, into the lavatory for what seemed like ages; and when she came from there she must have paused for a time in the lobby prior to opening the kitchen door. It closed and she paused again, before passing across the floor to boil a kettle of water. In a sense this was all thoughtful. She has always had particular ways of going about her business; thus Hines had planned nothing but assumed he would be staying silent. Then she was set to break the silence and he spoke. He told her of the need to understand how things would definitely be better in terms of himself, and therefore of her and Paul, the unit. There was no point really in talking about this because far better just doing things than talking about doing things. What was required was a bit of faith — not really faith, commitment; it was commitment they required, to the three of them, the unit. The situation they were in was bad but not a disaster. It was not beyond recall. A lot had to be done, practical stuff; Hines knew this. But she knew as well as he did that when it came down to it, when it came down to it he had never let her down, not really. If they were to actually split up just now it would be in a sort of uneven sense and fuck that for a game it was stupid, it really was. He wasnt bothered about this evening. He could figure out why it had happened and the rest of it. He just didnt see that it truly mattered, as long as it was perceived clearly. All he wanted was that she should understand.

Now sitting on her armchair Sandra had crossed her legs, and she was watching him, only partly relaxing when he smiled. He walked to her and stood between the wall and the side of the chair, and

107

smoothed the hair at the nape of her neck; she didnt move her head. It was the first time she had ever stayed out in this way and he could appreciate how she was feeling, how she would have had to endure certain moments of awareness while in the pub with her office friends. He bent to kiss her, and did so, on the forehead; but she was looking at him in too set that manner of hers. He shook his head, went to the sink, to await the water boiling. There was grub in the pot could be reheated but she wasnt wanting anything. Although she hadnt eaten she wasnt hungry. The others had gone for a Chinese meal but she hadnt felt like it.

He faced the oven when she seemed set to be continuing to speak.

And he was to get the coffee spooned into the cups, the boiling water from the kettle, and the milk to be poured from the bottle. His cigarette wasnt burning; he got it so from the pilot-light on the oven. Passing her a cup of the coffee he began telling her how bad he had been, cracking up almost; she has no idea, not really, she could have no real idea of how bad it had been, for the past while — almost cracking up it was so bad, really really bad. He was sitting on his chair now and making a flurry of movements with his hands and head, even his feet, and smoking rapidly, keeping her going and away, not to let her speak, needing himself to do so, to not be silent; but then, eventually, there was nothing to be said any longer. He apologised. She asked about the uneven. What was it about the uneven. He had said something about the uneven. What was it he was meaning? if they split up? in an uneven sense?

You must've meant something by it.

What.

When you said it, a wee minute ago.

He nodded; he studied the cigarette; he was holding it between fore and middle fingers, and the nicotine stains. He gazed at the ceiling, the mantelpiece. How could a gas-bill amount to so much. 1 gas-oven and 2 gas-fires, 1 of which was hardly used.

You were talking about us splitting up Rab.

What — naw; naw Sandra, what I was saying: it wouldnt be right if we split up, no just now, I mean christ sake it would be uneven, it really would, if we split up, it wouldnt be fair, it just wouldnt be fair, no to the two of us. And Paul. But forget about Paul as far as this is concerned.

O Rab.

Naw Sandra really; christ sake, we're getting fucked about; please
. . . I mean, a bit of honesty.

What?

A bit of honesty, let's have a bit of honesty; you and me; between
us, fuck sake, I dont care where you were tonight — it doesnt matter,
it doesnt matter Sandra, honest.

She was looking at him. After a few moments he glanced at the
fire, he inhaled on the cigarette. The clock that is ticking. I'm going to
bed, he said. And she nodded slightly without replying. They
continued to sit until at last he got up.

Dont go yet Rab . . .

He shrugged. Early tomorrow.

I thought it was your day-off.

Naw.

You sure?

Aye.

She glanced away from him; I've never heard you talking seriously
about us splitting up before.

A comedy. He made to speak but remained silent. She stared at the
floor. He felt himself to be caving in; he continued looking at her, and
when eventually she returned his look neither smiled; he sat back
down on the armchair.

They went on looking at each other, he with a vague smile on his
face but she had no smile on her face. It was terrible, and he got up at
once and across to her, and she was onto her feet, and they clung to
each other, her head at his shoulder. I am not playing a part in the
system of the British Greats, he muttered. And he became aware of a
something in her, that she was attempting not to cry maybe — she
hated to cry. He had to open his eyelids very widely to stop himself
from doing it.

It was a chuckle. She was chuckling. He grinned. The system of the
Greater Brits is neither here nor there, honest. He kissed her on the
lips. Your nose is hell of a cold.

She snorted.

Aw jesus christ. He laughed, I feel like getting the wee man up to
celebrate.

She kissed him.

It was him who broke the kiss. The swimming — I told him we
were going tomorrow, christ sake.

Well take him in the afternoon, get him out early from the nursery. I wont be back in time, I'm going out to the Drum when I finish.

She moved back a little, to look at him.

That's the trouble with maws and das, you've got to visit them now and again!

Her look became a frown for a moment.

Naw, he said, I've no been over for ages. I can get my tea there and maybe go out with the auld man for a pint or something — that's how I thought it would be best if I went myself, instead of . . . He shrugged: No think it's a good idea?

Well yes, I suppose so.

He pulled her into him and they kissed again but she had become absentminded about it. Christ, he went on, the things that were going through my mind! you and auld Buchanan off to the Bahamas for a winter week in the sun! No kidding ye Sandra, christ!

I wish you could actually see him.

He snorted.

No, really. You should come to the Christmas-do this year.

Ha ha ha.

You could give them a piece of your mind — it would be an ideal opportunity.

He glanced at her, then walked to his chair and lifted the tobacco tin, but replaced it; he sniffed and lifted the alarm clock, and set it for 0445 hours. A mistake making this coffee, he said, it'll probably just keep me awake . . . He drank briefly, emptied the rest of it down the sink and rinsed out the cup, leaving it on the draining board. I better go to bed.

She was still watching him.

I need a sleep, he said, while walking over to the recess and tugging the jersey up over his head and shoulders. It's okay.

What's okay?

What.

What's okay Rab . . . she was saying it isnt okay at all Rab, really. He had shut his eyelids. But in her set voice she continued on saying it to him, that it was not okay at all, as though she had decided long before that this would have to be said tonight but had only remembered this very minute or else had maybe just found the right opportunity. Ever since coming home she had been about to say it; he had been sidetracking her. She said: We cant carry on the way it is just now Rab, we cant.

I know.

Well then . . .

Well then something's going to happen, that's the well then, something's going to happen.

O God. She smiled, and shook her head.

Thanks, thanks a lot, that's smashing. He sat on the edge of the bed and took off his socks. Your ironic wee smiles.

I wasnt being ironic.

Naw, sorry, it was a genuine smile of a friendly nature, I just misread it.

I dont need any of your bloody sarcasm.

Good, fine. He had undressed and was now in bed, pulling up the sheets, and gazing at the ceiling.

That's it finished I suppose!

That's what finished?

O God.

Look I'm fucking tired Sandra that's how I'm in bed — I've been sitting worrying about you all fucking night.

Dont start blustering.

Blustering!

Yes, blustering, the times you've stayed out! bloody cheek, it's just different for me.

I've no done it for ages, ages; christ sake.

No, you just dont go to your work and never tell me and then when I ask you you tell me a bunch of lies, a bunch of bloody lies.

Lies. What was she talking about lies. It's because I dont want to worry you.

Why? what d'you think I am? you dont want to worry me, Rab! I've been married to you for 5 bloody years!

Hh; christ. He got out of bed in a movement and went to the lavatory; and back into bed, pulling the sheets to his chin, and turning to face into the recess wall.

Her chair had been shifted and she sat so that she could have been looking into the fire — although a magazine was lying on her lap.

ooo

111

Things passed sluggishly. All kinds of items. He was fancying a similarity between it and what was supposed to happen to people that instant prior to death. What a fucking jumble and yet also quite coherent. The idea of laughing aloud occurred, and made him smile. The clock. He raised himself to see the time: apparently 20 minutes had elapsed since the alarm clock sounded. It seemed like 20 seconds. Too late now to make any breakfast, not even time for a coffee, and coffee would have been delicious. What like would a coffee have been. Delicious. And Sandra; snuggling into her; what like would this snuggling into her have been like. There you have a body warm and soft; the woman you love and are sleeping with and want to sleep with, to continue this sleeping with; she's lying beside you not conscious. And not to be conscious of last night if abruptly wakened so that the possibility of breaching the divide through physical arousal must exist, the slightest touch on her shoulder, and moving to her.

He was out of bed, wanting a smoke. Smoking helped him get out of bed on bad mornings. Without that to look forward to he would be an even worse timekeeper. And yet he wasnt the worst of timekeepers because the worst of timekeepers had already got the boot. The Busconductor Hines has yet to get the boot. This should be remembered. As should the following proposition: The longer one remains in a job the more difficult it becomes to get sacked. They keep him in the job. Mayhap they have resigned themselves to the fact of Hines. He is already a fixture. In the years to come, when one-man-buses rule the roost, they will have him cast and hoisted above the garage exit, as an example of The Busconductor.

Before leaving he touched Sandra on the shoulder but decided against taking a look in on Paul — too sentimental. Life is difficult.

Crunch crunch crunch. The snow turned slush turned ice. What a transformation! And all the hand of that mutable nature as well! it makes you think right enough. Take the clockwork universe: aye, just pick it up and set the wheels in motion; tick tock etcetera; just lay it down now, aye, that's correct, the broad shoulders will attend to such a burden.

The brisk march along the wintry city streets at 05 something hours. The discreet tenements on either side, high and yielding efforts while straight above them the blankly grey clouds firmly, permanently, hanging there.

Pause.

The fellow rolls a cigarette. The charlatan did not accept his just reward in the house cum flat but employed it to advance himself towards his place of work. Now that he has come so far it would appear there is to be no turning back.

Glasgow thoroughfares can be mysteriously still, the slightest breath of wind seeming not to exist. The smell of fresh tobacco on the nostrils first thing is an astonishing item. Did you hear the one about the woman with the green lips. A disgusting verbal jape. There is no time for such knavery; come on there you there Hines! get crunching to your fucking place of work, the poor auld punters by christ they await, they stand chittering at bleak outposts, their pitiful attempts to retain body heat while where is the blooming bus. O for fuck sake but it's freezing man can you imagine lying in your kip, the breakfast in bed and that, brought by this amazing big blonde with no knickers.

Shut up ya cunt I'm going to my work.

Naw but imagine it man you're lying there sound asleep, right out the game, then a wee nudge on the shoulder, eh darling, eh darling, you awake, you ready for a bit of morning fare, here's the paper, the mug of piping hot coffee to get you going, your tin's at the side of the bed, aye, just reach across while she's getting off the clothes. Fucking nonsense: get to your work ya cunt ye.

Look at him stride! In the name of christ his legs might fall off. Naw but he quite likes walking — it makes a fucking change! Gaaa haaa ha. Ding ding. Heh you there laddie, the greyly black boots and brown leather cashbag; pick up these heels of yours, let's be having you, king and country laddie king and country; hup two three now hup two three, she'll be coming round the mountains when she comes, she'll be coming round the mountains when she comes, she'll be coming round the mountains, coming round the mountains

Life is too serious.

Hunch the shoulders and march. The furtively fast figure. One fine morning Hines R. was arrested. Crackle crackle crackle. We have this fantasy coming through on the line sir should we tape it and hold it against him or what. Naw but honest sir he's just a lowly member of the transport experience; he slept in a little and perforce is obliged to walk it to work, having missed the staff bastarn omnibus. A certain irony granted but nothing more, no significance of an insurrectionary nature.

He was chuckling as he pushed back the chair. His waybill remained blank. He had neglected to fill in the opening numbers and names and dates — it would appear he had always been allowing for just such a decision. He grinned, swallowed the rest of the lukewarm tea, thanked the conductor who had supplied the second-hand tea-bag.

The bothy was full of people all talking and not talking; it was great to see. Gathering his chattels he bade the cheerios and walked to the door. But it opened just as he arrived and he had to withdraw his hand to keep from being struck. McCulloch and Colin Brown. They wanted to chat a minute. A rumour about him jacking the job as a point for discussion. Returning with them to a table he sat down to recount the one about the woman with the green lips but that cunt Reilly had already told them it. He left immediately, along the corridor and downstairs where he paused to roll a cigarette. But could he afford to be seen smoking. Would going sick with a bad stomach retain the hallmarks of authentic reasoning if the subject were to state the case amid clouds of blue. He would be laughed off the premises. Into the washroom and into a cubicle in the lavatory area where an ancient *Sun* had been jammed behind a cistern pipe. But there was plenty of toilet paper. According to the retired conductor who cleaned the place the average amount stolen per week could reach to twenty rolls during a one to two month period. Having to account for this curious situation was one of the less gratifying aspects of his job, and Hines often had occasion to cheer the fellow up by pointing to the more gratifying aspects of which there were plenty in comparison to plying the decks of streetfaring vehicles of a public service nature.

The door into the lavatory area opened. Somebody shouting him by name.

He had been studying the marks on his knees, old scars, from playing football, actual dents in the skin, a sappy kind of surface, unlined; one scar in particular he recollected, the doctor or doctor's assistant having to scrub vigorously with a brush, to clean out the

114

flesh, getting rid of the dirt and gravel, using a red ointment substance that the patient could not tell what was blood and what was ointment. For the garage football team: what a business.

It was the driver shouting on him. Sorry, he replied; he was not able to fulfil the duties of the day because of the pains he was getting. Was he kidding. No. And the driver was to inform the Deskclerk about Hines having to sign-off sick. Would it not be better if the driver just waited a minute to see if maybe Hines began to feel more healthy. No. There was no chance of his making it through an entire shift due to the condition he was in. What condition was he in. A fucking terrible condition. In fact he had been up all night with it. The Deskclerk would have to get a spare conductor to take over. But Hines would go in and tell the Deskclerk himself just as soon as he felt capable of leaving the fucking cludgie.

When the door banged shut he made to leave; stupid — too early; he sat down again and made to unjam the *Sun* but it wasnt safe to touch. He rolled another cigarette. At length McCulloch and Colin Brown entered the area, to be standing on the opposite side of his cubicle door, shouting if that was him in there. We can smell your clatty tobacco ya cunt. Heh, how can you sign-off sick if you've no even started. Their laughter. Wait will Reilly hears this yin right enough. Heh, you really got diarrhoea. Just as well he didnt — fucking place, you're not even allowed to have a shite in private. He waited several minutes after they had gone; and when he walked into the Office he was massaging his belly.

The Deskclerk glanced at him then turned his back.

Hines sniffed and went back upstairs to replace his machine-case. The voices in the bothy could be heard in the corridor. The canteen would not open until 0730 hours; and a further hour from then until the snooker room opened. The thing to do was leave the garage completely and immediately, of course.

A lot of bustle outside in the yard. More buses departed the garage between the hours 0615 and 0700 than at any other time during the 24. Drivers checked radiators and conductors checked destination screens and waybills, then hung about chatting together and with members of the blacksquad who were ready to go home from nightshift. McCulloch was sitting at the wheel of one bus. Hines waited until its engine revved then he trotted across and aboard. He grinned at the pair of them. Perhaps a brief account of the future was in order. Then you're a grandfather and dead thank christ. He shook his head.

There is a road from Yoker goes near the Forth & Clyde Canal — across the Great Western Road which is an amazing road, stretching to the beautiful sights: from the centre of Glasgow it runs such that if a tourist asks how to get to Loch Lomond, Glen Coe, Fort William, Loch Ness, the Shetland fucking Islands, you can more or less tell he or she just to drive straight out on this yin jimmy and that's you — and leads right into the District of D.

He was not smoking when Colin Brown came upstairs but began rolling one as though preparing for a friendly chat. Colin likes to talk to him on serious subjects. He regards him as a potential force in garage politics. Recently he has been making hints about Hines accompanying Reilly on an electioneering campaign: with one as Shop Steward and the other as Branch Secretary what will be that which is not to be being accomplished.

But said Brown C. has accomplished something heretofore outwith the reach of said Hines R. He has attended the School for Busdrivers. The silly cunt failed right enough but he must be granted a second shot fairly soon. And he will surely pass then. McCulloch gives him a go at the wheel at certain remote terminuses at specific times of the late night and early morning and his confidence grows no end. Reilly has offered this to Hines in the past but Hines had been unable to accept. Why is that. Even just for the experience it might have been worthwhile.

This busdriving licence is a watershed for some folk. Apparently Colin and his fiancée have agreed not to name the day until he is finally driving his own wee bus. Incredible how it affects people. There was definitely a sparkle about Colin. It was the licence. Even while speaking of the licence Colin sparkled.

Then he stopped. He had become self-conscious. He glanced out the window, the bus had pulled into the kerb to collect a passenger. He changed his fare-stage. He was aware of the future of Hines and was experiencing a terrible guilt. Eh! poor auld fucking Rab the unfortunate bastard with his wife and 38 weans who, unless content to remain as conductor for the rest of his working garage life, is definitely best to chuck the job right now and get it over with. Eh! Fuck off.

Hines grinned, and patted him on the arm. There was a middle-aged man sitting a few seats to the front; he had raised his bunnet to scratch the back of his head. It was an amazing thing and obviously symbolic. Hines chuckled. He got off at Yoker.

He had begun by walking at an even stroll but gradually quickened to something nearer a stride while managing to keep it even paced. He could have changed buses earlier on the journey to avoid this trouble, but it was no trouble. It was fine to be walking. Brisk right enough; not a strong wind — more the sharp breeze which nevertheless went right through you and caused great pain to the ears. A balaclava would have been ideal. His mother had knitted one for Paul but not for him. This maternal neglect had not upset him. Still and all, ears are open entities, important items. One might have expected the Department of Transport to take care of such detail. Deaf conductors would certainly be a liability. Uniform hats are fine for parading but not much cop for the Arctic hike. Perhaps removable ear-flaps could be invented — clip-on fashion; the conductor to remove them during warmer weather, apply them during colder weather, and so on. A straightforward idea, awaiting a likely inventor whose patent of same would ultimately yield a cash return of infinite extension.

Hines could be that inventor. The Good Lord knows he needs the money. This week's wages for last week's workings amount to well nigh fuck all; and next week's wages for this week's workings is a ludicrous example of the parsnip. In the name of christ. And yet certain possibilities concerning future weeks are not, however, absent. Rumours of overtime being enjoyed by those and such as those continue to proliferate despite persistent denials from the crawling bastards in receipt of same. With maximum luck one could be netting a fortune. A week of backshift beginning at 1600 hours would allow some 11 extra working hours daily. If one were to be

117

granted another shift in the morning hours one could be earning double wages — in fact it would be more than double wages since overtime rates must operate. 5 extra shifts per week would throw a minimum of 40 hours onto the basic plus $\frac{1}{2}$ this extra 40 for the overtime time and a half rate. A round 100 hours of a wage. Plus if 2 of the days fell at the weekend there would be additional cash since to work a Sunday even as an ordinary day will throw time and a half. And the same applies to Saturdays after 1300 hours — which gives an extra 12 to be tacking onto the 100, plus of course the additional possibility of getting working both days-off, which at time and a half equals another 24 onto the 112 making 136 in all plus if the days-off chanced to be a Saturday by christ and it was after 1300 hours then the rate gets doubled to treble time which is 24 for working 8, throwing another 12 onto the 136 so what is that for fuck sake must be near about 148 hours, a hundred and forty-eight hours, of a wage, all rolled nice and tidy into the 1 week's wage-packet, the future being more than darkly.

Hines had slowed down; his pace now increased. Forces were pushing him. The uniformed employees and mechanics, the black-squad — even the office fuckers; they were all in unspoken league, edging him onto the brink and beyond. Having recognised the futility of certain methods of advance they had now chosen him as representative — leader was to go far too far. He was to represent them. By struggling ahead with life he would be showing the way. Could this be true. Did he have something they didnt. At an early age he had sucked in the ultimates. He had revealed a marked ability to steer clear of a special type of conventional motion. Nothing was, it would seem, being left to chance. Even the circumstances surrounding nowadays were part and parcel of the whole. All went to force the point's arrival, hence departure; and speculations concerning the when were irrelevant. That kind of stuff can be stowed away. There can be no settled moment, rather a mass of moments; because of this a great deal can be taken as granted.

Maybe his father would slap him on the back, as an indication his trip out had been expected, and lead him down to the *Glen* for a pint and a laugh over the bad quarrel they'd had that last time. Surely Hines had never taken it seriously! Aye. Well well well son an odd bundle of turnips. So you didnt even recognise it as part and parcel of the whole! well well well right enough. Never mind but all to the good, all to the good. What we had planned in fact because it was hopeless you getting here too soon. You had to be ready, in the precise frame of mind. And now everything is seen to fit. Settled from the hour of birth. Your maw always enjoyed a seascape son: now you know why — you couple that with my view from the window and there you have it, the A going to B that the C has become a picture.

That it has been revealed to Mr Hines that his son is the representative is fine, fine; but what about his own wee boy, Paul, what about him.

Just a son, just a son; another tomorrow, He could even have a more strenuous time of it, since Hines wouldnt be getting beyond the moment; by his not getting beyond the moment Paul would be obliged to account for much of what is to follow — although Sandra would see him through. It is down to her to show him the road. While what will she be doing. She will be getting ahead with things. What things. She will ascertain that which is to be done and go ahead and fucking do it. Fine. Not fine at all. At times like the present 1 or 2 items cannot be dwelt upon. Especially when cutting through from Y to D because of the route taking one to the outer skirts of High Amenity Zone K. He could have walked 20 minutes out his way to gaze in his parents-in-law's living room window. That would've been a fine how-d'ye-do. Pardon me, is that the nose of one's daughter's spouse pressed against the glass. Fuck off.

A sylvan setting. Around that area the snow lies at deeper levels for longer periods. In the gardens the grass is covered, toty holes indicating the shoots; trees to make you feel like pulling the branches to see the snow shower down. Hines hates the place. It is not to be wondered at. He has always been glad it is to always be beyond him. The fellow is quite weak. Entities like space could have demolished him. He might well have succumbed to a life of ease, growing old in the pursuit of vegetables.

But vegetables may be grown in D. A lot of people out there are also proud of their gardens, particularly during the long hot summers at which time it is a paradise. The weans go rushing off and enjoy themselves daily when the school hols are in progress and things arent falling from the sky so that rushing about bareheaded can be comfortable.

When he reached the shopping centre it was still early, only newsagents were open. He purchased a newspaper, entered a shop doorway to keep out the way of everything.

His fingers had become very cold. He pressed them against the glass to obtain heat from the interior Xmas lights. On the window itself a lot of frosty stuff and tinsel were pasted, and on the ledges and floor inside was a great display of goods built round a feature involving the Splendid Tassels of the Future Chief of the Britons. He winked. Then folding away his newspaper he put his hands into his trouser pockets.

Weans had begun to appear; and all sorts of dogs were prowling about in that unfurtive manner, having folk alter stride to allow them passage, and they werent noisy. There was little noise of any kind. He recognised a face, a woman who lived quite near his parents' place. She was cleaning in a big department store; she had pushed open the glass door at the side to attend to the wide tiled floor immediately outside. Steam rose from the bucket of hot water which she nudged ahead with her mop as she progressed. Obviously a method derived from maximum experience, she would be using less energy than others perhaps, and to more effect. Probably her mates were employed in different sections within. Shortly they would knock off for a quick cup of tea and a buttered scone, and a cheery chat, before completing their tasks for the day. It was great to see. She had a son 2 to 3 years older than Hines who used to be a terrible footballer, but played the pipes in a Boys' Brigade band; he rarely spoke to boys younger than himself but occasionally nodded to Hines because their mothers were acquainted. What was he doing now. Hines hadnt seen him for 10 years. Maybe he was married and now living in South Africa. Or he could have settled in England, in London probably, quite near to Hines' young sister.

The woman didnt see him at first. He had the tin out and was licking the gummed edge of the rice-paper. Sticking the tin back into the cashbag he lighted the cigarette and said, Hullo Mrs Noonan.

She started, frowning, moved back a pace as though to focus precisely, but she was not wearing spectacles. She said: You gave me a jump.

Ah, sorry.

How's your mother?

Fine. I just saw you there. He sniffed. Cold yin this morning, eh!

It is . . . She had continued mopping but wasnt signalling an end to the conversation, and she smiled that he should carry on speaking, instead of which he walked on without immediately looking back. He walked round to the front of the complex and stopped at a place where a few people were queueing for a bus, standing well back from the kerb though there was no slush about. Then he continued on, that instant prior to being asked questions on the scheduling of the city transport. If anyone was to give a derogatory mutter he would return at once to challenge the largest body to a fight. And so what if it should prove a woman! He could knock her to the ground and stick the boot in. That would teach the bastards.

He was gripping the cashbag; he relaxed. Yet he hadnt been angry at all — just tense perhaps. Seeing the woman there maybe had something to do with it. Aside from that, aside from that there was nothing of any real significance. Life is simply too bad to be true at times and there's a fucking end to it.

About to return into the shopping centre he set off in the opposite direction on to the top of the street, right across the road and along. Everything familiar of course, except the faces, but it was doubtful he would have recognised anyone bar a contemporary, which might have been weird — this part of the district used to be hostile territory. A bus approached. He waved it down. A 1-man-operated effort. He passed the man without comment, to sit near to the rear; and remained there until the terminus and back down the hill again where he got off and continued walking.

A boy dashed out a close, down the flight of steps in a jump to go skidding right out across a patch of ice, and he fell but was then on his feet and running; an elder boy pursued him and it was not until about 100 yards on that he paused to examine himself and rub his elbows and back. The elder boy also paused, probably wondering whether to stay in pursuit; he did, walking steadily onwards.

Quickening his stride Hines soon caught up with him and as he passed he murmured, Touch him and I'll give you a doing son I'm warning you.

And he strode on at the same stride, trying not to chortle but also aware of possible snowballs or bricks being heaved at the back of his head. The younger yin had crossed the road — this was Andy, his young brother, a cheery wee cunt always pulling some stunt or other and being clouted by the methodical big brother — and was frequently glancing back over his shoulder, the superficial bravado, while the elder yin — poor auld Hines — kept relentlessly on. By this time he would no longer be sure whether he had heard a genuine threat or just dreamt the fucking thing, an unknown voice of probable retribution all set to pounce towards the backend of the formative years; merciful heavens right enough. Yet the belting couldnt be avoided. The younger yin would be captured and that would be that. The poor auld fucking elder yin had to get a grip of him. He had to. That would be that. Hines had clouted his young brother quite a lot, not into the teens. During the teens he gave him a few terrible tongue lashings. One of them was so bad it reduced him to tears. It was a remarkable thing. Possibly it could have stopped a heart from beating. It was horrible. Such a power, making somebody

Dont tell me yous're on a bloody go-slow!

A pensioner of the male variety standing on a grass verge by a bus-stop. He seemed to be expecting an answer. This crabbit wee red face shouting on about timetables in a tone of voice that conveyed a total lack of willingness to hear a genuine reply.

But ice-bound roads are always irrelevant in this fucking city. So too the perennial shortage of able bodies. He had stared at Hines with a really fierce expression on the countenance. Abuse was out of the question. What would have been the point, the auld cunt, standing chittering there, a constant drip from the nostrils, in a patch of spare earth, the few thin trees in a kind of formation, waiting for a fucking bus.

Amazing but; how people are conned into thinking high unemployment means parsnips are not in demand. That's the trouble with the lower orders, they're a bunch of bastarn imbeciles. As though emphasising the point a girl was just then ejected from a close, being pushed out by a youngish woman — the mother — who forced the girl to march ahead by a series of sharp digs in the small of the back, displaying her scapegoat for the catastrophic state of the steel industry. That spot on the back is maybe his favourite on the whole of Sandra's body, right at the base of her spine, this wee bit which is always so warm. The mother was wearing slippers never-theless, and ice needing to be crunched. A right fucking headcase. She dug the girl on toward the small cluster of local shops. Probably the girl had been sent a message earlier and been short changed by the thief who owns the newsagent, or maybe she had purchased an incorrect item. What a performance! The woman quite wee, with long black hair, the coat unbuttoned.

All in all a scene to avert the face from.

Hines followed them into the newsagent. Pandemonium inside. Weans everywhere, and a few disgruntled adults — and these latters having astonishing sets to their bearing to indicate extraordinary emotional control, as they stared to the dwarfs jostling each other along the counter, poking around in the boxes of sweetmeats and generally ignoring all known rules of social conduct concerning orderly procedure. But the thief's trio of assistants was performing wonders, serving a minimum pair of adults to the 1 child.

He had bought a ½ ounce, rice-papers and matches; and he rolled a smoke in a shop doorway.

Along the street music blared from a 1st storey window, a teenage girl leaning out, chatting to three others at the long entrance to the close. Farther on somebody called to him. A man he knew. He returned a hello and continued on up the hill where on the road the grit should have been lying very thickly. He passed the close where he used to live.

One of Griff's three daughters opened the front door. She left him and came back with her mother. He smiled and made to speak but she had turned, and she showed him into the living room. Once she had gone the daughter entered, to remain for quite a while, just looking at him occasionally, pretending to be engrossed with the objects inside and on top of a glass display-cabinet; she was called away. Hines lifted a newspaper from beneath a coffee-table.

Several minutes went by till Griff appeared. Hines had heard him being shouted awake. When he came in he took a cigarette from a battered packet on the mantelpiece and switching on the electric-fire he crouched over it with his back to Hines. Then his wife entered carrying two mugs of tea. That can of lager, he said.

What can of lager?

Look I brought one back with me last night.

No to this house you didnt. And she went out, closing the door. Griff glanced at Hines, pursing his lips; then the door opening again;

Mind you've to sign-on this morning . . . And it closed immediately.

Griff stared at the door. How can I sign-on if you'll no give me the bloody bus-fare! Crouching back over the fire he rubbed his hands, inhaled on the cigarette, blinking as the smoke hit his eyes. These weans no away to school yet! he added. He looked at Hines, shook his head briefly.

Hines sniffed; he had prised the lid off the tin and paused, he sipped at the tea. Taking a paper from the Rizla packet, and the door opened: Naw, they're no away to school yet.

Griff had moved onto the nearest armchair and lifted the mug of tea from the coffee-table.

Hines said, How's your maw keeping?

They took her back into hospital.

Aye, I heard.

Ah she's okay, no bad, she was talking the last time I was up, a wee bit — you could make out what she was saying.

Good.

Griff yawned then shuddered, shaking his head: Fucking freezing man eh! A team of huskies you need for the hill. You should've seen them coming out the boozer last night! pantomime on ice so it was. O by the way man your name cropped up.

Hines looked at him.

Milligan.

Aw aye.

He was saying he bumped into you a wee while ago.

Aye — he's doing alright eh?

What! fucking loaded the cunt — these oilrigs man to listen to him you'd think they were 5-star fucking hotels or something — the grub they get. T-bone steaks man; and the cunts're leaving half of them on the fucking plate: right out of order so it is — all gets dumped into the fucking sea.

Ah well at least we'll get fat fish.

Griff snorted.

The door opened and the girl entered with her younger sister; they kissed Griff and said cheerio. On their way back out he asked them to see if the toast was ready yet. The door closed he said: So you're still on the buses!

Naw, grunted Hines, and he flicked the hat off the settee onto the floor and stretched to kick at it.

At least it's a fucking job man. Any vacs?

Aye, four hundred and twenty seven. Naw. Hines shrugged. No for conductors. If you could drive . . .

Ach I dont fancy these fucking shifts anyhow. Griff yawned, swallowed some tea. So how's the maw and da these days?

Away up and see for yourself.

For fuck sake man you've got to ask these questions; it's called fucking politeness I mean battering the door at all times of the morning when cunts're trying to kip!

Ah christ, I've been up for days.

Aye you get paid for it but.

Naw I dont; propaganda.

Griff raised his eyebrows and sighed, gazed briefly at the ceiling. On the wall to his left the small picture of King Billy on his white horse, athwart Boyne Water. Hines grinned and nodded to it: I see you still like the cowboys Griffin.

He had been exhaling smoke, and he smiled a moment. He glanced at the door and it opened. His wife and youngest daughter — an infant; she was clutching a blanket to her mouth and toddled to squeeze her way in beside Griff on the armchair. The plateful of toast on the coffee-table.

No cheese?

In the fridge. I'm going to the shop, she added. She paused, then she looked at Hines and indicated the toast.

Thanks Rita.

She nodded. How's the family?

Aw fine, okay.

We need fags, said Griff.

Is your da still working?

Aye.

It's just the one you've got?

A wee boy — four and a half.

That's right . . . After a moment she nodded then walked to the door.

Mind the fags, said Griff as it closed.

They munched the toast without speaking. The girl occasionally twisted to touch Griff's head then would stare at Hines, the blanket almost obscuring her face. And when Hines eventually prepared a cigarette she studied his movements, and he rolled it slowly, sitting

125

forwards for her to see more easily. Griff said, I could never be bothered with that — no patience.

It's no patience you need man it's skill.

Griff snorted.

It's an art.

Griff raised his eyebrows and he reached for the last piece of toast; then he said: How's the wife? what's her name again — Sandra?

Aye; ah she's alright.

Still got the wee job?

Hines nodded.

That's good.

Aye, it's a help right enough . . . He struck the match; he had been waiting for Griff to get another cigarette from the packet on the mantelpiece; when he had lighted his own he passed across the burning match. Heh how's wee Frank doing these days? you ever see him?

Hh. Griff put the match into the ashtray, he frowned: No if I can bloody avoid it. A Peter Pan that yin.

He's still going about but?

Aye, unfortunately. He's jumping around *The Glen* with a young team. When you see him you walk the other way. Naw Rab, a headcase, worse than ever he was . . . He sniffed, made to rise. How? you're no wanting to see him are you!

Hh; naw.

Griff had risen from the chair, holding the girl in one arm; he collected the mugs and went ben the kitchenette, and returned with refills of tea. The girl got up onto the chair before him. He shook his head as he sat down. That last time he got lifted, they'd stuck a blade in some poor . . . no reason nor nothing.

It wasnt him but, no as far as I heard.

Aw Rab, Christ sake.

Hines shrugged.

I mean you dont know him now man; he's no the way he was at school.

I'm no saying that; I'm just saying it wasnt him that actually done it.

Ah! Griff snorted, shook his head. He's a headcase Rab he's a headcase. A wean. Showing off to the young team and that, makes you . . . bloody sick.

126

Hines grinned after a moment. Sorry, sorry sorry sorry! He held his hands palms outwards.

Naw, these . . . Griff shook his head. He raised the girl and sat her on his knee, bounced her a couple of times then sniffed and lifted her up to smell the nappy. Away and get your potty hen. He put her onto the floor then got up and opened the door for her.

Christ, good for her age!

Aye. Griff smiled.

What is she anyway?

Just turned two.

What!

Aye, yaps like fuck as well — you can hold a conversation with her. He grinned as he sat down.

That's great man.

Aye well, you just having the one and that . . . he shrugged. The other pair talk to her so she picks it all up — she could be at the nursery the now. They've got her doing her sums. Ask her 2 and 2 and she'll tell you 4. She doesnt know what it is right enough but she'll fucking tell you anyway. Griff chuckled. He sniffed. Actually I better see she's alright and that.

When he returned he left the door ajar.

Hines had lifted a book from beneath the coffee-table and was reading the blurb.

Take it with you if you want. I finished it yesterday. No bad, it's about this guy's retired from the Secret Service, finds out his auld boss's been done in and that, so he rejoins to get after the cunt that did it.

Hines nodded. After a moment he reached to replace it but he sat back with it again, flicked through the pages; he grinned. I wonder if it's these pesky fucking commies to blame?

Griff glanced at the ceiling. D'you never give up!

How can I when cunts like you're still voting fucking tory!

Ach away and give us peace!

Hines grinned.

Griff laughed. The brainbox of 3c! He laughed again. Heh man mind that baldy auld geography teacher!

O christ! I wouldnt say he was a thingwi but you should see the way he thingwis his thingwi.

The two of them laughed for a while. Eventually the girl pushed her way in carrying some dolls along with the blanket. Hines glanced at the electric-clock on the wall, and Griff noticed.

Naw, said Hines; he reached for his hat. I just thought I'd take a walk up, since I was passing and that.

Griff nodded.

That's the trouble with nowadays, you've got to see the parents once in a blue moon . . . He stood up, buttoning the uniform jacket. Heh you fancy nicking down for a pint later on?

Naw no me, the time I get back from the broo and that. He stubbed the cigarette dowp into the ashtray, and rose from the chair.

Eh, etcetera, sorry and so on, getting you out of bed at godforsaken hours of the day.

Ah I was having to get up anyway. So . . . Griff paused, glanced at Hines.

Hines shrugged.

Take a run over the centre some Saturday, me and Hammy and a few of the boys, we're always there round dinner-time — the ITV 7 and that; if we're no in the boozer we'll be in the betting shop — collecting the dough!

Hines grinned, then snorted. I dont even know what a Saturday looks like.

Griff chuckled. Is it no about time you jacked it in man? I mean Christ, how long's that now?

Ah no long, no long, just a miserable 38 year. Hines got a 10 pence coin from his trouser pocket and handed it to the girl. Watch your auld man doesnt spend it on drink!

ooo

It was only because he was in the district that he was sitting in the home of his parents. It had not been the purpose of his visit. And if the auld man had been present the whole thing would have been beyond talking about. Bad enough with the maw. How to speak to her even. What is important concerning a mother. There you have the weans and their way ahead. Nothing wrong in that, perfectly

128

reasonable. Three of them to get worried about. The youngest a lassie working in England who telephones quite regularly and is the favourite of the dad; perfectly natural — and she and Hines were close in childhood; and then she got very upset on her most recent visit home, last Hogmanay, in company with her boyfriend. The discussion had begun in general terms but finally involved only her and Hines. Sandra, the boyfriend, and mother were present — father having previously retired to bed having consumed too much to drink. It was a strange kind of situation altogether and no one had seemed to feel at home. Apparently Hines acted badly but doesnt regret any of it. The boyfriend was working in a good job which wasnt his fault and he came from the English Home Counties which also wasnt his fault and he spoke with this fucking amazing English accent which also might not have been his fault but who can tell; one would require to know how the cunt's family, friends and neighbours conversed in order to settle the point. Anyway, that was irrelevant. What mattered was the wage (and Barbara's wage if it comes to that). It was an extraordinary piece of business. As an illustration of how Hines felt about it all he ventured that he might have to vomit when he saw the boyfriend being friendly to Paul. There was, of course, nothing wrong in being friendly to weans, doing your bit and so on, when they've become bored and tired in adult company. It was just a sharp sensation of nausea. He just didnt want the cunt playing with him — bad enough having to speak to him but imagine having your wee boy actually touched by the cunt, actually fucking touched; jesus christ, too much. It was nothing personal. Hines had explained how the thing was genuinely distanced from individuals as such. And to be honest, the boyfriend wasnt too bad a cunt. This is always the fucking trap. Hines was able to drink with him and shake hands with him at *The Bells* and the rest of it. But not for the actual future. That would have been too shameful.

His mother was uneasy in his presence. He was bothered and not bothered. Always when he spoke to her he had to underline everything in sarcasm. Terrible. He was not able to get free of it. Even now as she asked after Paul he was having to let her perceive how he regarded the boy's existence as a total waste of time. A silence developed and lengthened. He became embarrassed and annoyed with himself for getting her into the situation. He got up and went to the window, to gaze at the high-rise flats across the way. Before they had been erected the auld man used to sit here in the evening, the main light switched off, witnessing the shades of grey. Hines got held there by the elbow, a desperate attempt by the father to instil some peace unto him. He must have reckoned the view capable of curious tricks, tossing off rays of solace during the long hot summer evenings as the sun went down, that much needed glimpse of the indefinite for those who dwelled up the hill.

The contact was an embarrassment. Yet Hines cannot be certain the auld man was being totally serious — he always had a peculiar sense of humour — sitting there with the cutains pulled right back and making a great metaphysical issue out of this seeing and not talking.

This business of the evening window sitting was treated by the mother in the following manner: she gave the weans to understand that their daddy had to have his moment of contemplation daily in order that he might continue after the fashion in which he had allowed them to have him become accustomed.

What an auld man! Hines could jump for joy right out the fucking window. Instead of which he returned to his seat to await tea. When she had brought it she kept on the move tidying odds and ends, unable to remain still lest conversation became primary. Hines mentioned the Festive Season, confirming the presence of himself and family on the night of the New Year, the Holy Bells of Hogmanay. My my my he was really looking forwards to the celebratory practices. How's it going mammy. Give us a kiss for the morrow.

A sandwiched lurked on a plate. He had told her not to bother but there it lurked, and he was to eat it as one of many, as one for whom alternatives did and did not exist in the true scheme of things. He bit a large mouthful of the bread, and cheese, as though by blocking his mouth and respiratory system his digestive system would be forced into taking action; he sipped the tea to aid its progress. O christ he felt like chucking it. A good greet could solve everything. She would settle his head against her breasts, pat his back rhythmically, crooning an auld scotch sang till he toppled off the edge to go crashing on the jaggy boulders below. A mother's love is that which is required. Thrust me back in out the road for fuck sake mammy I need to hide away, away. It was awful the way she could look at him. Hard to tell whether she was allowing him to see she was looking — maybe she was being caught in the act. Or maybe she wasnt doing anything at all, just gazing in abstraction, this gaze chancing to alight on him while moving around on nothing whatsoever in particular for christ sake. No; she looked at him; and knew he was not now ever going to hit the High Spots. Too late. Even a mother's dreams will have faded.

And if he had spoken aloud: that strain on her face.

Downstairs a vacuum cleaner roared. New folk. In the past decade only one family has moved from the close. This is reason for pride. In other closes a constant toing and froing and general mutability but not here; here are permanent folk, the good tenants. He mentioned Griff's mother earlier on but the conversation had petered out because of Griff whom Mrs Hines did not care for, or rather his father, she didnt like Griff because she hadnt liked his father who used to be the talk of the immediate vicinity, some 15 years ago.

She had asked him where he was going. Having at last sat down, probably arriving at some sort of decision — she could be firm at times. That defensiveness. Hines made a point of looking at her eyes while saying: I dont know mum, Sandra hopes Knightswood or someplace but . . .

What a fucking lie! Sandra hopes nothing of the kind! She'll go to K. instead of D. but she has never actually wanted to go there at all. She would take the place if ever it was offered because it is the best available out from the situation but she never bothered about things like that, not really. All she wanted was — something or other.

Knightswood's nice, said Mrs Hines; not so much the new parts.

Aye.

D'you think there's much of a chance?

Hh! He was rolling a cigarette, knowing she would follow his movements with the rice-paper and tobacco. Her sadness. Not on account of the smoking habit. In fact she no doubt assumed he only smoked through perversity. The sadness was for the things coming to such a pass. Here you have a woman in middle age, then then, a nice looking lassie with mysterious dreams, who has always been enjoying seascapes. She marries a young fellow. They wind up in the District of D. And the first baby is to arrive, then the next two and they are all leaving school and now a grandmother, the eldest son sitting facing one, lighting his cigarette.

Getting a house in Knightswood isnt always easy.

For god sake mum.

Well it isnt Rab, she replied, as though he had been refuting the proposition. Obviously she knew they both knew it to be almost impossible for him to get going there. It was pointless talking. He exhaled smoke at the ceiling then inhaled another lungful. Sandra's mum and dad were lucky, she was saying, It was easier when they got married, not like when me and dad were trying. Well, you know, we were living with his sister at the time and it was a terrible squeeze so with you coming along we really had to find somewhere — and we were lucky getting here.

Hines nodded politely as she manoeuvred her tangent.

Why in the name of christ had he come up. He could have continued down the hill. He could have waited on and maybe gone to the broo with Griff. No. He was to be here and staying to listen to rumours concerning the housing situation in Glasgow of more than quarter of a century ago.

Come on mammy get to the present. No. She is to ramble. People need to reiterate their facts. It makes them feel agents of a verified set, whose clear-eyed vision of the world is justly recognised by one and all. On you go hen, your wee first-born's listening quite the thing, an ever-increasing belief in your continued integrity. No.

Stop the shite.

Who knows what she believes in. Most probably she believes in nothing, that her secret desire is death as eternal sleep. Perfectly sound. Anything else would be nonsense. It is true that she has no faith in external entities in the guise of benign personage. But what she may still retain faith in is absolute justice. What a fucking imbecile. Here you have an intelligent being such that she knows the earth as earthly but since justice is nowhere to be found it might simply be out of sight.

Come on mum: out with those mysterious dreams immediately.

Quite a good looking woman; she doesnt take great pains over her appearance but always looks okay. Sandra is a bit like this. Sons and their identikit mothers.

Hines grinned at her. She had stopped speaking. He leaned to rub his hands at the fire. Any word from Andy?

Not since the last time.

Ach well, it's no that long.

It's nearly 6 months, July.

O aye, still . . .

You havent heard?

Me! I've no had a letter off him for 43 years; brothers dont count nowadays.

She smiled for a moment.

You're no still worrying surely?

She smiled.

I'd have done exactly the same as him. Australia's a big place mum I mean, really massive; what a country! Hh; surely you didnt expect him to stay with Uncle Vic for the rest of his life?

Well at least he could write.

Ach!

She smiled.

Any tea left?

She was up from the chair at once. He hadnt meant her to go for it. But he should've known she would. It was the way she acted. Maybe he had known she would do it, and was giving her an escape. Jesus, it breaks your heart the way she carries on sometimes. There isnt any need for it. There is no need for it. He half rose to take the cup from her . . . How's dad?

O, he misses not seeing Paul I think.

Right enough, it's a wee while since we've been up.

She didnt comment which was irritating, but without inducing guilt. There was no reason for guilt. Obviously she thought there was but there wasnt. He remained silent as though implying he also did. That poor auld auld man, there he goes, making his way wearily through life with this eldest son who doesnt bring the one and only grandwean up on regular visits.

Does he still sit at the window?

O for fuck sake why did he ask that. He should never have asked her that. God forgive you Hines.

He prised the lid off the tin. He glanced at her. It's no the same with

133

the high-rise though eh? spoils the view.

O you get used to it; anyway if you stand to the side you can see right through. At first it was awful but sometimes I think it's better, the wind's not as bad now — remember what like it used to be . . . She had lifted a biscuit, she broke it in two and ate one.

Aye, well, I hope we get a view.

She had gone on to ask what time he started that afternoon. He compounded the earlier lie with another couple. She probably wouldnt bother about him taking a day off except insofar as it threatened his continued employment. The job meant nothing to her. All she worried about was him being stuck on the broo with the likes of Mr Griffin down the street. She rarely seemed to think things out very clearly otherwise she may have asked more awkward questions. And yet she wouldnt ask any question she thought might be awkward. It was something she didnt do. And anyway, he would just have told her more lies. Maybe this is what she was avoiding.

She was now asking after Sandra's parents as though some sort of bond existed between both sides. It was nonsense. She got on okay with them but his auld man couldnt stand them. Why bother. What was the point in such carry-ons. Life is too brief. This carefree lass with the mysterious dreams. And now look at her: fucked again, after her own parents. What is the answer. Not the weans. That had never been true for her. It took Hines a while to discover this but he knew it now. She had never set her life at the feet of the next generation. She wanted to fucking live. It was the auld man who made a cunt of everything.

How's the job? he said.

Busy. They're wanting me in full-time for the Christmas rush.

Dont fall for it.

She smiled.

Heh by the way, I saw Mrs Noonan down at the shopping centre. She was looking well. What was the name of that boy again? the one who played the bagpipes for the B.B. band . . . Hines grinned.

Donald.

Aye, Donald.

Donald Noonan! And then she laughed that peculiar laugh, almost smothered before it could be heard.

134

It was an ancient joke. At one time he thought it was only a joke between his mother and father, but it wasnt; almost every Protestant home in the area shared it. Mr Noonan was an Irish Catholic who had married a Scottish Protestant, but all the offspring had names like Donald, Angus, Morag or Fiona, and attended the Protestant School, and were led to the Protestant Church.

Mr Noonan was a Catholic?

Still is, she smiled. He was a nice boy though Donald, so were the others.

Hines shook his head with a grin, and then yawned. This set her to asking about the sleep he was getting on shiftwork and developed into the need for the correct clothes during wintry December weather. Eventually she left the room and came back with a brown paper parcel which she gave him. They're too small for your dad.

He shook his head.

No Rab they are, he's put on a bit of weight; you might as well take them and get the wear — it's just two vests.

He sniffed. Thanks . . . He laid the parcel on the floor; lifted the tin and opened it but closed it again, and made to rise from the chair.

How's Paul getting on at the nursery?

Fine.

He's clever.

Well, he's good at concentrating.

He's clever all the same.

He's on his own so much. Hines shrugged: It means he finds it that bit easier to concentrate.

The mother said nothing, gazed at the carpet. In this at least she obviously knew better than Hines. She would just say no more about it. But she knew all the same. Then she moved on her chair. That peculiar attempt to not say what she knew she was going to have to say anyway, and Hines would have to listen.

I didnt, he said, I could never sit still.

She wasnt hearing him. Maybe he hadnt spoken aloud. Had he spoken aloud there! Christ sake, maybe he was no longer able to tell when he was speaking or thinking! She was speaking herself of course, she was on about the possibility of things to come he had always shown signs of during his schooldays. All had been there for the grabbing. He had let himself down. He had never tried! Why had he never tried!

135

What? What did I not try?

Her smile.

Hines shook his head and took the lid off the tin.

But after a moment she had to continue: The Report Card, and that teacher saying you found things too easy.

But that was rubbish.

She smiled.

But it really was. It just wasnt true.

Well that's what he said.

I know he did but he was wrong. He might've thought it was true but it wasnt. I just couldnt do a lot of the stuff. Then I kidded on I wasnt interested.

She shook her head.

Mum, it . . . he sighed.

She didnt look at him while saying, You could've stayed on at school if you'd wanted.

I couldnt.

You could've. You could've if you'd tried. You know you could've Rab, you could've got your Highers.

Aw christ.

She was staring at the carpet.

Once he was smoking he said, Heh — that driver of mine; he's doing them at Nightschool. English and History. He wants to become a Shop Steward into the bargain. He's going to stretch the world the right way up.

Your driver?

Aye Willie, Willie Reilly — no mind I brought him up a couple of New Years ago?

O . . . She nodded, very vaguely, either switching herself off or having already done so a couple of sentences back.

His wife's at Teacher Training College. A rosily white outlook. They've no got any kids right enough. To be honest mum what I was thinking of doing was starting a revolution: Kirilov. One shot and one shot only. What d'you think?

She breathed through her nose; a method of not answering a non-question. And he had to stop himself from adding, Seriously, and continuing with something else altogether. He inhaled on the cigarette, glanced at the clock on top of the boiler-cupboard. Life is not too difficult. He chuckled. Heh! mind how granpa used to hide behind the door and fling his bunnet at us!

She smiled.

That time Andy ducked and it hit dad on the head while he was eating the bowl of soup!

She had no option but to laugh in the most genuine of manners. Hines shook his head, also laughing. And she added, An awful sense of humour he had — a real Highlander.

He must've embarrassed grannie.

O . . . she laughed briefly.

An odd bundle of turnips. He had wondered about such power on different occasions. Here you have a manic depressive bastard who can make cunts laugh more or less at will. A great deal of hypocrisy, of course, being inextricably bound in with it. Pure relief on their part; thankful they arent having to start committing dastardly acts. What a performance.

When he left his mother had forced another bag onto him, one of the plastic carrier type. He detested being given bags by her but methods of declining werent always available. Going downstairs he glanced inside: a tin of cold ham, a ginger cake, a packet of digestive biscuits, and an envelope containing £2.

If there had been any justice in the world he would have carted it all across to Griff. Who would have collapsed on the spot. Who would have flung the stuff in his face, stick the charity up your arse ya bastard. No he wouldnt, he would have shrugged and called for Rita. No he wouldnt. It would never have happened in the first fucking place thus as reasoning goes is absolutely nonsensical.

A man was pitching what seemed to be boiling water at the windscreen of his car. Surely the glass would break. It didnt break at all, the icy bit just having melted away. Shaking his head at Hines the man gazed at the white sky, clenched his fist at it, smiling good-naturedly.

The fates, grinned Hines, be careful.

The man nodded. Heh, he said, you got a light by any chance?

Hines gave him his box of matches, waited for him to light the cigarette.

I left my lighter up the stair, he said as he returned the box. Ta.

Farther on there was a wean's slide on the pavement; grit had been laid on it but it was still serviceable. It looked dangerous — should a wean have misjudged the thing it would be easy to go slithering right off onto the road and it being so steep the vehicles would have been incapable of an emergency stop. Shoving the cashbag into the carrier bag he tugged the hat firmly onto his head and taking a short run up went sliding down, travelling quite a distance but maintaining balance well. It was satisfying without being exhilarating — it was only a weans' slide for christ sake. Nevertheless, the sensation of risk, that slight awareness of devil-may-care-abandon and so on.

Halfway down the hill he glimpsed the pale sky over the Old Kilpatricks which were white at the top. If they were the Swiss Alps the District of D. would be being worth its weight in gold.

The fellow is cockahoop.

This can be explained simply. That brief reminiscence about the granpa cheered him up as well as his mother, and allowed the leave-taking to occur amid low-key scenes of mutual understanding. Does she really understand him. Of course. She knows fine well why he is not to amount to anything in their world. Her only problem is in agreeing his course is all that there is. Not that she has any inkling of it. But she does know him quite well, that if eventually he does do something then that something might turn out to be startling.

He grinned at the elderly woman; she was struggling along on the grass verge at the side of the pavement with two big shopping bags for ballast, her gaze to the ground as she passed. Probably she lived on the 19th floor of the fucking high-rise. But it isnt her fault she's a bastarn imbecile. She had to leave school at 13 years of age to go to work in a steamy ill-lit washhouse, craning her neck to read in the dull yellow glow at all hours of the night, her father lying exhausted in one of these 1930s labour camps down in Ayrshire, her maw in a fucking workhouse. Never mind auld yin: jumping jehova'll fix everything, a land of hope and glory right up there beyond the mountains. Terrible damp in winter but, it's these low-hanging clouds. Heh d'you hear the one about the 3-legged priest in Ballymurphy. A strange kettle of toadstools. The universe, however, need not be a bleak item. Unzip the 54th onion peel and the sturdy shoulders will attend the task. There is a song. There is a song, whose name Hines cannot recollect at present though no doubt it is appropriate. If truth be told his memory demands a thorough shake.

Other folk seem capable of conjuring the remotest detail in straightforward primaries. Maybe there's something wrong with the cunt. Even the pettiest of entities, certain nomenclatures for example, take flight out the fucking window at the most inopportune of instances. But he well remembers dancing with Rita long before Sandra stepped aboard his platform. She and Griff got married young and were in the position to throw a few parties without any real parental disapproval to worry about. She held her body close. It was fucking smashing. Poor auld Griff, the boys queuing up, the terrible lack of women as usual.

Yet this is no time for breasts.

And do such thoughts follow as a direct effect of the fellow's recent visit to mother. Yes, no, I dont know albeit in times of joy the male heart leaps.

Fuck off.

The mood darkly but, at the approach, then constant through the first part of the visit, then somehow less darkly till bang, enter granpa flinging bunnets at cunts' heads for no reason.

There you have it. He was not a bad old bastard. A bit doatty at the finish but fair enough, it's a hard life in the grey but gold city if you've had to come down from the freedom-loving highlands and islands.

He walked through the shopping centre, and then out the other end, in the direction of the library. But this was fine. And he entered. The walls were painted. The whole lay-out in fact, had altered. He found an empty seat and left the carrier bag on it, went to find something to read.

The bag was on the floor when he returned. He glanced round but no one acknowledged responsibility. He pushed the bag beneath the seat and sat down, studying the words on the page of this large book. He took off his hat and placed it on the carrier bag. His head was acting up, a sensation of thickness about the upper regions of the nose and eye-sockets, a slight ache in the temple region, and his feet were itchy — in reaction to the sudden shift in temperature perhaps; it was hot and stuffy; the boots were soaking. And his nose now streaming. Plus the necessity of smoke. He needed a smoke. He hadnt smoked since leaving the house and now he wouldnt be able to. What a time to be without a hankie. He was sniffing continuously. He called a halt, it was out of order. He remained motionless, resisting all manner of urges; the water gathered; he raised his arm, the cuff of the uniform sleeve to be capturing the drops before hitting the book. O for a pint of milk. Milk is great for runny noses, causing the liquid to thicken into mucus thus the stuffed rather than streaming effect. Reaching beneath the chair he extracted the brown paper parcel. He would use only the paper. Sacrilege to even consider the vests — although he would never ever wear them. No; those vests would definitely never be worn — not unless he reached a point where the tallboy drawer was empty of T-shirts. And Sandra seldom allowed that to happen — although on occasion it did appear as if his laundry needs took third place in the Hines' household. Too late to go home. By the time he arrived she would be leaving to stick Paul into the nursery. Before heading on to the office. No point thinking about that.

They would all have hangovers, diarrhoea with a bit of luck. The girl whose birthday it was would be at the centre of things. It's your fault we've all got the sore heads and the red hot arses, you ninny you. Obviously it all took place as she said. If Sandra wanted to leave she would leave. Dear Rab, Our life to date has not been sweet. With this in mind I've taken the boy and skedaddled. Yet she is so honest she would be forced to leave Paul behind. And he would be forced to give up the buses, to allow him the proper attention, at least until he started school. And after that: infinity. Measureless space. Emigration to Australasia. Uncle Vic would see him okay for the first couple of months, just till he got a few quid together, then off into the outback to team up with Andy, one of these wee sheep-shearing stations.

Fucking rubbish.

He blew his nose into the brown paper and stuffed it into his jacket pocket, then took off the jacket and draped it over the chair. A woman had glanced at him — the librarian probably. It must have been her that took his carrier bag from the seat. She was wearing a dress of a soft clingy material.

He examined the book. Big illustrated pictures of an anthropological nature. It was a mistake to have taken it out, he would probably end up with a hardon, and she would see him, and report

140

him to the authorities. Come into the office you and just wait there till the wagon arrives, bloody cheek, getting hardons in my library, why dont you fuck off to a bus where you belong. But buses are bad as well. You can be sitting there minding your own business and the next thing bang. That's what happened with Sandra. It was an old backender — one of these with the passenger entrance to the rear, no doors. Freezing in the winter but great in the summer. It was almost empty and Hines sitting there having a quiet puff at a Players' Plain because at that time the idea of rolling one's own had yet to present itself. The seat he was on was to the side, one step up from the platform — the conductor to be positioned that he could twist and with minimum effort be applying the ding ding when necessary; the big drawback being the punters' ability to jump aboard at will. And Sandra must have known this as well as anybody, that of all things hated by the busconductor/tress, this uninvited jump onto the platform took the fucking biscuit. And it explains why she should have immediately parked herself down on the side seat facing him. She was too embarrassed to go farther. She was flushed, an effect of this platform jumping at the traffic lights. Then that was it that Hines was blushing. What did she look like at all. Christ knows. The flushed face, the set face; Sandra through and through. She had taken the purse from her handbag and was footering with the coins. But Hines was finished. It wasnt even possible to collect her fare. Having to sit there staring at the window, then the twitching, the throat feeling about one hundredth of an inch in diameter, and the face of course, so fucking purple. And becoming aware of how uncomfortable it was making her feel; her hand, travelling to her neck, to fidget with the collar of the thing she was wearing, probably that it was arranged okay or something, while the bus went vibrating on its way out to the famous K. Theretofore had her life been sheltered. That's these fucking High Amenity Zones for you.

He got the brown paper out of the carrier bag for another clearing of the nostrils; then stuffed it into his trouser pocket. The dampness through the cloth. It might be an idea to start wearing tights. Quite a few male wearers of the green already did so — drivers mainly, to combat the draught whizzing up through the cabin floor. Or longjohns. Apparently such efforts were still being manufactured — although Hines could not remember having seen any in the shops. That's the trouble with nowadays. And with 3 months of winter looming ahead a couple of pairs could be well worth an investment.

These fucking buses with defective heaters: 60% of the fleet in other words. O for the sandy beach and the sun beating down; secluded dunes; that time they went across to the East Neuk of Fife with her stupid brother and sister-in-law in the sharp Cortina car, but then when they had gone off somewhere, the beautiful screw, so slow, so painstaking, the sounds in the distance through the stems of the long rushes, close your eyes and listen, that slight stickiness of contact, skin on skin.

The book was closed. He raised it a little. The woman was probably hiding somewhere and watching. He studied the floor. For some reason his shoulders were astonishingly tense. How does such a thing transpire. One minute you're fine and the next it's as if something or other, a definite reason why you are not to be fine though this reason is impossible to discover. And he was onto his feet now and getting the uniform jacket from the back of the chair and stuffing the cashbag back into the carrier bag with the folded vests and the grub and returning to replace the book. He nodded to the person at the check-out point and down the steps and out jesus it was fine, but he was having to go quickly now and no option whatsoever. But it was fine, the shoppers and everything, familiar faces about also no doubt.

Crossing to the pub his pace altered in mid-stride, to a kind of slow quick-step; he felt like calling a halt altogether, to see if he was okay, was he about to collapse or something, the way things werent in order, the concrete slabs even, as though shifting at the edges, not vertically, the boots holding them down. The way he had been in the library he really could be coming down with flu, those first throes — the rapid movements in temperature and him not wearing the proper winter clothes too always the same be it summer winter spring or fucking autumn the things always the same that the possibility of at long last the system reneging and no wonder, no fucking wonder. The door. What happens now. In.

He was fitting the scene so well. He had carried his pint to a good place near the rear wall, went back to collect the hot pie and beans. While serving him the bartender had continued a conversation with another customer exactly as if he was acquainted with Hines in some fundamental way. And yet, all he had to do was announce himself and somebody was bound to step up: Aw aye, Boabby Hines' boy. No bother son, he's always talking about you.

O christ.

It is fine. It is a simple matter. Frank! How's it going man! long time no see. So this is where you're drinking then eh! Small world right enough. Hines was to drop the pint of heavy the next time the bartender glanced his way, the crash onto the floor, the instantaneous spread of beer and broken glass. Right you ya handless bastard get to fuck out the door and dont come fucking back either. Heh wait a minute you, heh a wee minute there, heh you that's Boabby Hines' boy, you cant start throwing him out the fucking door! Eh? blooming cheek. Come on son, back to your seat — another pint? Just sit down, you'll be alright in a minute. A bit dizzy there, the head and that, getting thickly. I know son, I know I know I know, the way things go, items on the mind and the rest of it, naw, you just get settled down there a minute, it doesnt do to go rushing into things.

With all the money they make the breweries should at least be laying on decent heating. To not do so is self-defeating: the hotter you get the thirstier you get.

He was touching the pie, that it might still have been too hot to eat. In fact he just wasnt wanting to eat the thing. His teeth chattered. He stopped it. He can have them chatter at will almost. It is an odd item he had often though of enquiring after. Can everyone make their teeth chatter or is he singular. Then he was yawning and it seemed to indicate a calm. He had enough money for a whisky. He got up and walked to the bar to buy one, and he received it and change from a £1, the bartender nodding when he asked if there was lemonade to go with it. The liquid jerked in the tumbler when he sat down and held it on the table. Were the nerves responsible or just the shivering. And if the latter were the nerves the cause rather than the lack of heating. He appeared to be in a hell of a state. He rolled a cigarette. But before lighting it he swallowed the first drop of whisky. He could have retched at the smell. Yet though the shivering could have appeared uncontrollable he definitely felt better. He shuddered audibly and tasted the beer which was become insipid after the spirit but quite good in that; and he smacked his lips, prepared to enjoy the smoke, and maybe even the pie. He bit a piece. Not so good. The scotch pie is an overrated article. But the whisky isnt. That's one thing we can do ya bastards. Jesus christ he was needing a shite. What a time to pick.

And all the stuff in the carrier bag. He could take it with him, though that kind of thing looks ridiculous, as if one was not trusting strangers.

Incredible: the urge now become irresistible. How in the name of christ does it happen. The Department of Transport must bear much of the blame, the way it fucks about with one's body-clock. For the average greenly member the movement of the bowels is a daily adventure, for here is no 9 to 5 worker whose amenities are a permanent fixture; on the contrary, one can find oneself performing weighty deeds on the toilet bowl at 0330 hours if one can find a fucking toilet bowl, such items not being part and parcel of an omnibus's furnishings and fittings. Few passengers appreciate the existence of the problem hence the bemused glance — and even the incredulous gape — when one's bus parks outside a public convenience, if you're lucky enough to get one open for business. Nor do they comprehend how the advent of an Inspector fails to expedite matters, and will only occasion a somewhat sheepish encounter between said official and luckless greenly member.

Hines may have gone mad. The state has always been a threat. For the latter while he has been watching his movements, viewing them in relation to faces, in apposition to his method of survival over the previous years. What he has now accomplished is to have become ridiculous. Yet the circumstances are peculiar. Maybe he is just pathetic. Pathetic and a little ridiculous.

Mad. It is truly mad. It is absolutely fucking ridiculous; it is stupid, crazy, he is a crazy cunt, and the second step, it is to not now be no longer be being articulately; it is not any longer, being part and parcel

Reilly's reaction would be total disbelief. Reilly would say: I do not believe it. And at long last the gap between himself and Hines would have become concrete, that the route of the latter can and cannot encompass a thing that may be descried as evil.

Fucking rubbish.

He watched the door and footered with the empty beer glass, the whisky also being finished, the pie discarded, congealed. There was more than enough for a third pint but he would not be getting one. Three pints and a whisky could be too much. Sometimes not but sometimes yes, it could leave him feeling half drunk. There have been times when he has taken only two pints at a meal-break and then conked out on the rear seat, boots up on the one in front and who the fuck knows how things worked out, how the passengers managed except that he has never been called into the Superintendent's Office to explain himself on that account.

The alcohol had definitely affected him. He knew it the way he was feeling. He actually had pains in the belly as well. The shite had turned out to be something approaching diarrhoea. Maybe he really did have an ailment of some kind. Tramping about in a pair of 6 years old boots, getting hit by all manner of temperature shifts, and just generally being run-down, needing a genuine break from the job if any fucking doctor would have had the sense to realise it but no, while cunts like Reilly just have to walk in the fucking surgery door and they get hit with panel lines for a week or a fucking fortnight for christ sake the inconsistencies man really baffling, within the Health Service, the doctors the bastards, having it all their own way on that particular question. They hadnt had a genuine holiday since the year Paul was born. Just a few days away from it all was what was required, a glimpse of different horizons, the chance to be together and alone, by the shore, quiet, a passive method of getting by, and then strolling back to some place afterwards, a rare coal fire burning, Paul asleep for the night, with the two of them there, just playing cards or something, the radio to its minimum volume, and toasting bread with a long fork and upstairs to the attic to bed then waking first thing in the morning to the surprise of it all, being in such a place, the whiff of seaweed and jumping out of bed to rush down to the water's edge. Sandra's dream. It is what she wants more than anything. Right away from Glasgow altogether. She doesnt want to be in Glasgow, not Drumchapel and not fucking Knightswood, she wants to be away, right fucking away and out of it, to not worry about the things that make the head cave in, that narrowing, the pain, while it contracts and gets you thin. Hines feels like something — a retch perhaps, being sick maybe; he feels like being sick. The fucking belly. The nerves of course. He should be relaxed. The shoulders have been so fucking tense. And still tense. They get tense immediately, after relaxing. He cannot get them relaxed. Each time he makes the attempt he is having to make a further attempt as though they are just not capable, of being relaxed, not at present.

At tables nearby the chatting and not chatting, a game of dominoes in progress. All the auld cunts there sitting having their fucking tourny, do not disturb for christ sake we might fucking wake up, shut the door and keep out the blooming draught we've no time for the likes of you ya cunt ye I mean what d'you think it is at all coming in here drinking your fucking beer and challenging the lieges to fight.

Amazing to see them sit there in that eternal manner, fixed in their places, the lives assumed on the strength of it, the sitting, while all around them the fires fucking burning and the stench of it engulfing every fucking thing under the sun, the cries and the screams of the cunts being tortured, the bellies, of the fucking weans there and their grandparents, their fucking ribs for christ sake look at their ribs, jutting out. That mark of distinction, it is all one to him that which may be said about him, it is all too transparent. The sun does go down and the whitely grey sky. One can climb the high-rise and wave down at the auld man, there he is, the healthy 50 years of ager at the parted curtains when the lights are out, bon voyage captain. Hines was rising from the seat and collecting his chattels; if Frank was somewhere it wasnt here. There was no relief but, if it wasnt to be now it would be the next time.

ooo

On the run home from the nursery Hines pretended they were being chased by ghoulish creatures and Paul enjoyed it. Then he roped him into the cleaning and tidying before preparing the grub, and when Sandra arrived everything was fine. He was nonchalant about generalities but she was quiet. She was tired right enough, obviously surprised to find how the house was, glad to see the food set for serving. He didnt tell her he had not been to work but since she wasnt

146

bothering too much about conversation he didnt have to go to any lengths.

They sat down to eat.

If Hines had not been hungry he couldnt have stomached the food. And Paul seemed in a similar state, just sitting there bashing his potatoes about with a fork.

Then she appeared to have been not speaking for quite a long while and the sound of cutlery on crockery more audible than usual, as if some terrible news was set for revelation. Often she chattered throughout the evening meal. The workaday antics of people amused her. She could make Hines laugh when speaking about it all. Occasionally she became self-conscious, effacing herself from it, that making him laugh had nothing to do with her but lay in the actual antics of the people involved. She would be very popular in the office. And obviously she was good at her job, otherwise Mr Buchanan wouldnt have regarded her so highly. If she wanted she could start full-time. This meant if Hines wanted. If he raised no barriers. If he didnt make it hard for her she would be starting full-time, after the New Year perhaps. Things slot into things; it's the sadness makes it so terrible. Sandra never used to be sad but now she has been sad for ages. He noticed. Why was he not able to do anything about it. He used to make her laugh. He had been good at making her laugh. He still does it. Not so often. Yet this is the thing for a good marriage. Who said that. An uncle of hers, at their wedding. He whispered it to Hines. If you make her laugh you'll never have anything to worry about. That was Lex McLean's secret, an audience full of women, all roaring and laughing. That's the way son, that's the way to do it. Look at Sandra's maw, you'd never think to look at her but that lassie used to love a laugh.

Things were not good. She was definitely not talking. She had been talking when she came in — quiet, but she had been talking. She was talking about what. Drumchapel. She had mentioned it about last night, in terms of today, as an interesting link to the previous day. The petering-out point of the conversation. What was he doing exactly about that. Drumchapel. He was not taking Paul with him because he was wanting to go himself. He would have been taking him to the swimming baths except he couldnt, because he was going to the Drum. He had postponed the swimming because he was going to visit the parents, by himself, going out for a pint with the auld man maybe. He wouldnt be collecting Paul from the nursery either so she would have made arrangements with one of the other mothers. And when she went up to the other mother Paul wouldnt be there, because Hines had collected him from the nursery, instead of being out at Drumchapel. So, then, here she was, sitting facing him.

He winked at Paul. What would happen to him. It was definitely best he wasnt extrovert, the withdrawn side maybe allowing him to survive that bit more easily.

He got up from the table, to pour the tea. He laid her cup next to her plate on the table and went to sit on his armchair.

She was talking to Paul.

He should be getting up to massage her shoulders, to smooth back her hair. Even the way she had been smiling recently. And then last night.

On the rear wall in the recess there was a rectangular space where a picture used to be. Hines took it down a couple of days ago. It was a picture he liked. He took it down and crumpled it up and dumped it into the rubbish bin. How come he did that. That was daft. It was a way of getting back at himself but maybe she thought he was getting at her. She also liked the picture.

Why had she not said anything about it, it being absent. He wasnt getting at her, christ, only himself, it was only himself. He was disgusted, with himself. For telling her something that was not true. He took the picture down from the wall to get back at himself for having told her a stupid piece of nonsense. He had signed-off sick during a late backshift in order to return home.

But told her something else altogether. That he had landed a shift with a big long mealbreak. Why had he done it, it was fucking stupid. He wanted to come home. He had to sign-off sick to get home immediately because it was just not possible to stay there.

But he should have just fucking told her that instead of the nonsense, the lie. Why did he fucking lie to her about it: it would have been fine. It would have been more than fine. She hates these late late backshifts even more so than he does and she wouldnt have minded at all, his signing-off sick, in order to return home, to be with her.

He withdrew his hands from his face, they had been covering his face, the fingertips pressing into the corners of the eyes, the lids shut. At first he had covered them with the middle sections of the fingers and was using force, but then this had eased and the fingers moved slowly down, as though he was just rubbing his face, and then the

148

hands being withdrawn altogether.

Willie was saying eh . . . he lifted a cigarette from the ashtray and put it into his mouth, struck a match and lighted it . . . if we fancied going up to his place, for a meal, a kind of party I suppose, him and Isobel and that — if she's talking to me — I think they've invited a couple of folk from her college or something I'm no too sure. He said we were to bring Paul if we wanted, it'd be okay, if we cant get a babysitter, just to bring him.

O . . . she nodded. When is it?

Saturday I think, a week on Saturday. I'll check tomorrow.

Is it not your day-off tomorrow?

Naw. He sniffed and reached for the *Evening Times*, paused before opening its pages. He glanced across when she rose from the table, pushing her chair back and saying to Paul about not bothering to eat everything if he wasnt feeling up to doing so.

In the name of christ.

He shifted in his chair so that he was facing the fire, studying the shapes within it. Their voices in the background. It was like something or other, bad, it was like something bad.

The clock on the mantelpiece. And the fucking wallpaper: so shabby — even a coat of paint might have done the trick, making things that bit more cheery. He got up to switch on the television.

At some time in the future Paul would be elsewhere and involved in something totally removed from it all when for no reason whatsoever the memory of the babybath. There are bathrooms in Drumchapel; Hines was never bathed in front of the fire. This experience will remain with the boy for the rest of his days. Maybe of that very evening, the mother and father sitting there and the silence — that tenement silence which encompasses vague bumps and bangs while cisterns empty and refill — and he might wonder about its cause. Had there been an actual row he couldnt quite remember. If not, what. And was this the usual state of affairs. No, for it wasnt always like this. In many respects it felt to have been a happy home. Is this true. Not untrue. Hines maybe a bit quick to strike at times, bad tempered on occasion, and probably inconsistent. But all in all not too bad.

And surely no worse than his own father; maybe even a bit better when it comes down to it, a deal more honest in many ways, a great many ways.

The flames are bluey grey. For each of the 3 sections there are 24 miniscule rectangles concealing hundreds and hundreds of toty wee pointed items of the colour white, and that toxic vapour, always seeping.

Sandra was looking at him. He grinned, then relaxed to be smiling, an encouraging kind of a smile. After a moment he raised the book.

It was time for his bed. He had an early rise. He had to go to work extremely early tomorrow morning. She could trip while carrying the huge soup-pot. She wouldnt; if she wants to have a bath while he's out on a backshift, she has to do it on her own and she never trips. He can wait until the thing has been filled. Then he can go to bed. Good christ. The words on the page are very fine, those little tails on individual letters, most pleasing to behold.

4

There's that instant a fraction before the alarm belts out and you've grabbed the thing and managing to shove down the stopper just at the warning click, knowing you're as fit as a fiddle and right up the lot of them; pushing out of bed and dressing in the black yet so swiftly, everything successful — the jersey in particular, seeming to pull itself on, settling round the trunk without even needing a tug. Pointless to eat; far better out on the road and walking. And the quick laying on the lips of lips for christ sake what does that mean —

kissing one's wife softly on the lips: that's what it fucking means. Then swallowing a half pint of milk prior to the silent farewell; an unknown moment of magical togetherness. Poor auld Sandra. Never to have felt these lips at that actual moment. Serves her right for being sound asleep. Women shouldnt go to sleep, it's a spoiler and we dont want that kind; what we do want is the fragrant aroma and soft flesh to be encircling one that one is pulled back beneath the sheets against one's will. Come on you I want to go to my work, stop it, stop it! let me get out into the harsh wintry wee hours of this my next moment of doom, that black black black of the

Jesus christ alfuckingmighty.

But it was almost halfway to the garage before the staffbus appeared he had been walking so quickly.

The driver was an imbecile. To talk to such a being is often out of the hands of Hines. And yet it was miraculous to have been there as it slowed to just that point beyond where he was standing that he had to be quickening to be jumping else no chance of getting aboard the thing. The public service omnibus is an amazing article. To be the driver of such a vehicle must certainly be a novel kettle of cabbage. Hines would have liked a buzz at it. Had his overall conduct been less

151

abysmal he would easily have fulfilled the function quite as adequately as anyone.

He sat down.

Other members of the green were there. He greeted them cordially albeit with a concealed smile of supercilliousness at the thought of himself there sitting there at this exact moment in the eternal scheme of things. Consolation was his, however, deriving as it did, via his experience, oftimes verified via countless other mornings whence the ragings of a darkly brain had indeed given way to a calm but firm detachment. Had a mirror been handy he could have watched his face. It would have been interesting to witness the outward appearance.

The staffbus stopped in the garage yard and the greens strolled along into the office with Hines bringing up the rear in company with a driver by the name of Davis who has the fine habit of not talking for shifts at a stretch. It is astonishing how quickly the place could fill with smoke; Hines had been about to prise the lid off the tin but he returned it inside the pocket. An interesting observation: places used to smoke fill up with it more rapidly than other places. Take the topdeck of a bastarn bus where the eyes actually smart — although of course you've got the diesel fumes as well as the smoke, plus the extraordinary smells of the cunts farting, sorry jimmy, been on the guinness last night. Smoking is a malpractice. Consider the youthful Paul, how his lungs must resemble the inside of a fucking chimney, and him hardly $4\frac{1}{2}$ years of age. Terrible. And the same goes for one's spouse. Although, having known of the habit prior to accepting the band of rolled gold, the question of an individual's freedom to form genuine decisions of an autonomous nature must enter the reckoning. The Deskclerk.

Davis had just signed for his duty and was walking to look at the duty-sheet on the wall. The Office was almost empty. Hines had taken the pen to sign for his own duty but he kept from pulling the book towards him; at last he looked at the Deskclerk: What's up?

The Deskclerk was smiling in a friendly manner.

Hines grinned.

Naw. I'm just wondering what you're here for.

Eh?

I mean there's no point signing the book, it's your day-off.

Hines sniffed; raising his right hand he scratched his hairline which seemed to be containing an enormous quantity of flaking skin nowadays. The Deskclerk continued to smile. He stopped the scratching, passed the hand over his forehead gently, as though not wanting to disturb the skin there lest it also flaked.

Honest Rab I mean that's what diaries were invented for; so folk can mark in their timetables!

Hh.

Anyway as it turns out, you've knocked it off, I'm short a couple of conductors this morning; you can switch days-off if you like.

Aw christ Harry ta.

16 duty; okay?

Great, aye, ta, thanks a lot.

The Deskclerk had pushed the book towards him and while Hines was signing he said, How's the stomach by the way?

Better.

The Deskclerk nodded, then he sniffed. Aye, I never heard till later on. You'd been stuck in the toilet for an hour because of it?

Well no quite . . . Hines grinned.

Look eh . . . I thought you were chancing it yesterday. That's how I eh . . . He sniffed. I mean I didnt know it was genuine, when you came in to sign-off, otherwise I wouldnt've eh . . .

No bother Harry.

The Deskclerk nodded. Right, day-off the morrow then — or Saturday? To be honest Rab it'd suit me better if you made it Saturday, you know what like Fridays are in this place!

Hangover day!

They both grinned.

Eh . . . Hines was rolling a cigarette.

Aye?

Naw, just wondering, I mean yesterday and that eh I dont suppose I mean, changing it; what I mean, to a day-off.

What?

Naw I mean yesterday and that, you know how I had to go sick; I was just wondering, if it could be changed to a day-off I mean, so I could work Saturday as well . . .

O Christ naw, naw Rab, that's no on, sorry I mean, it's just no on; it's through the books and that and you cant go back over it now.

Aw.

153

Aye, Christ, sorry.

Naw naw, okay Harry honest, no bother I mean I was just eh . . .
He sniffed, signed at the space appropriate to 16 duty; he lighted the
cigarette and coughed sharply, and added, Thanks again Harry.

Aye eh . . . The Deskclerk was gazing at a sheet of paper lying in
front of him on the counter; he raised his head briefly to nod.

It has never been acutely necessary to think. Hines can board the bus
and all will transpire. Nor does he have to explain to a driver how the
bus is to be manoeuvred. Nor need he dash out into the street to
pressgang pedestrians. Of its own accord comes everything. Not only
are the passengers to be congratulated, so too must the creators and
current administrators of the Public Transport System. It is all
superb. Hines simply has to stand with his back to the safety rail
beneath the front window and await the jerk of gear or brake to effect
his descent to the rear and, with machine at the ready and right hand
palm outwards to take in the dough, the left hand is extracting a
ticket and dishing it up to the smiling person. Then though it be busy
a lull always arrives, during which he can return to the front for a fly
puff at a relaxing roll-up and, if of a mind, he can engage such as a
Reilly in conversation. But a driver can be new. The Newdriver is a
problem. One should tread warily in gabbing to such a being lest a
lapse in concentration causes the bus to crash. Hines seems to get
more Newdrivers than is his fair share. It is as though the Higher-ups
view him as the "deep-end" and thus they toss him the Newdrivers
whenever available. They say to themselves: This Busconductor
Hines is a difficult kettle of fish; should the Newdriver survive a shift
alongside him then this Newdriver is indeed the man for us. Hines
will show them that which is the ropes. He will advise them what is
the what. Let us continue to ensure that he remains the busconductor as opposed to a busdriver that we may continue to
toss him the Newdrivers whenever he and his own driver are not on
together. And gentlemen, let us also take pains to ensure that he and
his own driver are not always on together.

Fucking shite.

But it's funny how he always seems to get lumbered with the cunts
when Reilly's on the panel or whatever. They're all fucking idiots as

154

well, this is the thing. 90% of their naivety is not connected with being Newdrivers; it is connected with being alive as persons. Hines cannot fucking understand how they have survived to the present. He signs for a shift and senses the proximity of a starched collar and tightly knotted black tie and there, in a quiet part of the Office, lurks the graduate, rocking back and forth on his heels while pretending fascination with the duty-sheets. What is the fucking point of such a carry-on. Useless talking. Hines leaves them to get on with it — which is no doubt why they get tossed aboard his bus. Some of them are cheery and some of them are not cheery, they chat and dont chat, but as the day progresses the latter always takes precedence. Because Hines doesnt fucking chat back! You think he wants to fucking die! Jesus christ!

Never disturb Newdrivers.

Even experienced drivers should not be disturbed. Back during the 1st term of transport Hines was feart to glance suddenly at the driver in case he caused a draught which might interfere with the steering mechanism. Absolute nonsense. But the quick glance into the cabin could have the driver reacting hastily that the possibility of disaster as reality. Hines tries never to speak without firstly having made his presence known. People can be deep in reverie. Some drivers have no idea where they are at certain points on the road. They say, Christ I dont even remember driving the last couple of miles! And these miles can embrace peak-hour city centre streets. It makes you quite jumpy to consider. Imagine a bus crowded with punters, standing room only both upstairs and down, all giving each other the time of day under the mistaken apprehension their lives are in a safe pair of hands. Now, these fucking hands might only be 2 days out the Training School for Busdrivers and some of them never sat behind a wheel in their lives before arriving there for fuck sake. Hines is sick of it. Apparently it isnt the fault of the Newdrivers themselves. But the poor auld conductors are having to carry the burden. No wonder certain shoulders will wilt. One pair should not have to support that kind of thing.

Weans are the main hazard. Newdrivers feel able to be at home with them. It is an error. They drive folk crazy. Newdrivers are simply misjudging the situation. Experienced conductors have no truck with weans. Weans are to be avoided at all costs. The most hair-raising journeys involve them. On they pile maybe 6 to 8 at a time so that they wind up getting jammed in the doorway and you have to be there to poke here and pull there. And they are out to con you into losing your temper. One must tread warily. Three years ago a conductor by the name of McManus had a stand-up fight with a team of them because they were drinking wine on the rear seat of the topdeck. The full facts have never come to light — although Hines has a hunch it concerned moral outrage. McManus was an alcoholic. He always carried a half-bottle which he wrapped in layers of toilet paper and stowed in his machine-case. According to garage rumour he lost his temper because they refused him a gargle but McManus was a whisky drinker and it was a bottle of wine the weans had. Far more likely he wanted to warn them off the wayward track. Anyway, whatever it was he was out of order and the weans were right to object. So poor auld fucking McManus suffered a beating, then lost his job into the bargain. The Department of Transport is opposed to the boxing games where members of the green are involved. There is no excuse. No circumstances are singular enough to warrant such action. But obviously the beating was sufficient; he shouldnt have lost his job into the bargain. And he wouldnt had the Union sorted it out properly. But the Union is not for discussing. Hines cannot discuss the Union. Yes he can. No he cant. Best leaving such a carry-on to the likes of Reilly who is able to attend meetings and even get involved in the proceedings. Life is too elongated.

There is a road; and on this road there is much traffic.

He was journeying home by omnibus having spent the past hour watching snooker-pool. Greenly members play for cash. Hines doesnt; he has no money to play at snooker with. He can hardly play the fucking game anyway. During his earlier terms he failed to master it and has continued to fail ever since. Usually he gets the chance to play only when Reilly has nothing better to do. Reilly is good and prefers to play others who are good. He can win money. How does he manage it. He plays and then people give him money. Off he goes to buy cigarettes or rolls and fried egg—or maybe home to weigh in with Isobel who then sticks it all into the building society.

The sun has set; the streetlights have been on for a while; the slush, almost disappeared from the roads.

Hines sits on a damp bus, on the lower deck, having lacked the whatever necessary to climb to the top deck. He is being glanced at complicitly by an imbecile of a conductor who must have started in the job yesterday morning — he is upset at having a busy bus. Everybody gets a busy bus. There is nothing unique in the situation except that it may be so for him. Hines feeling obliged to raise the eyebrows occasionally, to convey interest, not wanting the cunt to suffer any sort of mental breakdown lest he is forced into donning the machine as substitute, until procuring an Inspector, and the ambulance. What a performance. At one stage the conductor slumped onto the seat beside him and began loud-mouthed complaints about the passengers he was getting. This loud voice going on and on and on, seeming to list the names and dates of birth of individual persons, in this voice which was grating on everyone — the heads of passengers twisting slightly to signal their awareness of what was being said.

Hines has enough on his plate. But there is no way through to some folk. A lot of drivers carry on in the same way, gab gab gab about the trials and tribulations of driving buses. Who's fucking interested. Hines is always getting cunts like that giving him their worries. Who wants to hear about irate punters at Hillington Estate. You finish your work and you expect a bit of peace, not some fucking imbecile battering your ears. This is what happens when you sit in the *Vale*; they all start yabbering about the morning's nasty events.

The wind was strong; he had to stride in a semi-sideways movement, frequently halting to catch his hat before it blew off his head; at one point he took it off but had to put it back on again because his ears got sore. Then the heat inside the nursery lobby, like a hospital. Even the smells of the place. Wiping his boots on the several mats he wandered down the corridor, seeing the work the weans had done pinned up on the walls. The hum of voices from the main play-area. He was still too early.

The Supervisor appeared; her tits very uncomfortable looking the way they seemed squashed together in the thing she was wearing. He nodded, stepping to one side as she passed, but she was frowning and barely noticed him. It summed up the place. Being a wean in the dump must have been no joke. Poor auld Paul right enough.

Near to the play-area door he paused at a print of the Chieftain of all the Britons. It was spendid. On the wall opposite were companion prints also splendid, of long canines with short legs, ideal goals for the kids. The Supervisor again. She hesitated. Hines raised his eyebrows, indicating the prints. Then she said: Paul isnt in today . . .

Although it wasnt a genuine statement it was nearer to that than a question. And she continued to look at him. Hines nodded, Aw aye, hh. He grinned, What a stupid . . .

As she pushed her way into the play-area he could hear her call to a child, or adult perhaps, before the door shut.

Along the corridor, ben the lobby, and out.

There were problems in what had been said but there might not be. There were other items — people for instance, as well as different things, needing to be considered. Plus the experiencing: the actuality. Even the pavement, dry bits and damp bits, hardly a sign of the snow now at all; and the condensation, on windows, of tenements and buses and other vehicles — those clear patches behind which the gazers, gazing. These fucking scary closes! Some of them are really evil. Strange dripping noises. Is it a burst pipe or what. A broken gutter. Just a tap with a faulty washer. And the concrete all cracked and treacherous for folk's feet. The auld yins there, having to tread with great caution, the lights in the close dim or not working except in periodic blinks; and that dogshit in dark corners — the floor just swept too and suddenly littered with a mysterious black matter which is picked up for inspection, O my it's awful soft this whatever it is: Shite! help ma boab right enough. No wonder the auld yins crack up. Half a lifetime spent scrubbing and whiteclaying the concrete only to have to finally admit the uncontrollable stuff going on behind their stooped backs. It is a pity.

Two teenage girls at the corner, probably on the game the way they were standing, conducting a form of non-conversation, their gaze everywhere — even to Hines. Too early; they have no doubt forgotten today is only Wednesday, that tomorrow is the day when members of the putrid can be worth a glance. In fact they probably werent prostitutes at all, just girls having a chat before going up the stair for tea. But the district is definitely going downhill fairly quickly and not even a dyed-in-the-wool native of the dump could say any different. Hines is no dyed-in-the-wool native; he's a fucking incomer.

He clearly distinguishes the candlelight at certain windows, and the women resting their elbows on the sills, watching you walk by. One's offspring should not be reared in such a den. And yet according to local gossip it was once a sought-after area, green grass in a few backcourts; and all the local wee shops, a hive of bustling, good-natured activity. Evelyn Donaldson's mother had been born and bred here. And if it was good enough for her etc. it was certainly not good enough for sane citizens.

He paused at the traffic lights, staying very still, as though trying to remain untouched by the sharp gusts and eddies from the passing vehicles. One minute you can be heading along the street nice as nice and then the next you're fucked as usual, care must be taken. You get the poor auld fucking animals; they go hopping about with broken shoulders and backs with the punters yelling at the conductor to put them out their misery. What are they supposed to do at all. Smash their heads in with the fucking machine!

Darting out suddenly he made it to the other side, just as the green became amber. It is a habit he has picked up from them, the cats and the dogs. Dogs are better at it. They cross the busiest thoroughfares in a fine trusting manner, trotting quite the thing as though the space they occupy is bound to stay constant. Not so the cats. They know fine well there is no such thing as constant space and off they scud in the surefire knowledge the course they have chosen is 90% guaranteed to fail. What is astonishing is how neither species, once safely across, will pause to glance back over its shoulder. This fatalistic approach to life: no, it is not so good. At least once per month Hines sees something killed, animal or person. Being the best friends of people the deaths of dogs are reported to the polis so the van can arrive to cart them off. But cats are regarded like rats. On the first journey one gets run over and killed and coming back from the terminus its body is obvious. On the next journey out the shape can still be verified but returning in less easily so, and onwards, till with a bit of luck the rain is falling.

He ignored the newspaper vendor outside the pub. Another thief. He short-changes blind pensioners.

He rushed past the butcher and fruiterer.

All a load of shite. Ha ha ha.

159

Naw but, seriously, the depressed rectangles can be vicariously aloof. Pneumatic drills go blasting somewhere. Here you have this yin and there the other. What about the head though. The head is fine, fine. The head is a finely honed item; merely restricted at present. A gap-site is a delicate absence; a hunner years ago it was a brand spanking new section whose brightly white sandstone was quarried in Aberdeen perhaps, carted down by rail, the labourers and masons singing lustily, giving vent to their earnest endeavour via the traditional scotch worksong, while delivering then assembling the goods prior to collecting their wages and religious tracts from the builder's daughter at the end of the contract, a rosebudly wench of prim but lovely exterior, getting some practice in with the lowly before shooting out to the African jungle to sort out the converts, beautiful stuff, with the laced bodice and so on.

It would be hard to say what he was playing at. The volume control on the music-centre might have required decreasing, as also the gas-fire. He was still wearing the uniform, standing at the windows in the front room, the curtains parted as though night had yet to fall. His lips moved. He could have been mouthing the words of the song but if the song stopped he would be talking to himself if still doing it — maybe still singing right enough. The cashbag lay over his left shoulder. Although right handed he always carries it thus. A point for possible discussion: do left-handed conductors carry their cashbags on the right. Or is it only those who smoke. Very few people dont smoke in the garage. Hines could have named almost all of them — at least those who worked on the same side of the shift as he did. Such people may have stronger personalities than the rest but they might just be stubborn. It is also noticeable how less eager the nonsmokers are to spend their dough willy-nilly. Or is this a case of yoicks tally ho on the part of Hines. In other words is he a bad loser. Because he still smokes and is aware he should not be. But if a poll was conducted in the bothy perhaps the percentage of nonsmokers who carried homemade sandwiches would be higher than that of the smokers. While the percentage of nonsmokers purchasing prepared food in the canteen would certainly be minimal. On the whole then, it would appear that nonsmoking members of the green are less inclined to spend money willy-nilly.

He continued to stand there once the LP stopped playing. Then he frowned and went ben the kitchen, and walked to the window. Some demolition equipment was lying about. It is surprising this should have been the case. Probably there was nothing of value else it would get stolen. The demolition men could even steal it themselves and say it had been stolen by nightprowlers. They could steal it each time it was replaced, until steps were taken. The firm would end up having to employ a nightwatchman and maybe even a daywatchman cause what would stop them stealing it during daylight, so the daywatchman would then follow them about during working hours ensuring the stuff stayed on the premises.

He switched on the television, the gas-fire; returned to the front room and put on another LP record, switched off the gas-fire there. Before going back to the kitchen he listened to the opening of the first song. He drew his armchair nearer the fireplace, then hunched over it, sitting on his ankles the way Griff had done. What would three daughters be like. A quintet. A unit of 5 — plus the mother when she got out of hospital. If she ever got out. People rarely get out of hospital. They get kept in. They have their own wee incinerator down in the basement.

Amazing.

Hines can see their double chins, the way their jowls droop, the eyes saturated, while the bodies, groping towards each other in an effort to feel. Is that veins there. Actual blood pumping behind the greyly shadows. Living organisms of a reflective nature. Aw look, heh jimmy, a stain on the mohair suit, the cunt's pished himself and might rub against us; quickly quickly to the basement with the bastard or we'll never be the same again.

Hines can get closer in to them by flitting into Paul's usual kneeling position. Fine to drag a needle across the flesh, that thin bubbling line of blood, stripping them of their garments and sticking them into formation, tallers to the right and shorters to the left, single rank: size! Just so we can study them properly — see: here you have this yin and there the other. Essences: this yin's the essence of this and that yin's the essence of that. Out of it all you've got the individuals who perform the feats. Poke and you'll see them quiver. They hate getting poked right enough. And they dont like quivering in public either. And see how affected they get when you break their glasses, that sudden inrush of air; their eyes widening in terror, the streets coming jumping up at them — the accelerator james: let's get to fuck rapidly.

Or simply rearing questions, the answers of sociological interest to such as the adolescent Paul. And did you act in honest naivety. Or with thought malevolent beforehand. Or just as a genuine agent for whom the no-nonsense lack of shilly-shally is to bring forth universal benefit, as between two industrial captains — a singular contract for mutual expansion (if the sun doesnt rise tomorrow a balanced scale might simply slide, eh!). And how was it up there. Slippery. No time to relax. Aesthetically irksome, but compromise to some degree is always imperative if one is to gain a foothold, that footholds are seen as essential, that they are to be being continuing.

The uniform off he got into bed. He had turned off the television and the music-centre. He could have put on his jeans and a different jersey but he didnt. He was sitting beneath the quilt, on Sandra's side, with his back to the interior wall. From the recess the kitchen can be a peculiar experience since while being inside the subject is also outside. Should he have witnessed another Hines enter and go about his various bits of business it would have been very scary indeed, and yet also relaxing perhaps. Especially if the event took place during a long hot summer spell and he made straight to the sink to sluice cold water on his face and neck, washing off the sweat.

Steam issued from the kettle. The water was for his feet. He was going to wash his feet. He never bathes in the babybath. It is too small for him. One time he nearly got stuck in the thing. But it was a good buy, no question of that. And another time for fuck sake when Sandra was in it he saw a mouse. He was sitting on his armchair half-reading a book, half-watching her soaping herself and the mouse there, it must have come in beneath the door and it started along towards the tallboy but then stopped and stayed where it was, before returning to the door, and out. It was a bad yin, really, really bad. He didnt tell her; he has never told her: it is something beyond the pale.

He poured the boiling water into the basin, adding cold from the tap. It was as much to heat the feet as clean them, their being really fucking freezing for the past 12 hours or so. Is it 12 hours since he left the house. It must be. Time shifts. That's the fucking trouble with nowadays; back when Hines was a boy

The water wasnt cold enough for the feet to enter immediately; he would be balancing them on the rim of the basin for the next 10 minutes at least, allowing the steam to get at them while enjoying the anticipation of actually sticking them under. He sat down on the armchair and started to greet. It was a strange thing. His face didnt alter and nor did his eyes redden, and he stopped it right away, balancing the soles of his feet on the rim of the basin, the water far too hot. He always allows the water to cool in the basin rather than adding too much cold to begin with. He likes to just sit there, the soles of his feet on the rim, sometimes with an additional kettle of hot water positioned at the fireplace which he can pour from, to protract the affair. He twisted the chair slightly, his shins having turned red from the heat of the gas-fire. O christ, he said and opened a book.

Hines is of the opinion that men have every right to greet though so far he has been unable to accomplish the practice in public. His most memorable bouts to date occurred after the death of his last surviving grandparent, and after his young brother had left for Australia. During the actual occasions he was the life and soul of the company; it was only a few days later the greeting took place.

He had brought three books from the front room, they covered a period of some 2500 years and spanned three continents. To plop them into the basin would be adjudged unusual. In itself his method of book-reading if not unusual would be adjudged irregular. He used to have a method he regarded as pertinent, as proper for the thing. He would place the book at the bottom of the basin and read the title page while rippling the surface of the water, gently, with a pinkie. If he had worn spectacles he could have placed those beneath the book.

Hines is an honourable fellow; if his wife has decreed the necessity of not being with him then she is entitled to have arrived at such a decision, even though it is to be taken literally i.e. that such a decision is irrevocably bound in with action. But they have survived bad patches in the past. And although he would probably argue that this is the worst yet, it is by no means certain this is true for Sandra. Nor is there anything to suggest that the current situation is a form of climax for it may yet prove nothing more than a further bad patch in a developing relationship. But it must be admitted that certain elements, unique elements, have already appeared. Prior to the other evening she had never stayed away without prior notice or something like it. That was the first time she had ever done that. Why did she do it. She knew he would worry, it was really strange, not like her. Tonight was like her. It was not like her. More, it was not, it was like as if, it was considerate though.

The note was propped against the wall above the mantelpiece, next to the gas-bill. His feet had entered the basin and he jerked them out, they had become red to the ankles.

There was no need to hold the note because he had read it at a distance. She had written 11 a.m. at the top as if this was the kind of information he would need to know at all costs. Maybe he did. What did it tell him. It told him she probably couldnt have managed it out to Knightswood and then got back into town in time for work. Was that anything. She could just have gone in late.

The soles of his feet were touching the water but he allowed them to remain there, the hard skin and so on. He lifted the tin and prised off the lid. Not much tobacco left but he had retained the price of more from the cashbag. Plus she had left £3 beside the note. The £3 for him.

This sort of escapade is beyond belief. Was it to be taken seriously. Of course, shouted a voice. Whose fucking voice was it. Funny how voices come along and shout, just as if they were something or other, knowledgeable fucking parties perhaps, that knew what was going on. Because Hines doesnt. He doesnt fucking know. It is a joke. It is beyond talking about. Yet one obvious factor exists to substantiate the thesis that this is Sandra who's fucked off. This factor.

Wednesday is the fucking factor. Other women would have waited till wages-day. Not her. There is only one day out every seven she can leave and this day is never to be Thursday. She can only leave that he is to be being fucking okay. He is such an imbecile he cannot be trusted to survive unless he has a full week's wages in the pocket. Such cash is not necessary for her and Paul. It is him who needs it.

He had the towel in his hands, raising the soles from the water. He dropped the towel to the floor. His feet were yet to steep. But he had been aware of this. It was not a moment of absentmindedness. Quite often he dries his feet without having washed them. Sandra nags at him and no wonder. Imagine being too lazy to wash your feet when you've gone and prepared everything, when you've sat for quarter of an hour with the cunts suspended above the bastarn basin, only to towel at the bottom portions, and see how the poor auld fucking skin goes skiting off into the basin because you havent washed them right.

Terrible.

There ticks the clock; if it hadnt been wound then the ticking etc., it wouldnt be happening. And anyway, he had forgotten to bring the soap so this is a genuine reason not to wash them. Often it is the fresh socks he forgets to bring and sometimes the towel and sometimes more than the one item maybe even the fucking lot so that Sandra, having to get whatever it is, for him. O christ. And he doesnt like having to ask her if he has forgotten, he gets so sick of it, this forgetting, and the dependency. What happened last night. He came home. Things were not as they were. He comes home and things arent as they were. The things that should be fine. He of course did not go out to the Drum because he had been earlier on, christ, having advised her he was going in the evening which was why he couldnt take the wee man to the swimming like he'd been promising, always fucking promising, he had promised, to take him, but then couldnt, he was not able to do it, because he had to go out to the Drum and see wee Frank. Wee Frank was the thing of course. He had had to see him and he didnt turn up which was — fine really, because the next time it would be in the evening, definitely, and it could be sorted out with him. Not wee Frank, just Frank.

What is up in his head. As heads go. He told her a lie, another fucking lie, a non-telling of the truth; and not even to explain, even attempting it, to give something almost, close to it, something as close to what was really the case, something that was the truth.

Yet once upon a time

It should be remembered, however, that Robert Hines has accomplished nought. Even the present circumstances could have been rendered more amenable. A lick of fresh paint for instance, to hide the terrible wallpaper; a bit of polyfilla round the skirting board. He could have been getting rid of the mice. He could have called out the rodent exterminators. They would have sprayed their stuff. While awaiting their arrival he could have filled in the cracks. The last time they came it was a lassie along with a middle-aged man. The lassie was in charge. She spoke with authority and must have had qualifications in rodent control. She stealthily peered at the plethora of books while in the front room. Perhaps she would return alone: cups of coffee and a doughnut, a quiet conversation, with a brief account of the current problem, how items are not always going properly, becoming a wee bit overpowering at times. You can just go along okay, keeping upsides the world, not doing anything except taking part in a low-key kind of manner; you go to your work and so forth, until getting punched in the fucking mouth. An old story right enough. It happens to everybody now and again, you've got the incinerator at the foot of the stairs, a thing to be encountered every so often. The lassie is probably the same herself. Here she is having to chap at the doors of strangers, to wipe out their rodents and the rest of it.

Odd she should have taken Paul so readily.

That is definitely a something. One would have expected such a matter to be worthy of a little discussion.

Why is last night not this evening. She doesnt go last night and isnt here this evening when the actual item, the spur, is of last night. She goes this morning, first thing almost — 11 a.m. She goes to Knightswood, the home of her parents. Imagine going to the home of your parents! She must've been upset, otherwise, christ, the home of one's parents.

She goes to the home of her parents and takes her wee boy, leaving her man to accomplish that which he finds to be necessary in view of the current situation, whose circumstances though astounding are nevertheless not too astounding should one pause to consider the various eventualities. Now, these eventualities, are to be considered. One can consider them. One can sit; one's lower portions dangling over the hot water, one's tin etc., by one's side, and the trio of books, the towel and fresh socks. There are many items. A certain pleasure is to be gained from the world, its items, you have this yin here and a few more over there. Although predisposed toward the speculative musings, one is bound to say, having regard to that which is having gone before. One considers the Busconductor, Hines: now, here we have a fellow, from a spruce district.

How does she leave. How does she even fucking think a thing like that. How can she even think it for christ sake even think the fucking thing. Imagine it. For fuck sake.

It's beyond belief. It's actually beyond belief. Sandra makes it worse. This isnt her. She must've been really fucking, upset. When it all comes down to it, the way she is, so set in her ways, determined, thinking things out. Not like him. Hines is a fucking idiot: but she isnt, she's fucking — the way she thinks things out. This is what's so fucking ridiculous. Then just to grab Paul. Even doing that. The fucking selfishness, that's not her. Christ.

Hines had grinned. He stopped it, it wasnt right. He had dried the heel of his left foot. He gazed to there for a few moments. Then up to the clock, and then was drying both feet, and across to the tallboy, looking in at the drawers where she kept her stuff but they were always so jampacked it was difficult to know if she had taken extra, except if she had it couldnt have been much.

He was dressed and stuffing the tin and matches into his jerkin pockets. Before leaving he got the £3 from the mantelpiece and dumped the note into the rubbish bin then retrieved it, laid it face down on the mantelpiece.

And the front door key.

ooo

There was no point in phoning. You go there and phone and nothing is to be said. Best just having a couple of pints and then going fucking home. You stand there having trouble finishing the first, giving nods now and again to this old cunt standing next to you who keeps on making comments on the weather etc. Finishing it off and ordering another, the natural thing. A load of shite. You grab a hold of his lapels: Here auld yin my wife's fucked off and left me I mean what's the fucking game at all, your fucking daft patter, eh, leave us alone ya cunt for fuck sake. This isnt Hines who's talking. It's a voice. This is a voice doing talking which he listens to. He doesnt think like it at all. What does he think like. Fuck off. He thinks like anybody else, anybody else in the circumstances, the circumstances which are oddly normal. Here you have a busconductor by the name of Hines Robert whose number is 4729 and whose marital status. What's the point of fucking about. You leave half of the second pint and get off your mark.

Glasgow's a big city, all the life etc. The scraggy mongrels, they go moseying along near the inside of the pavement then to the outside and maybe off across the street to sniff other pastures. Hereabouts the district is a melter of sniffs. A myriad of things at your nostrils.

167

The decayed this and the decayed that. A patch of tenements set for the chop. Imagine being drunk one night, as if that which is not to be doubted is on high authority, such that its existence can only be assumed, such that the body is duty bound to endorse that assumption, fine, and sneaking into a derelict block for an illegal pish and tripping over a lump of concrete, cracking one's head on the floor, not badly, just enough to lope out of consciousness for an hour or so, to awaken in the wee hours, lying in the black, the smells surrounding you, then engulfing you the more aware you become; but not wanting to move in case your noise arouses other noise from a different room or maybe even the same one, that dark bit in the corner — it is your awareness sets it all going because these fucking noises man they were ever present, you just hadnt fucking realized them and now they come crashing in on you, indescribable noises; and how to escape how to escape, without your movement activating other movement. Better off razing the lot to the ground. And renting a team of steamroadrollers to flatten the dump properly, compressing the earth and what is upon and within, crushing every last pore to squeeze out the remaining gaseous elements until at last that one rectangular mass is appearing, all set for sowing. The past century is due burial; it is always been being forgotten.

There is a crack in the pavement a few yards from the close entrance; it has a brave exterior; it is a cheery wee soul; other cracks can be shifty but not this one. Hines will refer to it as Dan in future. Hello there Dan. How's it going? Cold yin the night eh! This fucking weather wee man. Never mind but, the ice and that, helps you expand. Pity cracks dont wear balaclavas right enough eh! One good thing about these old tenements, however, is the way they refuse to allow snow to hang about. A tough set of bastards so they are. No messing. None of your fucking good king wenceslas rubbish with them. The more mockit the better, where the air stinks and the absent horizons, the backcourts of a sturdy obscenity, these disused fucking washhouses whose brickwalls are liable to collapse on the offspring's skull at any moment. Fuck off.

Hines dislikes being a laughing-stock. The people he works beside are laughing-stocks. He is a laughing-stock. They are all laughing-stocks. Occasionally this being a laughing-stock is something not to be borne. He can lie awake at night, the head having started to bang. It is strange how they are content to remain objects of derision. Hines can see the faces. He can hear them discuss their children. What else does he do. He does a lot of things. It all gets a bit much. Very little time is left. There isnt the time to accomplish much. Should much be accomplished the time has shrunk. Should little be accomplished the world expands. To accomplish the little demands particular heads. Hines has not got a particular head. In his head the things go scratching against the outer shell. He can lie awake at night and breathe deeply, regularly, for the scratching to cease.

Sandra was in the kitchen. It makes no difference. With the gun in his possession movement will accelerate. The main problem is money. Hines was relying on his knowledge of Frank Sinclair to overcome this. A gun would probably cost 2 or 3 weeks wages but maybe as much as 4. Hines had no way of obtaining such an amount. The sum of £80 lay in the bank but could not be withdrawn by him. Yet no genuine reason exists for this situation. It is as much his money as Sandra's and Paul's. He just felt he should not be withdrawing it for selfish purposes. With £80 in hand he could probably get the gun quite easily, the additional cash to be advanced later on. Frank would arrange that.

Although in an obvious sense the £80 would have to be used for the gun. It belonged to the unit. As a symbol of that unity the money should be used to real purpose. Once Paul was old enough he would understand that. He could understand right now. If rupture within the home was the only alternative the boy would know fine well what had to be done; it would scarcely be a case of understanding or anything like it, just the natural order of things, that which the adult is obliged to do.

Of course Sandra was looking great, the jeans and the jumper, so reminiscent of how she used to look when pushing the pram; she used to push it down by the river to meet him coming home off early shift.

If the day was fine they did this rather than him just taking a bus home. He used to run up the road, all the way from the garage, then down through the park. It was still a surprise seeing her shape, her lack of belly, fitting into the old outfits again. She looked really well, and sometimes he felt a bit of a cunt to be meeting her in uniform, an embarrassment, the daft cashbag and hat while she was looking the way she did, and the wee yin babbling away; walking home, along past the old flint mill, the trees and the bushes, the grass: right smack in the heart of the city she had found this place, an amazing spot where you could walk in a valley by the side of a river; an enclosed place, road bridges high overhead, no traffic sounds whatsoever.

Hines grabbed her. He increased his hold of her, he laughed abruptly, relaxing the hold and increasing the hold; again laughing and she began laughing, that chuckling sound; it begins from way deep in her throat and makes a noise like gloogle gloolg. He kissed her on the lips, his tongue along her lower teeth; he felt her relax, returning the kiss with genuine aggression, the kiss mattering in itself. She liked kissing him. This was the great thing; and probably an explanation of why their lips always fitted together so well — a kiss can be really erotic, one kiss and one kiss only, if that kiss is right, is enough to get things moving immediately. Her skin through the jumper; the actual texture of the jumper, lamb's wool maybe or something akin; the size a bit big for her, the upper trunk slenderish; her tits through it as though she had left off her bra altogether but probably because she buys good bras that their material resembles flesh almost or maybe just so thin the skin through it cannot be concealed. She could get him from nothing; just sitting in the same space and it altering, naturally enough, an inter-something-or-other connected with radiation or something giving off from each other that one hand is moving to the other's hand, this drawing together as reaction, then the fitting together so exactly right. All parts of her. Those dances they used to have in just that kind of awareness, playing, dancing towards and dancing away, circling, an occasional touch, the tremble; then another record and sometimes when it was a slow one and they danced holding he got hard and they had to move from the floor, her shielding him.

Paul . . .

Asleep; he was dead-beat.

They kissed again. Over her shoulder he saw the gas burning in its

170

steady flame; the arrangement on the mantelpiece seemed different, the note either not there or lying so flat it couldnt be seen; and the blind drawn at the window. She had maybe given the whole place a going over. She moved and he was aware of her jumper again, of how slender her body was, or just the jumper being that bit too big for her. But he felt he could put his arms right round her and still be touching the sides of his own body, as though she was eating less than she should be — skinny, not slender. He moved to look at her and they both smiled. He shook his head. Aw Sandra.

I'm sorry Rab.

Jesus christ. He clutched onto her now, his chin on her shoulder, his eyelids shut; she shifted to kiss him, she was beautiful; his hands beneath her jumper and lightly on her skin, his fingertips to that spot at the base of her spine, and moving upwards on her spine, to beneath the strap of her bra, then out and he brought his hands out from her jumper. Fancy going to bed?

She smiled.

What is it?

O . . . She shook her head as she stepped to the armchair and began to undress.

How come you're so beautiful?

She stuck her tongue out at him, chuckling as she released the catch on her bra. Her tits jutted out as she turned to lay the bra on top of the chair.

He undressed and switched off the main light; she switched on the bedlamp. Lying down on his side he cupped his chin in his left hand, gazed at her until she moved nearer to him and he shifted so that she could lie above his left arm, it lying exactly beneath the pillow, within the space between her head and right shoulder, comfortably. She looked at him before they kissed. That can be a strange look. A look to see something or other — as though she isnt a hundred percent certain who he is. And when he broke the kiss she looked at him in the same way, before it continued, now pulling him more closely in to her. Sometimes he was unsure about holding her too tightly in case her breasts got too squashed by him, by his chest — one time years ago she gave him a kind of punch there, on the chest, and winced and rubbed her knuckles, not having been aware of how hard male chests can be. He manoeuvred her onto her back and they looked at each other. He kissed her throat and down to kiss her nipples, reaching to take down her pants; her head rose a little, her right arm lying over his back, to nibble at the lobe of his ear; she laughed and lay back on the pillow. Her legs parted as he positioned himself to enter. The opening felt so narrow.

God Rab you feel huge.

Hh.

It's because it's a while.

I'm no hurting you?

No.

You sure . . . christ . . . He breathed out and relaxed a moment, then pushed up slowly. He opened his eyelids but hers were closed; he kissed the tip of her nose and settled onto her, but taking his weight on both elbows. He grinned. Dont move or I'll come.

O.

Ssh.

She made as though to speak.

Ssh . . . He was having to smother a laugh. He placed his head on the pillow above her left shoulder. Think of churches. That old lady in the blue skirt walking up the path — Auvers, somewhere in France; where the sun shines. Going down some Rue, in the early evening, just the pair of them, heading for a meal, then onto some cafe for a chat and maybe a dance or something, Gaite Parisienne, the lassies kicking out, wee Toulouse with the sketch pad, the Seine in the moonlight, picked out on the ripples. Careful.

What d'you mean?

Nothing — a twitch, you twitched.

Sorry.

He was suppressing laughter.

Sorry! She began to chuckle.

They kissed now and he was moving and not able to stop, christ and he was having to thrust and come almost without an orgasm but having to cry out all the same.

He lay on her, still taking the weight on both elbows. It's okay, she said but he continued to take it. After a while he grunted and she said, Dont come out yet.

Okay.

God Rab it feels like the Niagra Falls.

He grinned and kissed her.

I forgot to bring in the tissues.

Use the sheet.

. . .

Naw, it'll be okay. Either that or you'll have to walk on your hands
to the fucking cludgie.

O God.

They both began laughing until she cried: It's coming out, you're
coming out. And he felt himself slipping out then was unsure whether
he was maybe still in. He moved onto his side and got out of bed at
once and dashed to the tallboy, into the top drawer for the box of
tissues. She took a couple. She wasnt rushing. It doesnt matter now,
she said. I suppose it's time the sheets were changed anyway.

Aaahh.

She glanced at him.

It's great to be alive.

She smiled.

He stretched, his fingertips to the ceiling, on tiptoes, muscles as
tensed as they could be. He relaxed enough to breathe out deeply,
prolonging it then breathing out again, the final old air, before
gasping in the fresh. Aah. Christ. Fancy a coffee?

She nodded. See that bag over there . . .

He went to the kitchen-cabinet, the pull-down section lying out
and the paper bag, containing two chocolate covered doughnuts.
Absolutely fucking disgusting. I dont know how you buy this stuff
Sandra I really dont.

Cheaper than tobacco.

Aye but christ sake I mean! When the water had boiled he made
the coffee and placed the doughnuts and cups on the television set,
beside the bed. Back between the sheets he stared at his doughnut
and frowned. I have reason to believe that in certain sections of
America one daubs one's erogenous zones with honey and one's
partner licks it off.

Sounds interesting.

Aye, strange fucking place America; it's a doughnut-loving
nation apparently.

It was me told you that.

Very sorry.

They dont have ordinary cakes, just assorted varieties of
doughnuts.

Monopoly land, what d'you expect.

No but it's funny . . . She studied the doughnut before taking the first bite. She was aware of him watching but continued as though indifferent, and she was managing to eat without getting any of the chocolate onto her face, except where a spot stuck to her upper lip, then out poked her tongue to ensnare it. It's actually quite tasty, she said. When he grinned she made a face at him.

How much were they?

I'm not telling you.

Dear but?

Yes.

A moment's silence; then he laughed and she grinned. Aye, he went on, life can be a startling item at times — I was just saying that very thing to a crabbit auld cunt who stepped onto my platform the other morning. Excuse me mrs I said I'm well aware your complaints are justified but in regard to the startling nature of the world, the ascendancy of certain stars and so on . . . He grinned and ate his last mouthful of doughnut. He got out of bed, collected the tin from his jerkin pocket and paused to slap at the soles of his feet before returning. It's great to see you.

Hines had said it while prising the lid off the tin. And he added, I didnt expect it I mean eh.

She handed him her cup and while he leaned to put it on top of the television she put her arm round his back; he closed the tin and placed it next to the cups. How come you're so beautiful?

You're a terrible flatterer Hines.

Hh; cant even get telling the truth nowadays.

She slapped his chest.

Ah! She's beating me next!

They rolled together until she was on top of him and she raised herself, her tits drooping so well and perfect and he craned his neck to meet them, taking each nipple in turn between his lips; she moved onto her side eventually, then onto her back, Hines managing to shift position while keeping mouth to nipple. He came away and they kissed, her hand now between his legs and their tongues touching within the other's mouth; he was attempting the insertion and she moved for him. They were still kissing but his head now rested next to hers on the pillow, and his left foot steadying against the bottom wall of the recess. He began the thrust, she going with it. A rhythm was settled into. Later he was set to climax and halted; she had also halted. He listened to her breathing. A few moments just, then it would be right to resume.

ooo

That sensation of dread, that terrible feeling, the alarm clock having failed to be set, it had stopped long ago, he had forgotten to set it. He was out of bed and lifting Sandra's wristwatch, which had also stopped — sometimes she neither winds nor wears it for days at a stretch. The light told him nothing; it could be 4.30 a.m. or maybe as late as 8. Ben the front room he gazed to the street, a man walked to the corner, the sound of a heavy vehicle passing away up on the main road. About 7 perhaps but not later than 8. He crossed to the cot, arranged the blankets over him, went to the lavatory. He could not go to work. He had missed the shift by two hours. He could go in and ask to sign spare. They would not allow him to sign spare unless desperately short of staff. But they would not be short of staff — not on a Thursday, wages-day. He would stand at the counter. He would stand there. He would roll a smoke. He would be standing. Harry Cairney was the deskclerk this morning; he was better than most but insufficiently so; he was not able to be as good as all that. Hines would be at the counter, smoking, and having to speak. He was not going in. He was not going in.

Time is it?

Late. He sniffed, I forgot to set the alarm.

O.

Terrible. Terrible.

What're you going to do?

Ach.

You going in? it cant be that late surely?

He said nothing. He went to the sink and filled a kettle for tea or coffee or whatever the fuck. His record was too bad to be true.

Should you not go in?

Aye, suppose so. Jesus. He gripped the edge of the sink. He took his hands away, he parted the blinds to see out. It was just too bad to be true.

175

When were you supposed to report?

The back of 5.

What time is it now?

Eh.

Switch on the radio.

Aye . . . He walked to the mantelpiece to get it and he lifted it. The water could be heard heating. It's getting bad really, he said, the timekeeping Sandra, it's out the window just now I mean . . . he sniffed. She took the radio from him and fiddled with the knobs. I cant seem to get into it. That's eh. And my day-off tomorrow as well, the wages next week I mean, hh. It's bad but Sandra, really bad. He was shaking his head. He shrugged.

Would they not give you a spare?

He shook his head.

Are you sure?

No on a Thursday. Afternoon aye but no the morning. It would be a case of well, turning up just, letting them see I've showed the face, so my name doesnt go into the book — well it still goes in right enough but no as bad, no as if I've just taken the day off without telling them I mean, without letting them know; that's the worst thing. But even then . . . even then, the way things stand.

7.27. She switched off the radio. You could be there for 8 if you hurried.

10 to.

She was waiting for him to say something.

10 to.

At least to show your face.

Aye. He sniffed, Coffee? Tea?

And you can get your wages at the same time.

Aye . . . He returned to the sink with the cups from last night, rinsing them out from the tap. He spooned in the coffee powder, waited for the water to reach boiling point. He got the tin from the television and rolled a smoke. He sneezed when the sulphur reached his nose. And he continued to sneeze while pouring from the kettle into the cups.

You should've put something on.

Aye, bloody freezing. He paused to sneeze again before carrying the coffees across, and he put them on the television before getting into bed. She snuggled into him. He put his arm round her, sitting up

176

with a pillow behind his back.

They sipped their coffee.

What was it you did again? last night. Over in Knightswood I mean.

Nothing — just put on my coat and left.

Aye but did they no say anything? I mean surely they said something.

No. I just told them I forgot you were coming home early.

Hines chuckled.

They didnt believe me of course. Dad's eyebrows: you know the way he can look, as if he's done everything possible and now he's powerless.

O christ!

They laughed for a time, then Sandra went on: They did know something was up, the way I wasnt talking. The afternoon was fine. Just after tea-time, that was the worst: I knew you'd be home. O God, I couldnt stop thinking about what you'd do when you found the note.

Hh.

I cant imagine not living with you Rab.

. . .

What'll we do?

He said nothing.

I was thinking if you went on the broo I could go full-time and you could find something else — anything; part-time, it wouldnt matter because we'd be able to save either way. It wouldnt be for long. Once we had enough gathered we could leave, leave Glasgow I mean, just go away.

Right enough.

Even if you couldnt find anything you would still get money, from the broo.

For a year, aye.

A year's good; we could save in a year.

D'you think so?

Yes; we would live on my money.

I doubt it.

Well I think we would. And even if we found we couldnt we'd at least manage to save something.

Aye, true.

Well then?

Hh.

Sandra was looking at him.

What happens if we get the dangerous-building notice next week?

We wont.

Aye but we could.

They've got that whole side to do yet.

Aye I know but still I mean, it could happen; anyway, even if it doesnt, it'll happen in a couple of months. Then these council rents, hell of a stiff so they are. I doubt if we could save much.

I disagree Rab.

He nodded.

We would manage on my money; yours would go straight into the bank.

Aye . . . He nodded, his lips pursing; and he nodded again.

She sipped coffee then passed him the cup and he placed it next to his own on the television.

So, he smiled, what do we do then? once we've got the sum, assuming we can save the fucking thing — what do we do?

We leave.

Hh.

She smiled.

He turned and kissed her forehead. Aye but where to?

God I dont know, anywhere.

He laughed.

It doesnt matter Rab, not really; just as long as we get away from here.

The ice-bound plateaus of the southern reaches.

It doesnt matter.

Hh.

It doesnt.

Naw, I know.

Well then!

Okay okay. He laughed and kissed her forehead. Just so's I've got it: I get the boot or I jack it; I go on the broo and you go full-time; we're saving the dough and arriving at a certain sum; once we've got it we leave; we just fucking leave. Right?

Why not? We just decide on a time really — say a year. By that time we can work out where we'll go.

It could even be Australia.

Yes. You get the forms beforehand. Andy said he'd get you a job easily.

Aye but no now; he's left.

Well your Uncle then.

Hh.

She chuckled.

I smell a rat.

Yes I know, it's too simple for you, that's the trouble.

Europe. What about Europe? could we go to Europe? France or someplace?

Yes.

Yes! Ha! Christ! He pushed down beneath the sheets and tugged the quilt right over his head and laughed loudly. Out he came to sit where he had been sitting. No we couldnt, no really.

Why not Rab? We would just arrive. We would just make sure we were arriving at the start of the summer. Remember that person in Isobel's college? Northern France, for four months. We would just need a tent, and my brother's got one; he would loan us it.

Hines laughed.

And if you stopped smoking . . .! She rapped him one on the shoulder. He had been prising off the lid of the tin. He replaced the tin on the television and took her head onto his chest.

She grinned, shaking her head slightly. Her left leg came to lie in between his. He already had an erection. Oho, she said.

Hines laughed.

Paul was chortling, his frequent shrieks could be heard. Between him and where Hines was at the oven, Sandra had arranged the clotheshorse with towels so that she could use the babybath without the boy seeing her.

The bacon grilled while the eggs crackled in the frying pan; on a plate to the front of the grill compartment lay a pile of buttered toast; the tea infused near to the frying pan. The table was already set. Hines glanced at the label of the cornflakes packet then flicked the hot grease onto the egg yolks to get them turning white while at the same time keeping them runny. Paul's shriek. Hines walked round the clothes-horse. Actors on the television. He watched for a moment. One actor had biffed another on the head; and this other was bouncing about then doing a cartwheel which carried him across to the first whom he kicked on the bum, and then cartwheeled out through a doorway. It was well worked.

Sandra had begun drying herself.

Are you sure he's just to get toast?

Ask him and see.

Aye, well, if you leave it to him he'll no eat anything.

He had cornflakes.

I know that, but it's hell of a cold outside; he could be doing with something hot in the belly.

Fine, make him an egg then.

Aye but he'll probably no eat the fucking thing.

Well . . . Sandra shrugged; she finished dressing and made to lift the babybath. But he did so instead; tipping the water into the sink. She took the bath from him and rinsed it out. Dont worry about it, she added.

Aw naw, naw, I'm just eh . . . He grinned. See when I was a boy! He chuckled and lifted the thing to lift the eggs out the frying pan. Bacon though, he said, I mean you'd think he'd go for that. Christ, how often do we have it!

Sandra poured the tea.

Surely he'd eat a slice of bacon?

She glanced at him.

And he grinned, Just kidding. Honest.

Thank God.

D'you believe in God? He sniffed. What I mean is an item such that it is more powerful than finite items, such that it makes them tick? Cause I dont, let me tell you, I think it is all a load of shite, a load of fucking codswallop, just stuck there to mislead the workers. That's the trouble but, they're all a bunch of bastarn imbeciles, the workers, the lower orders. Eh! He grinned, lifted the bacon from the grill to lay on the plates. Sandra also grinned; she cupped his right hand in her own.

He nodded. I like the way you do that it eh . . . makes me feel something or other — great; it makes me feel great.

She kissed him and walked to clear the clothes-horse. He laid the food on the table. She said, If you dont go in what'll happen?

Nothing; I'll just have to go up to Head Office for the wages. After a pause he added, I'm going in but. Anyway, with a bit of luck I'll just march in, get the dough and march back out.

I hope so.

I'll play it cagey, boxing clever, sidling through the door, up to the counter — in my stocking soles so they'll no notice . . . Heh! the wee man; I've got the wee man with me! Psychological warfare for fuck sake I'll sit him on the counter. They wont give me a sherriking in front of him surely! Eh I mean how can they humiliate a man in front of his boy? I ask you, is that the done thing!

Sandra smiled as she took a slice of toast across to Paul.

Potato scones, he said, it's the one thing missing from this breakfast.

Well I told you to buy them.

Aye I know, but you've got to buy the whole fucking packet nowadays, they'll no let you take a couple.

We would've used them up.

Ah. He shrugged and pushed the plate of toast towards her as she sat down. You'll be okay about yesterday afternoon? about taking it off?

She nodded, then she looked at him. And he wont deduct any money from me either . . . She paused, then began to eat.

He studied the food on his plate.

Sorry.

I wasnt getting at you Sandra.

O I know you werent.

He reached over to hold her hand for a short time. Last night . . . I didnt expect you, I didnt expect you to be back like that. I mean I never really thought about it, what I would do, if you didnt. Too much . . . he shook his head.

I'm sorry Rab.

O christ shut up.

ooo

There are parties whose attention to a variety of aspects of existence renders life uneasy. It cannot be said to be the fault of Hines that he is

181

such a party. A little leeway might be allowed him. A fortnight's leave of absence could well work wonders. A reassembling of the head that the continued participation in the land of the greater brits

Fuck off.

Hines is forced into situations a dog wouldnt be forced into. Even a rat. It is most perplexing. Hines has a wean and he treats this wean as a son i.e. a child, a fellow human being in other words yet here is he himself being forced into a situation whence the certain load of shite as an outcome, the only outcome, an outcome such that it is not fair. It is not fucking fair. Hines is fucking fed up with it. He is not to be treated like this. He has already decided not to be.

As also his wife. This very morning she has suggested things may yet prove brightly. And even prior to that he himself

Paul tugged on his hand, wanting to stop at a shop window. There was a fine display of toys and games, the tinsel and Xmas paper, coloured lights and the rest of it. Paradise for any kid, to be locked in overnight.

He rolled a smoke. It was good being without the uniform. Worthwhile paying the busfare just for the privilege. Although the pockets of the jeans were hell of a tight for the hands to rest inside comfortably so he had to put them into the jerkin pockets which were far too open to the elements. Nothing was dropping from the heavens thank fuck but the wind was really powerful. Paul was okay, having the mittens and balaclava; warm hands and ears. Adults dont wear balaclavas. They seem to regard them as childish. Balaclavas for adults could take a trick; fashionable designs perhaps, manly for men, womanly for women etc.

The nearer to the garage the more people he was nodding to. On wages-day this area is full of them. All going off with their cash to here there and everywhere. It's an astonishing life. You see them all doing this that and the next thing. Hines seldom does this that and the next thing. What does he do. Fuck all. He's always skint. How come he's always skint. A grave A and a grave B but still quantifiable.

Aw christ though it can be fairly disquieting, how one's belly reacts to mental shudderings, especially when aforementioned shudderings are an effect of the utmost cabbage kettles. One fine day Hines R. was arrested. It was like this man: there he was heading along nicely nicely when all of a sudden bang; right out the fucking door. And for

182

what too! fuck all. Screwing the wife and forgetting to set the fucking alarm clock cause he fell asleep. Terrible. Really bad, bad, really, really bad.

A sweetie shop. Inside he pointed the lollipops out to Paul. But Paul preferred a packet of sweeties then outside he paused to stare in the window again. Hines stayed to let him look for a time then he picked him off the ground. I know you're a bit big for this lifting son, he said, but I want to talk to you. This is one of these wee moments in life which you're earmarked to remember once I'm dead and buried. You're dad's going to get a telling off. More than that; he's probably going to get a line — maybe even a Head Office line. And Head Office lines arent good, they're bad in fact, murder polis. Actually I'll probably be getting the boot if that happens, the chop, doomed to a life without buses. It means — hopeless really, bad. Here . . . he put the boy back onto the pavement.

Only a few people were in the Office. At this time of the day the vast majority would already have collected their wages. He took his place at the counter behind a queue of three, and rolled a cigarette. Paul wandered off, chewing his sweeties and gazing at the objects of interest. Harry Cairney was the Deskclerk on duty earlier this morning but he would have finished by this time. It was for the best. He would maybe have been a bit irritated by the sleeping-in; he could even have taken it personally, the way some folk do. That's a strange thing, how people take things personally.

The Wagesclerk had pushed the sheet of paper across the counter. Hines Robert 4729 being underlined in red ink. The Wagesclerk muttered, Hang on a minute, and walked away over to a small room at the rear of the area, where the Deskclerks went for their tea and so on. The red line had been done free-hand and wasnt too straight, not squiggly, but not straight either.

Campbell. Hines inhaled and exhaled. He was eating a roll as he came over, not glancing in the direction of Hines, not acknowledging that this was Hines which was fine really because they disliked each other very greatly. He pulled out a drawer, humming to himself, bringing out a slip of paper; then he brought out another slip of paper which he laid near to Hines. Sign there conductor, he said; they want to see you at Head Office directly.

Hines nodded; he frowned. What d'you mean directly?

Directly, right away, they want to see you just now; you better go home and get into your uniform.

Hh; I'm no working but.

Aye I know you're no, you slept in.

Hines nodded. Naw eh . . . how can I put on the uniform?

What you on about?

Well if I'm no working; how come I'm to put on the uniform?

Campbell gazed at him. Look, just sign there for your line, they want to see you at Head Office.

Aye I know but I'm no actually being employed the day I mean so . . . Paul was beside him, trying to edge his way in between Hines and the counter.

After a moment Campbell said, Either it's the day or you've got a 10 o'clock for tomorrow morning: suit yourself.

Hines sniffed. It's my day-off tomorrow.

Well the bloody next day then.

The next day's Saturday. I didnt know they worked Saturdays up at Head Office.

Look Hines just sign and take your line; they want to see you right away.

Aye but what I dont understand is how it's to be accomplished.

What're you bloody on about! Campbell had whispered this; but the anger was apparent even to Paul and he was gripping Hines' hand. Hines inhaled and exhaled, he patted the boy's head. Naw, he said, it's just eh . . . I dont see how I can go to Head Office the day. And it's my day-off the morrow. Then next week I'm backshift so how can I get a 10 o'clock line for then, unless it's a 10 o'clock at night line.

Campbell took a cigarette from his packet and lighted it; he looked at Hines.

I mean as far as I can see I'll no be able to go for another week at least — no unless they agree to see me in civvies. But even then, it means I'll be going when I'm no actually working i.e. I'll no be getting paid. I mean tell me this: if I was working the morrow and got taken off my shift on a 10 o'clock, would I still be getting paid while I went up to Head Office?

Campbell exhaled smoke. Go and see your Shop Steward.

Aye but . . .

Go and see your Shop Steward.

Aye I know I mean I'm going to but . . .

Here. Campbell pushed the slip of paper nearer to Hines.

I cant sign, no if it means I've

Look Hines I'm no going to stand here arguing with the likes of you. Either you sign for this Head Office line or you dont. What's it to be?

Naw eh . . . I'm no being cheeky or anything; I just dont understand how it's to be accomplished properly. I mean how it's actually possible for me to go. No unless I'm wearing the uniform and I can only really wear it when I'm getting paid to.

Campbell snatched the two slips of paper from the counter and strode back to the Deskclerks' room. The Wagesclerk was examining his sheet of paper with all the signatures. Hines ground out his cigarette on the floor and moved along to him; he nodded and turned the sheet round, signed his name. The Wagesclerk hesitated a moment but then gave him his wages-envelope. Hines checked the amount. The pay-receipt and money were always arranged so that the contents could be counted without opening the actual envelope. He put it into his pocket and took Paul by the hand, turning to leave. Barry McBride walked over, grinning slightly; obviously he must have been witness to some of the proceedings. Behind him came another driver — Scott was his name and he was a bit of an idiot.

Hines shrugged. They're trying to give me a 10 o'clock line . . . He grinned: I mean it's half-past fucking twelve!

Barry chuckled.

Scott said, Sammy's up the stair. You going up to see him?

Suppose I'll have to. He grinned again and left the Office. Upstairs in the corridor he waited by the notice-board. Paul gave him a sweetie. He chewed it, staring at the notices; then the door opened downstairs and he could hear Scott's voice. Quickly he bent to Paul. Listen son, he whispered, you probably dont know it but this is great fun. Just look and listen and you'll be fine. But dont worry. Whatever you do dont worry, okay?

Paul looked at him in that straightfaced way he has.

Hines smiled. It'll be quite hard to follow. But if you just watch the faces . . . Okay; just watch the faces. Whatever you do dont worry — you're a hell of a worrier for a 3 year old!

I'm four.

Four! Jesus christ right enough! Hines winked and led him along the corridor. In the bothy the Shop Steward was sitting at his usual table, reading a newspaper. How's it going Sammy?

Ah no bad Rab; how's yourself?

So so . . . He lifted Paul onto a chair and then sat down on another. Naw, he went on, a wee bit of bother with Campbell there.

Sammy paused, and nodded; he folded the newspaper away into a side pocket and bringing out his cigarettes he offered one to Hines who declined. He lighted his own while Hines began rolling one. The door opened and in came Barry, Scott and a couple of others; they sat at a table not too near and not too far from them. Sammy glanced at Hines.

Ach it's daft really. I just wouldnt accept a Head Office line.

Sammy nodded and waited for him to finish rolling the cigarette, then struck a light for him.

See I'm no working the day and they want me to go up and see them this afternoon. I mean I'm supposed to go home and put on the uniform.

Aye.

The point is: if I'm no working what in the name of god should I go and put on their fucking uniform for?

Aye. Sammy sniffed, glanced sideways at Paul.

I mean surely if they want to see me on garage business they should be doing it on garage time i.e. I should be getting paid.

Sammy looked at him.

Eh? What d'you think?

Well . . .

Christ sake Sammy I mean they're wanting me at Head Office and I'm supposed to go on my own time and wearing their fucking uniform. And if I dont go the day they'll hit me with a 10 o'clock the morrow morning, right? so I get pulled off my shift to go straight up. But I'll still no get paid. My time stops as soon as I step off the fucking bus.

Aye. Is that how you never took the line off Campbell?

Hines nodded.

What's it for? your line.

Ach. Couple of sleep-ins and that. It doesnt matter, no really.

Naw I'm just asking . . . Sammy glanced at the water-boiler; Scott had gone across to make a pot of tea, he was rinsing out a few cups under the cold water tap.

Hines shrugged. What d'you think?

Well, Christ, I dont know to be honest. Eh . . . Sammy sniffed. What makes you think you'll get hit with a 10 o'clock the morrow morning?

Campbell told me I would.

Did he . . . Sammy scratched his chin. Just for sleep-ins?

I've had a couple of bookings as well right enough.

Aye still, you're no expecting a 10 o'clock line unless it's bad Rab I mean you know as well as I do, 10 o'clock lines, pretty serious.

Ach I dont . . . probably just wanting to get fucking rid of me. Sammy snorted.

Hines looked at him.

That's no the way they work, come on.

What d'you mean come on? all I know is I'm back here 18 months and I'm still no up the fucking driving school!

Aye well you know the reason for that. Your record's bloody hopeless — that's how you've got the line. Christ Rab I mean the other day you've signed-off and no even been out on the blooming road! I heard about it as soon as I walked in.

I had a bad stomach, diarrhoea, ask anybody — Harry Cairney'll tell you.

Aw I know, I know; I'm no saying you were at it . . . Sammy stopped and sat back from the table as Scott laid down two cups of tea, murmuring, I've put in the sugar . . . I mean look at it this way, continued Sammy. if you say to me, Sammy — will you go and find out my chances of getting up the driving school.

I wouldnt say that.

Naw, hold on, I'm just

But I would never say it.

I know you wouldnt, I'm just trying to show you something.

What you trying to show me?

Well your record for heaven sake it's murder. If I walk in to fight for you what happens: they bring out your file. End of story.

Aw good, good, that's you told me my record's bad.

Sammy looked at him.

My record's got fuck all to do with it.

Aw that's a good yin. Sammy folded his arms for a moment; he then reached for his tea and sipped at it; he lifted his cigarette from the ashtray, and glanced sideways at Paul . . . I mean what're you wanting me to do Rab? I mean if you're wanting me to come up to

Head Office with you then I will — course I will, it's my blooming job.

I'm no asking you to do that.

Naw I know you're no and I'll tell you something for nothing: you should've been up that driving school years ago. And you would've been if you'd screwed the bloody nut — so there's no use coming in here with your complaints.

What're you talking about?

Aye, you know fine well what I'm talking about. Sammy sipped at his tea and then put the cup down; he glanced at those at the other table. I've heard your moans and groans Rab, I've heard them.

No from me you've no! you kidding? I've never fucking said a word about it. Hh.

Aye well I've heard it. That mate of yours, shouting his bloody mouth off. Dont think I dont know cause I do.

You talking about Reilly?

I'm no naming any names.

Hines shook his head. Paul gazed at him. He reached to pat him on the head. You too warm? he said, and tugged the balaclava down to lie on his shoulders. He glanced at Sammy who had been glancing at him; each glanced away. Hines inhaled on his cigarette; it had stopped burning; he struck a match to relight it; then he said, Look Sammy I've got nothing to do with Reilly; if I was wanting to make any complaints I'd come and make them.

Sammy nodded.

I'm here to see you about one thing and one thing only. If I sign for that line downstairs then I've got to go home and change into the uniform; then I've got to go up to Head Office to see them right away. I'll no get paid for it. I'm doing it all on my own time. What I really want to know is whether the Union is happy to let this happen to the members?

Sammy sighed and scratched his neck.

I think Rab's got a point, said Scott.

Aye I know he's got a point. I just dont think there's anything we can do about it right now.

How d'you mean? said Hines.

Sammy shrugged. He laid his cigarette on the ashtray. Look, d'you want me to go down and see Campbell or what?

How?

188

Just to find out the score.

In what way?

Well for one thing I mean, to find out how serious the line is. For instance: did he actually say it'd be a 10 o'clock the morrow morning if you dont go this afternoon?

Hines shook his head. Then a tapping noise sounded from the intercom; the breathing noise from the microphone . . . Conductor Hines. Conductor Hines. If you're on the premises, report to the Office. Conductor Hines.

Paul's amazement. Hines winked and asked him for one of his sweeties; and then indicated Sammy. Paul offered one to him. Sammy took it and swallowed it, following up with a quick mouthful of tea. Hines grinned. It's no a pill.

Sammy smiled briefly.

I'm no signing for the line.

I'll come down with you.

Heh Rab, called Scott; you want to leave the wean here?

Naw it's alright, ta.

It's up to you. Scott shrugged.

Ach I'll just take him with me. Ta anyway.

Sammy had finished his tea and rinsed the cup out; he went to the door and held it open for Hines and Paul to exit. Out on the corridor he said, A wee bit warmer the day.

Aye, I thought that myself.

Sammy snorted. There's quite a few having a bet on snow for Christmas. Mugs — every year they do it — what they forget is it's got to be snowing at midnight on Christmas Eve. Otherwise they lose their money.

Christ.

Aye; it's a stupid bet.

Hh.

An Inspector was standing by the counter-hatch when they entered the Office; he raised it for them; but noticing Paul coming through he frowned, You cant take the wee boy in with you.

I'll have to but.

He'd be okay here, said Sammy.

Naw, he'll just no stay by himself. Hines ruffled Paul's hair then made to continue but the Inspector raised his right hand. Better wait till I check, he told him.

189

I'll come with you Bob, said Sammy.

Thanks a lot, muttered Hines. And the Shop Steward looked at him before carrying on across the Office area behind the Inspector. Hines hoisted Paul onto the counter. 1255 hours. Nobody queued for the wages. The Wagesclerk had begun clearing his stuff away. Hines gestured at him and said, That's the guy who dishes out the money to the drivers and conductors son; remember I got mine off him? the envelope with the money?

Yes.

He took a last drag at the cigarette and ground it out on the floor. The Wagesclerk hadnt glanced across. Towards the rear of the Office area a girl came from one of the larger offices near to the Deskclerks' room, and walked along towards another. That's a girl who works in the Office, he said. She earns more than I do for fewer hours.

The Wagesclerk paused.

Hines sniffed and nodded in his direction. That man there, he earns an awful lot more than I do; and he works fewer hours as well. He's a Clerk, the Wagesclerk. See: he has to wear a shirt and a tie and the rest of it . . . Hines glanced away from the man and asked Paul for a sweetie.

The girl was returning. She was nice to look at. She would be wearing perfume; if she wasnt wearing too much that good smell of skin would be overriding. Short skirts had been in style last summer and she still wore one; her legs werent as good as Sandra's but they were fine all the same. She walked in a studied manner, her sheets of paper flapping as she opened the door, she entered, disappeared.

Sammy came from the Deskclerks' room not long afterwards; he also wore a shirt and tie, and he kept his uniform well pressed although not as if in an effort to emulate the Inspectors, more as if he paid extra heed to Head Office memoranda in the belief that Shop Stewards should set an example. His eyebrows were raised. You could tell he wanted to speak but was having to restrain himself. When he got to the counter he said, Rab — you never mentioned it was your day-off the morrow.

Aye, I told Campbell.

Sammy nodded. You're definitely best going up this afternoon then. I'll come with you but. And listen, between you and me, it's very doubtful they'll give you the bullet. Your record's bad right enough — you've got to admit it — but I think you'll get away with 2 days and a severe reprimand.

You sure?

Well no guarantees, but eh . . .

I had a feeling I'd be out the fucking door.

Naw; doubt it. You've been too many years in the job.

Aye but my service is broken Sammy.

Still and all, it must go in your favour. Mind Billy McCann? Christ I had to go up with him once and I'm no kidding you, if you think your record's bad!

Hines nodded. Will I be on time then? if I go up.

Ho!

I'm no going if I'm no.

Look Rab, to be honest, I think you're making a mountain out a molehill.

Well I dont I mean I'm no really; it's a point of principle. I dont see why the Union should be willing to accept a load of shite from Head Office.

Ach.

Hines paused then took out the tin, began making a cigarette. Barry McBride had entered with Scott and a couple of others; they were standing out of earshot but occasionally gazing over. Look at it this way, continued Hines: if you and me go up to Head Office this afternoon I'll be the only cunt no getting paid. You'll be getting paid and so will them wanting to see me. I'm the fucking imbecile. No just me, every busworker who's ever in the same fucking boat. It's always the same Sammy. Christ sake I mean either everybody should get paid or no cunt should get paid.

Sammy sniffed and nodded slightly. Then Hines grinned, Away and tell Campbell I'm willing to go and meet them in a fucking pub if we're all wearing civvies and it's after working hours!

Sammy smiled briefly. But what're you wanting them to do? you've got to see them sooner or later.

I know, I know . . . He lighted his cigarette. I'm just no willing to put on my uniform and go on my own time to do something connected to garage business. Nobody else does. I dont see why we should — do you?

Sammy looked at him.

Hines shrugged and exhaled smoke.

Is that it final then?

Aye.

Okay, I'll away and tell them.

Sorry.

What d'you mean sorry?

Nothing.

Listen Rab, dont try any of your fly patter with me.

I wasnt meaning anything.

Aye you were . . . Sammy sniffed. Avoiding the faces of those standing out of earshot he turned and headed back to the Deskclerks' room. The Inspector stood at the door; he opened it for the Shop Steward then followed him in.

Paul began swivelling on the counter, propelling himself like on a roundabout. Hines pushed him for a time, then returned him to the floor and moved a couple of paces nearer the group. Eventually Scott approached, wanting to know what was what. Just the same, said Hines.

A conductor asked, What's it actually about but. Are you refusing to take a Head Office line? is that it?

Well aye, but no really. I'm just refusing to go home and put on my uniform then go up to Head Office when I'm no working.

Aw aye. The conductor frowned, Quite fucking right and all.

Heh Rab . . . Barry nodded to across the Office area; and Hines turned slowly and became engrossed in checking the buttons on Paul's coat. The Inspector was attempting to beckon him on through. Hines continued footering with the coat buttons.

Eh conductor . . . The Inspector had arrived at the counter. Come through a minute.

What about the wean?

Eh — can you no leave him there? it'll no be long.

Hines nodded after a moment. Just wait a minute, he said to Paul, I'll no be long. Okay?

Paul nodded. Hines winked and patted him on the head, before following the Inspector across to the room.

Campbell and Fairlie were both there. Fairlie was another Deskclerk, a man in his late fifties and about 20 years older than Campbell; he appeared to have just eaten the remains of his dinner; a full mug of tea lay in front of him on the small table. Campbell sat along from him and Sammy was standing to the side, near to a wall. And directly at the door stood the Inspector, arms folded. It was a small room; Hines had to take up a position closeby the table, quite near to the elderly Deskclerk.

Campbell spoke first. You're still refusing to take the line?

I'm no willing to put on my uniform and go up to Head Office on my own time.

Campbell frowned. He glanced at Fairlie who was studying his mug of tea, then said: So you will take the line?

Aye, as long as I dont have to go up when I'm no working.

If you dont go up this afternoon it's a 10 o'clock tomorrow morning.

It's my day-off tomorrow.

Campbell glanced at Fairlie and folded his arms.

This afternoon or tomorrow morning, said Fairlie. Suit yourself. He raised the mug of tea and sipped, making a slight slurping noise. Hines glanced at Sammy who pursed his lips. Then the Deskclerk placed the mug on the table and looked up. What's it to be then?

Eh . . . will I be on time?

What d'you mean son?

Well I'm no working the day and I'm no working the morrow.

Aye, so you've plenty of time.

I know, but it means I'm no getting paid.

What exactly is it you're talking about?

I'm being asked to put on my uniform and go up to Head Office. I should get paid for it.

Hh; that's a good yin. Fairlie half smiled to Campbell who snorted. Then he looked to Hines again. How d'you work that out?

I'm having to put on my uniform and go up to Head Office: I should get paid for it.

No you shouldnt.

How no?

Fairlie raised his eyebrows then frowned, he lifted the mug to sip at the tea and peered at Campbell over its rim. Campbell replied, There's no point trying to talk to him.

Fairlie said nothing. Sammy cleared his throat; he sniffed and glanced at the elderly Deskclerk. What he says Tom, in a way he's got a fair point.

Dont you start!

Naw but if you think about it.

For God sake Sammy. Fairlie shook his head. You mean he's to

193

get paid for going up to Head Office with a bloody line!

Aye I know, but if you think about it.

Campbell snorted. I know what I effing think about it. He sat forwards on his chair and he stared at Hines, then seemed to relax, and he chuckled slightly. Fairlie was sipping tea again; he laid the mug on the table and gazed at Hines. You get paid for conducting buses son. Your trouble is you dont conduct enough of them. That's how you've got the Head Office line, your timekeeping's a bloody disgrace — your record as a whole for that matter, no two ways about it. In fact either you take the line or you'll be out the door.

Hines looked at him. They exchanged looks. Then Fairlie lifted the mug of tea.

That's a bit strong, said Sammy.

A bit strong! Fairlie glared at him. D'you know the kind of record we're talking about here? I'll be surprised if he's worked a full week since he came back to the bloody job. I'll tell you something for nothing: I dont think he's got a leg to stand on. And I'll tell you something else Sammy: I'm surprised at you!

What d'you mean?

Well, this bloody nonsense. Fairlie shook his head and swallowed a mouthful of tea. His face had reddened. So had Sammy's. After several moments Campbell sat up and took a packet of cigarettes from his dustcoat; he passed one to both the men and flicked a lighter to light his own; the other two lit their own.

Hines gestured with his tin and murmured, Okay if I . . . And he rolled a cigarette and struck a match and lighted it. When he exhaled he did so to the floor, and he held the cigarette cupped in his right hand, at his side. Campbell had been watching him. There was a large pictorial calendar of Canada on the wall above the table. Hines coughed and studied it, then inhaled.

Fairlie nodded in some significant way; and the Inspector opened the door and murmured, Eh conductor, will you wait outside a minute . . .

The door clicked firmly shut behind him.

Hines shrugged across for the benefit of those behind the counter. Although Paul wasnt tall enough to be seen he would be thereabouts of course. More people were there now. Hines glanced about to see the time. There was a large electric wall-clock; according to it he had been in with the Deskclerks for less than 10 minutes. He puffed rapidly on the cigarette to get it burning properly. He walked a few paces, and leaned with his back to the wall. Soon the door opened. Sammy gestured at him to go with him in the direction of the counter; they stopped about halfway across and he stood side on, so that he was speaking a few inches from Hines' left ear; and he spoke very quietly. Tom Fairlie meant what he said there Rab. If you dont take the line he's going to try and sack you on the spot. He's waiting for McGilvaray to come back from his dinner and he's going straight in to see him. I'm no kidding you, Sammy shook his head, you're really stirring things up.

What?

Sammy nodded. I mean you've got a good point, I'm no saying you've no. I'm just saying I dont think this is the way to go about it. Christ sake I mean Rab, bring it up at the next Branch Meeting — if you dont I will. And I'll be bringing it up at the next Shop Stewards' Meeting as well. Eh?

Hines inhaled and glanced towards the group behind the counter. I cant take the line, he whispered.

How no? the two of us'll go straight up Head Office — I'll come with you and that I mean . . . He sniffed. You're making an issue out of nothing.

I dont agree.

Come on Rab I've known you for years; I know you've got your principles.

It's got nothing to do with that — honest I mean I'm just fucking sick of getting messed about.

Sammy sniffed; it became a sigh. Wiping the corners of his mouth he inhaled deeply on the cigarette, retaining the smoke in his lungs for a long period. Is that it final? He exhaled.

Hines shrugged.

You're refusing to take the line?

I'm no willing to go up to Head Office in my own time, aye.

Sammy nodded. He inhaled again and muttered, Right you are then. And he returned to the Deskclerks' room, chapped once on the door and entered immediately, shutting the door behind himself. Hines walked to the counter and raised the hatch. Before anybody could approach he held his hands palms upwards mouthing, No.

Paul came trotting up to him. Lifting him up Hines placed him on the counter. You been good?

Paul didnt answer; he was staring out into the Office area. Then Scott strolled over. What's happening Rab?

Nothing. I think they're giving me the bullet.

Fuck sake.

Hines nodded and turned from him, gazing in the same direction Paul was; and when the boy swivelled back to look at the faces in the group so did Hines. He caught the gaze of a conductress called Irene and grinned. The suspense is killing me!

An outbreak of mild laughter; and conversations began. A conductor offered cigarettes till his packet was empty. Scott stepped in with his own packet to the few who had been left out, and got jeered. Hines ground out his own and took one from him and the laughter was quite loud.

When Sammy came from the Deskclerks' room he did so very deliberately; he crossed the floor in the way people do when there is only one goal to be reached and that goal by the one route. Scott moved to raise the hatch for him.

I'm calling a Meeting, he said generally. The bothy in 20 minutes. I want a couple of yous to go and see if you can drum up a few folk.

I'll try the *Vale*, laughed somebody.

So will I, said Barry and with a grin at Hines he added, This thing's cost me a drink so it has!

Sammy said, The more the merrier; we want a good turn out. He sniffed and glanced at Hines: Fancy a cup of tea?

ooo

Somebody had given Paul a cup of milk and he seemed content to sit next to Hines, listening to the voices of those at the table. Nothing was being said that could be linked directly to the cause of the bother. Sammy appeared to be saving it for the Meeting proper. More people gathered than Hines had seen in the bothy for a long time. Normally Branch Meetings took place in one of the rooms of the local Masonic Hall; attendances rarely numbered more than twenty. Two members of the Committee arrived and went to sit at a nearby table; they glanced at Hines and glanced away when they saw he had noticed.

196

They were probably talking about him. They dont like him very much. He doesnt like them either. Well, he doesnt not like them, he just thinks they're fucking idiots. A variety of animosities exists within the garage. Quite a few people, including Hines, find it impossible to talk to those who werent staunchly opposed to the introduction of one-man-operated buses. The issue disrupted, totally, garage life towards the end of his first spell in the job. It is the root cause of most of the present disharmony. And now that the poor old fucking conductor/conductress is becoming absent things can never be the same.

Why worry. Hines doesnt. He's given up the fucking ghost, it is too ridiculous, it is a joke. Most of the carry-ons in the garage are a joke. People who eat in the bothy consider themselves superior to those who eat in the canteen. They regard the latter as a bunch of ne'er-do-well fly-by-nights while the latter regard the former as a bunch of infirm pensioners whose one aim in life is to secure a gold watch. It stems from the simple fact that the longer a person remains in a job the more habits and possessions he or she will acquire. And since habits demand further possessions and all possessions require space, bearing in mind that the bothy has lockers and the canteen doesnt, the bothy becomes a home from home for those who remain attached to the job — but there again: a lot of folk like to drink tea or coffee whenever they are on the garage premises and they can only do so in the canteen between certain hours of the day such that they are forced into using the bothy outside of those hours even though they would prefer not to do so because when all is said and done it is much better sitting drinking tea in the bothy than standing doing nothing in the fucking corridor.

He stopped himself from rolling another cigarette. If this was a different occasion altogether he might have decided to stop forever. The atmosphere was thick with smoke, stifling. No windows open, the condensation dripping down the walls. Yet if anybody was in a position to get them opened surely he was, the life and soul of the affair, the bone of contention, the one of whom it might be said etc., that the present dispute and so on.

Once upon a time he was ejected from a Branch Meeting for applying the term Shite to a Chairman's summing up. That kind of thing should be beyond belief. The incident occurred midway through his second stint in the job. What a shambles. It was his own fault for having allowed himself to be dragged along by Reilly. And very recently Colin Brown asked him to come back again because things were getting better. But Hines declined, he wont return till muffins are served. He doesnt have the time to spend. It may seem as if he is better than others by not doing so. Occasionally he does see himself as better while at other times he sees himself as worse. He simply doesnt have the time. He requires to move. Other people apparently do not require to move. Maybe it is hypocrisy alone keeps them from it. Other arguments arent good. Things that are wrong are seen to be wrong when eyes are not shut. And eyes cannot be shut when people are working otherwise buses would crash and conductors would trip over outstretched feet.

He stopped himself from rolling another cigarette. Heh Sammy! fancy a bit of air? hell of a smoky in here . . . He nodded at Paul.

The windows were raised a little.

Then moving his chair backwards Sammy rose and paused for the two Committee men to join him; they made their way to the rear where tables had been placed end to end, with a row of chairs immediately to their front. The Committee men stood on chairs to either side of the row while Sammy climbed up onto the centre table and clapped his hands for the chatter to cease. He began to speak but many of those seated had their view restricted and had to stand; the ensuing noise of furniture being banged about could have seemed deliberate. Hines was aware of his heart thumping, his irritation — anger perhaps. What a time to collapse with a stroke. Yet Sammy took it all in his stride. Probably Reilly would manage this kind of thing in a similar manner; his temperament is right for it. Somebody next to Paul had hoisted him onto the table. Ta, muttered Hines and he took the boy's hand and continued to hold it.

Sammy had been given a cigarette. By the time he was smoking the racket died; he started to speak. Eh I've had to call this Extraordinary Meeting. A thing's just happened and it needs to be discussed. Most of yous'll already have heard about it by now. What it is: Rab Hines there, he had a Head Office line waiting for him when he collected his wages this morning. Campbell was on the desk. Anyway, Rab wouldnt take the line. He wouldnt take it because it means he would have to go up to Head Office this afternoon and he's no working. He told Campbell he wasnt going. The thing is: if he doesnt accept the line they're saying they'll sack him on the spot. It's a genuine threat. Fairlie. No messing with him as most of yous'll know. He's going right in to see McGilvaray. Now as far as I'm concerned he's went over the score, and I told him that. The point is but — let's no kid ourself — McGilvaray's going to be right behind him . . . Sammy dragged on the cigarette.

What're they wanting to sack him for? called somebody.

Cause he'll no take the line, replied somebody from the crowd.

The brief chatter halted when Sammy raised his hand; he went on: Now as I say, this thing's got to be discussed. That's how I've called the Meeting.

What was the line for? called somebody.

Sammy raised his hand to stop anyone replying. We cant have the Meeting lasting all day, he said, for all we know Fairlie's in with McGilvaray right at this minute. So it's a possible strike situation; that's the kind of thing we've got to talk about.

Someone had passed Hines another tipped cigarette; his mouth tasted like burnt paper; smoking is bad for the health and requires immediate cessation.

Now as I'm saying, it's no a strike situation at the moment but let's no kid ourself, we might have to start thinking along these lines. The point is: Fairlie's out of order. He's threatening to sack Rab Hines on the spot if he doesnt take the line and go up to Head Office this afternoon. Now he's got no blooming right to carry on like that. What I'm saying is: if Mr McGilvaray backs him up then we should be prepared to withdraw our labour. And I think McGilvaray will back him up; he'll go the full road. So we've got to be ready to go the full road as well.

Sammy inhaled and gazed round at the faces, then turning to a Committee man he nodded and stepped down onto a chair. The Committee man got up onto the table. The Meeting's being thrown open, he called. Remember to speak through the Chair.

And just to remind yous, said Sammy. We'll need to keep it short.

Somebody tugged Hines by the sleeve. What's happening Rab?

Hines shook his head, indicating the Committee man on the table. Towards the rear someone had raised his right hand and called a question. Speak up! replied the Committee man.

Naw, said the man, I was just saying if Sammy wanted us to strike? It's no a question of that.

Well what is it then? cried a voice nearby Hines. We've just come in off the street and we dont even know what the hell's going on!

Aye same with me. I just came in and somebody said we were striking!

An outbreak of chatter followed. A voice kept repeating: What did he get the Head Office line for? that's what I want to know.

The Committee man was frowning. Order! he called. Order! Come on now, yous'll have to address your remarks through the Chair.

The chatter continued. Again he called for order. A person down from the tables asked a question but it wasnt acknowledged until eventually the chatter ceased. Both Sammy and the other Committee man had climbed onto the tables. When they stepped back down the person raised his hand: Eh brother, I think the members here want to know the score and that. Now from what eh the Shop Steward said Tom Fairlie's wanting to sack somebody on the spot. Is that right?

Aye, called Sammy.

But he's no sacked him yet?

Naw, I told you that.

What the hell's he wanting to sack him for? called the angry voice nearby Hines.

He refused a line off Campbell, replied somebody from the rear.

What for? cried another man and the chatter resumed.

Sammy moved quickly onto the table again. He called: I'll tell yous once more, for the benefit of those who've just come in. One of the conductors — Rab Hines — he had a Head Office line waiting for him this morning. He was supposed to go right away. But he objected, because he wasnt working . . .

Sammy paused for a drag on his cigarette. Immediately Hines raised his hand aloft, waved it. Just a wee word, he called; and when Sammy nodded he said: Just to get it clear, what I objected to. See I'm no working the day. If I took the line off Campbell it meant I'd have to go home and put on the uniform then go away up the town to see Head Office. I dont think I should be forced to do that. I mean I'm no objecting to getting a line — I'm just objecting to having to go up to Head Office in my own time. I think it's out of order that we've got to. I mean if they get paid to see us we should get paid to see them.

Muttered approval followed. Sammy was nodding.

That's all I'm saying, added Hines.

What was the line for? called somebody.

It doesnt matter what it was for, replied an irritated voice.

That's right. Sammy held up his hand to prevent further comments. And what really matters as well is the way Fairlie's wanting to sack Brother Hines on the spot I mean that's really out of order. And I really think we should lay it on the line for them.

D'you mean strike? called somebody.

Well aye Brother; if we have to. But that's up to yous to decide. That's how this Meeting's been called, so yous can discuss it and take a vote . . . He glanced about, looking for somewhere to stub out his cigarette dowp; eventually he dropped it to the floor and someone trod on it . . . What I want to know is if yous're backing me; cause then I'll know where I'm speaking from.

For a moment he glanced round the room then he stepped down onto one of the chairs. Okay, called a Committee man. If anybody wants to speak, now's the time. But mind and address yourself through the Chair.

Brother . . . the angry voice from behind Hines. I dont think there's any bloody need to take a vote. They're trying to bloody mess us about down there as usual. I mean if they bloody get away with this then . . .

A bit easy on the language there, called the Committee man.

Aye, sorry; but I mean if they're going to you know, Christ I mean we're no going to sit back and let them. I think it's a disgrace!

Aye, shouted somebody. Away down and tell them Sammy.

An outbreak of angry muttering.

Hold on a minute, cried a voice. There's got to be a vote.

Hell with the vote, shouted somebody.

Aye, no fucking need, shouted another.

Other voices began to be heard as the Committee man called for order, and the second Committee man climbed onto the tables, also calling for order. The clamour stopped almost at once. Does anybody object if we take the vote just now? asked the first Committee man. Nobody answered. People were looking about. The Committee men exchanged glances and the first went on: All those in favour of withdrawing our labour, if they try to sack the Brother; will you raise your hands!

The response was immediate.

The Committee man grinned: I think that's unanimous.

A few cheers and applause. The Shop Steward had climbed onto a

201

table and he raised his hand. Good to see the support, he said, and I just want to point out that things'll probably no go that far now they see where we stand. Sammy sniffed before continuing. I'll go down the stair and explain the position . . . He nodded.

ooo

Reilly had come into the canteen, smiling and shaking his head at Hines, as he queued for something to eat. A constant toing and froing of people both in and out of uniform, walking from the bothy to the canteen, to the snooker-room. Hines would gaze up from the table and find somebody turning away, emabarrassed at being caught staring at him. To pass the time he had been borrowing newspapers. One of them he folded and ripped methodically into shapes that multiplied as the paper unfolded. Paul was bored to the point of sleep but not beyond, and Hines had arranged two chairs so that if he did sleep he wouldnt roll onto the floor. There was no chance of getting him to the nursery now but what did that matter; just one more petty point with nothing to do with anything. Sammy was downstairs; he would be addressing McGilvaray as Mr while he in return would be addressed as Sammy. Was that of more importance than the nursery. Obviously. Obviously it was. What a strange fucking question. That is the kind of thing Hines has to be wary of. Maybe if people would talk to him. But people dont talk to him. Of course there are reasons for this. Most of the crowd attending the Meeting worked the opposite shift from him; when he was on earlyshift they would be on backshift. It was only now, when the earlyshifts were finishing, that folk were coming in to whom Hines could really chat. But not many of them were chatting to him. It was probably his own fault, when all's said and done he is a negation. Being a negation is peculiar. Hines can see himself as this and it makes him think. What he thinks is nobody's business. This is why he left the bothy as soon as possible after the Meeting broke up. The majority had remained there to get their thoughts on the tables. It wasnt Hines' place to be there during such an occurrence. He would be a point of

202

discussion and was duty bound to vanish. If he had shirked his duty and stayed, and become involved in laying himself out for inspection, what would have happened. To begin with he wouldnt have done it. He would have lied. It is pointless lying. Hines gets sick of it. A wee boy sits facing him. Probably Hines will become his greatest influence. So what. There isnt much to be said about that. Lying wouldnt make any difference. It's all a load of shite. And what about auld Boabbie. Is he Hines' greatest influence. Hines cannot talk to him and vice versa. What has that got to do with it. So fucking stupid. There are matters in hand of an important nature. Reilly has been talking with great excitement. What is there to be excited about. The thing has finished before it has started but he cannot understand. Reilly cannot understand. In a year the fare to Australia can be achieved. Reilly would give a year's wages to be in Hines' shoes. Hines would sell his part in the dispute. He doesnt want to be in his own shoes. There are practical reasons. He is not able to shout. If Reilly was in his shoes then he could shout but as things are he is unable to do so, because he is directly involved. Reilly can shout. He could be ben in the bothy doing shouting instead of eating soup in the canteen. He could be downstairs shouting. They should all be downstairs shouting. None of them are downstairs shouting. They let Sammy go down to speak and he will address McGilvaray as Mr and in return be addressed as Sammy. What is the point. There is no point in any of it. They do not understand. There is no point in speech. How come they speak. What do they speak for. It is beyond belief. How come people are content to act in this manner. Are they fucking crazy. McGilvaray is the type of fellow for whom a no-nonsense lack of shilly-shally goes down a bomb. If you trace a knife line from the adam's apple to the belly button his blood'll spurt in wee bubbles. If I had a gun I'd blow McGilvaray's fucking brains out. Hines grinned. To be honest I wouldnt — ever see his daughter! Eh, christ sake, murky nights at Yoker terminus.

Naw, said Reilly, it's Campbell gets me; I'd love to have seen his face when you refused to sign for the line.

Hines nodded. It was yet another lie. How come you nod to such nonsense. You spend your life working such that you cannot say what the things are. An apple a day keeps the doctor in clover.

Reilly smiled. He likes to smile. He is a humorous fellow. He shall be a more agreeable Shop Steward than Sammy; he shall address

McGilvaray as Mr and in return be addressed as Willie — or Bill. From now on I'm going to call you Bill Bill. Hello Bill, how's it going?

Your patter's really degenerating ya cunt ye.

Is that right Bill?

Reilly grinned. He finished eating by wiping his soup bowl with his last bit of bread.

Bread had been the highlight of the day so far for Paul. Hines had bought them both soup and bread; and he was amazed to see the bread being served dry, without margarine. He thought it was a joke, grinning his disbelief at Hines and it had taken him a while to make the first bite. Now he was munching away on potato crisps, bought for him by Reilly. It was good to have bought him the crisps. Hines could have done it himself if he had thought about it but he didnt. Reilly is good at thinking of things like that.

I've got one question for you Bill, one question and one question only. How d'you make a petrol bomb?

Reilly's look!

Naw seriously man; d'you know?

Others were sitting at the table. This made matters complicated. Hines grinned and glanced from face to face. I mean surely that's a fucking legit question to ask a potential Shop Steward? I mean if I was fucking Shop Steward I'd want to know such things in the off chance of helping out the Members.

If you were Shop Steward there wouldnt be any bloody Members, laughed a fellow with a large nose.

Hines has nothing against people with large noses. His own nose isnt small. Nor is it large. It is just right. The nose that juts from the face of Hines is just right. Heh you ya cunt, he said, see if you were fucking Shop Steward!

The expectant faces.

Hines laughed briefly. Naw, seriously, I want to be a cowboy when I grow up.

I wish to God they would sack you, chuckled somebody.

Reilly nodded, grinning.

I didnt even have time for a pint! laughed Barry.

Well fuck sake man, said Hines, neither did I . . . He glanced at Paul and winked. Give us a crisp.

Paul gave him one.

Heh Willie, said a conductor, you missed yourself; best Meeting I've ever been at. See when the vote came! totally unanimous. Everybody in the room man it was really good.

Aye, I'd like to have been there, I must admit.

Admit fuck all, said Hines, just keep it to yourself Willie; that's my advice to you.

Ohh! Reilly rubbed his forehead. Anybody got a fucking aspirin!

Christ sake ya cunt ye one minute you complain about me no talking then the next you're fucking . . .! Hines shook his head. I'm definitely going to Australia now.

I wish you would and give us all peace, laughed a driver. Bloody strikes! Christmas coming and no wages! murder polis. *You* can go and explain it to the wife.

Aw here we go, said Reilly.

I'm only joking.

Hines muttered, Is he — is he fuck.

A short silence. The driver shook his head. I was only fucking joking.

Hines raised his right hand. The man was only joking. Anyway, to be perfectly fucking honest with yous all, I dont want anybody going on strike on my behalf. I want to do it on my tod. It's my strike, yous can get your own. I mean they're fucking easy to find.

Here we go! Barry smiled.

Naw, said Hines, the job's so fucking lousy you can choose anything you like, just at random. Same with me. That's what I'll do, I'll go down the stair and tell them I'm on strike for something else altogether.

Such as? said Reilly.

Look ya cunt you started at 5 this morning and finished at the back of 2. I mean it's alright for you and that, no weans or fuck all — you can jump into bed with Isobel whenever you fucking like. But no me man, I'm beat. How come we dont strike about that!

Shut up ya fucking idiot.

Did that no make sense?

Heh, said Barry, what did Fairlie say to you? you never told us.

Ach . . . Hines shrugged then said: Tell me this Barry; how come we dont go on strike about these Office cunts? I mean they're earning more than we do for fewer fucking hours.

Barry shrugged.

No reply, see. Hines shook his head. Heh Bill, what about you? One question and one question only.

Aw give us peace Rab for fuck sake.

Hines looked at him and nodded.

After a moment Barry said, I wonder what's keeping them.

Nobody replied. The driver who had only been joking got up and said he was feeling like a cup of tea, and went to buy one.

Hines said to Reilly, You were asking about the line and I never told you. I just never took it because it meant I would have to put on my uniform and I wouldnt be getting paid for it; basically I mean that's it. But as far as Sammy's concerned — and every other cunt — it's got nothing to do with that; they're going to go on strike if I get the boot and that's all really.

Naw it's no, muttered Barry.

It is but; look at what he said in the bothy, the main issue, it's Fairlie being out of order. I mean . . . Hines snorted. It's a load of shite. I'm on strike because garage business isnt my business outwith the sold hours.

Reilly grinned. How can you be on strike if you're no working? Eh? you're outwith the sold hours right fucking now ya daft bastard.

Hines looked at him and chuckled. He lifted the tin and prised off the lid. Your patter's improving Reilly. Heh, your turn for the tea.

Naw it's no ya cunt ye!

No time for tea, said somebody.

One of the Committee men had appeared in the doorway. Hines had turned away; he asked Paul if he was doing okay, if he wanted a cup of milk or something. When the Committee man arrived at the table Hines glanced round at him, aware of the faces looking from elsewhere in the canteen. They're wanting to see you down the stair.

He nodded. Who was it asked?

What?

Was it Sammy told you?

Eh; naw, an Inspector — Bob Docherty.

Is it McGilvaray I've to go into?

Aye, come on, they're waiting.

O sorry, I better run. He got up, glanced at those round the table. How come McGilvaray doesnt go into the fucking bothy to see me? I mean I've got to go into his fucking Office and face him and Fairlie, and Campbell, and that stupid fucking Inspector. It'll no do. It'll just no do. What d'you think Willie? point for discussion?

Reilly didnt reply.

Should we go on strike or what? Hines grinned and followed the Committee man to the door. But he had forgotten about Paul; he returned quickly. I'll no be long son, just stay here with Willie eh!

The boy wasnt looking too keen. With a bit of luck he'd get a chip on his shoulder — probably against Hines; it wasnt him bought the potato crisps! That's the trouble with weans, a selfish bunch of bastards.

He followed the Committee man in silence, occasionally smiling when somebody they passed called a comment. At the counter-hatch downstairs in the Office he said to the Inspector: I dont feel like this. The Inspector shrugged. He was just doing his job. You run messages for Deskclerks and garage Superintendents whenever necessary. Hines smiled, It's my angina acting up.

He followed the Inspector across the Office area and through into a corridor, along to the Office of the Superintendent — a room Hines knew well, having made frequent visits to the place over the years, in order that he might explain certain conductorial deeds of a nefarious nature and be brought to account for same, that a rightful retribution might be passed upon him, set against him, as further Black Marks in the File, to be noted against his name, a name which has long been frowned upon when matters pertaining to the recruitment of new men are discussed within the School for Busdrivers. The Inspector had chapped the door and waited. Hines smiled at him. Then a noise from within which amounted to Enter!

Ah, fish. That was the smell. Fairlie must have had fish for dinner. There had been a particular tang in the Deskclerks' room earlier on. Hines had caught a whiff of it but laid the cause to himself; he had neglected to wash the genitalia after the sex of last night and this morning. Sandra had forgotten to point it out to him; normally she reminds him of hygiene. He was too busy cooking the breakfast. It was a good breakfast, a great breakfast; a breakfast in celebration. They had celebrated by having a cooked breakfast. They had celebrated a coming together, a renewal, a case of fuck them all. Why should people worry about things, petty things. Hines cooked the breakfast, cheerily but not cheerful at all, not really; he was too busy worrying about this fucking matter in hand. What he had been hoping for — he had been hoping for something. What in the name of fuck had he been hoping for, he was hoping for something. Hope. What a strange fucking word. Hope. Here I am, hoping. I am hoping. Hope hope hope, little bunnies, hope hope hope. Poor wee fucking Paul right enough. Strange how things fucking happen. There you are etc., then and so on. Christ almighty.

The Superintendent was writing into a folder. He was sitting at his neat desk, bent over a folder, writing away. This is what he does. Meanwhile Sammy and Fairlie were standing a yard apart, to the left side of where Hines stood facing the desk. Campbell had become absent. He would be off for his dinner, or maybe away holding the fort of the Deskclerks. The Superintendent sniffed very slightly and turned pages in the folder. He shook his head and glanced up: Do you have any idea how bad your record is? I mean you must have some idea: do you? The last time you were in here I told you if you kept on the way you were going you'd be right out the door: d'you remember that? I'll be frank with you son, I think you've got a damn cheek. Mr Fairlie says you're refusing to accept a Head Office line: is this true?

Eh.

Is it, is it true?

Hines shifted his stance a little, he glanced at Sammy.

D'you realise you might be right out the door? The Superintendent sat back on his seat. I mean I dont think you realise how serious this is. Do you? He sat forwards again.

Yes.

Yes . . . The Superintendent looked at him, nodding. The last time you were in front of me I had to give you a 7-day suspension: d'you remember that?

Hines paused.

Well?

Eh . . . he sniffed. I think the Shop Steward should speak.

Do you. The Superintendent nodded. After a moment he said, If you ask me you regard yourself as a bit of a barrackroom lawyer son; is that how you see yourself?

Hines looked at him.

Is it?

No.

No . . . The Superintendent nodded. He glanced at Sammy.

Well as I was saying before Mr McGilvaray, he wouldnt take the line for Head Office because he's not working and he'd have to go this afternoon.

That's right, he slept in this morning, said the Superintendent.

Fairlie smiled slightly, he gazed at the floor, arms folded.

And it's his day-off tomorrow.

Day-off; you mean he's not suspended?

Hh. Hines shook his head, and he smiled.

D'you think it's funny Conductor?

No.

No . . .

Sammy sniffed. Eh but like I was saying as well Mr McGilvaray, I think there's a fair point involved.

Do you; well maybe there is and maybe there isnt: but d'you think this is the way to go about it?

No. No I dont — but at the same time I mean . . .

Och come on Sammy, muttered Fairlie.

Naw Tom I think it's a fair point and it needs discussing. Aye, I think it does. And I'll tell you something else: I think you were right out of order the way you threatened him with his books.

Do you, well I dont.

Sammy had his arms folded; he gazed at the floor. Fairlie had glanced at him then at Hines, before he too gazed at the floor. Probably he would like to strangle Hines. And what a fine how-d'ye-do that would be! staff strangling hourly paid workers; where would it all end. These petty squabbles gentlemen! play up and play the game for fuck sake.

The Superintendent had been shaking his head while appearing to reread the Bad File. Eventually to Fairlie he said, D'you know — I doubt whether they'll have time to see him now . . . He indicated his wristwatch. No, he said, it'll have to be tomorrow. And he looked to Hines. Give me your line a minute . . .

Eh.

It's still in the drawer, said Fairlie.

Yes. The Superintendent shook his head slightly. Right Conductor, it'll have to be a 10 o'clock for tomorrow morning.

Hines looked at him.

I really dont think you appreciate how bad your record actually is. I mean you dont, not really. Do you?

Yes.

O you do.

Hines nodded. Can I just say something about why I wouldnt accept the line?

With your record son, once upon a time, you'd have been straight out that door. D'you know that?

Yes eh . . .

The Superintendent gestured at the file for Sammy's benefit. You should take a look at this.

Aye I know Mr McGilvaray but like I was saying earlier on I mean it's the principle of the thing eh . . .

Uhhu? The Superintendent nodded.

Fairlie was staring at the floor.

Hines hadnt looked at Sammy. He said to the Superintendent: I think I should remind you, I've been in the garage since about half 11 this morning. I'm no getting paid for it: I'm here on my own time. And something else — I'm supposed to be looking after the wean; he's sitting up the stair with a bunch of bloody strangers. I think it's a disgrace, to be honest.

Do you?

Yes.

Eh Inspector! would you go ben and get that Head Office line from the drawer please . . .

Hines sniffed. I wont be signing for it if I've to go tomorrow: it's my day-off.

O is it?

Yes; it seems a peculiar idea to ask an hourly paid worker to go about his employer's business when he's no getting paid for it.

Uhhu? The Superintendent leaned his elbow on the desk, res ed his head on his hand.

Aye, said Sammy, I mean that's the point.

O is it?

Well aye I mean

Hines interrupted: Would you sit there talking to me if you werent getting paid for it?

Dont be bloody cheeky, said Fairlie.

I'm no being cheeky.

You are, said the Superintendent.

O; very sorry.

And now you're being sarcastic.

210

Hines paused. I beg your pardon sir . . . He studied the floor during the immediate silence.

The silence continued. Sammy was pursing his lips and had folded his arms and then unfolded them. Meanwhile Fairlie seemed at great odds with himself, alternately frowning and not frowning at the floor, and he reached into his dustcoat pocket — for his cigarettes perhaps, although he didnt bring out the packet. Look son, said the Superintendent, carry on this way and you'll definitely be out the door, and I'm no kidding. Go and get the line, he told the Inspector.

The door opened and closed.

I'll tell you something Hines; I just dont know why you started back in the job. Eh? he glanced at both Fairlie and Sammy.

Jobs are scarce.

Jobs are scarce! The Superintendent snorted. He shook his head and gazed at Hines for a moment. I think I know what it is with you, he said. You fancy yourself on the soapbox. Eh? is that what it is?

Hh.

Eh? The Superintendent snorted again, shaking his head.

Sammy moved, from foot to foot. The proceedings were to be brought to a conclusion.

I think we should call it quits.

O?

Aye, I'm away home; that's me resigned. Hines turned at once and walked to the door; he opened it and stepped out, shutting it behind him. He walked along the corridor and didnt look at the Inspector while passing him going out into the main Office area. A few Members were behind the counter. He walked out and along into the washroom; but he halted at the entrance. He was to leave the garage immediately. It was the thing to do. Nothing else could be right. It had to be right now, otherwise, otherwise things would not be for the best. He went upstairs at a steady pace, avoiding the gaze of the Members milling about. From the canteen doorway he beckoned Reilly to bring Paul. I blew it, he grinned. I'll tell you downstairs. And he lifted Paul to his shoulder and set off downstairs. Upon reaching the yard Reilly paused but Hines led him on out to the pavement beyond the garage exit.

That's me jacked it at long last, he grinned. The sheriff's cleaning up the town. The land of the regal brits is to let sleeping dogs lie.

Poor auld Reilly's face.

211

But what about Hines! He was having to stop himself from bursting out greeting. He felt absolutely defuckingplorable. An actual fucking blockage in the gullet causing him to gulp drastically, hanging onto his son for grim life, pulling his head down closer onto his shoulder so he could be having no option but to peer anywhere except at the old man, anywhere except seeing his auld man's fucking kisser. What a performance.

What happened?

Nothing. Hines shrugged. Naw, listen Willie I'm away home. You better hang on but, to find out the score and that, from Sammy.

Christ sake Rab.

Ah it's fucking hopeless — well no exactly hopeless . . . Hines shook his head. Ah! fucking bastard, I blew it. He turned and walked on up the street. He stopped to call: Sammy'll tell you better man I'm fucking . . . he shook his head.

Reilly had his hands upturned, a gesture of despair, of indecision, of sympathy maybe — wanting Hines to wait there a minute, not to be leaving at this precise moment, not without telling him, his one true mucker etc.

Sammy'll tell you better: he called, and he looked to the front as he walked now, not letting Paul to the ground till having rounded the corner into the main thoroughfare.

ooo

A nasty wind was blowing, rending the very heart of the backcourt asunder. The debris reeled and the huge puddle was extremely choppy. Patrons of the midgies staggered as they made their way, bent into the blast, their bags of rubbish tilted against it, but these sudden draughts, the bastards, whirling out old bits of paper and stuff, high into the air. It wasnt possible to measure facial expressions but it could be guessed that a certain perplexed, rather absent-minded frown was the order of things.

The kitchen was a cosy place. From the front room the music sounded loud and strong, a rhythm and blues equivalent to the

Marseillaise. Hines felt as fit as a bastarn fiddle. A match for anything or anybody. No more getting fucked about.

And there knelt the wee man watching television, untoward happenings in a rural English village. A proper joy. Two winters ago a television got heaved out a window directly across from here. A domestic quarrel. Nothing to do with political affronts though Hines has related the event in that colouring to various parties both within and without the garage. He doesnt regret having falsified the tale. Why should he. Lying is no concern of his. Truth is. He seeks the true. Fling the telly out the fucking window and be done with it. Not for him the lush pastures. He is in favour of the bottomless depths, however, which are good when clear. Clarity for a policy. It arrives via silence. Silence is a remarkable how-d'ye-do. Hines would wish to maintain it. His mouth gets him into difficulties. His language contains his brains and his brains are a singular kettle of fish. He often feels like slitting his head open to have a look at the mess in a mirror. It is a peculiar notion. Hines is, however, peculiar. And genuinely regards himself as such. He is a picnic. A pic nic. Anyone who refers to himself as a picnic must be certifiable.

— But the winter is a time of madness. Hands up those who get carted off in straitjackets when the sun is shining and summers are long and hot. Not many I'll be bound. No, the summer is a time of pleasure, relax and breathe in. Just take your sausages and fry them, browning the skins all over, then add the water, the salt & pepper, the seasoning, and soon they stew, to be served with mashed potatoes and cabbage, a fine tasty meal. Obviously Paul prefers them fried and served with chips but he isnt the fucking chef and what Hines says is this; tell the wee cunt to go to a cafe. And anyway weans are weans; they prefer what's bad for you.

Hines likes order. Order. Line them up and shoot them down. He takes a dash of this a pinch of that and then goes out the window. You see them down the backcourt, cutting through a wind that chills to the marrow. What is marrow. It is a stuff which comes out your bones, of a gelatinous nature.

Who wants to know. There is a voice such that it cuts about discharging commands and stuff. In a square rectangle there lived a triennial unit once upon a time. The head is a strange item. Hines cant get into his. He gives it every opportunity to produce the goods but does it ever pay heed!

Tomorrow is another day. It dawns, then you eat your breakfast, and have had your wash then shave perhaps, if you can be bothered. If you can be bothered to shave. Paul doesnt shave. He is a wee boy. He wont be shaving for another ten years or more. By that time a Hines will be reaching the approaching forty years of age stage. Forty years of age is a blockbuster. When Hines gets to that age the world will have become something or other.

He will be dead though, for years perhaps, before thirty probably. He will have bowed out, cut short at the prime. Well well well right enough. This is a scream, a genuine scream. What you do is toss your bunnet at cunts while they're eating their soup. You get them laughing. Even Sandra's maw was a laugher and that's saying something. I wouldnt call her a thingwi, but see when she thingwis her thingwi! Gaaa haa ha. An astonishing bowl of parsnips.

Say something to the boy.

Hines cleared his throat. The boy was engrossed in the television programme. But it was the news that was on. Imagine watching the news at $4\frac{1}{2}$ years of age. Definitely a sign of genius. Perhaps he'll become a Statesman. Yes, back home in Scotland my father was a bit of a radical. In all honesty one is bound to remark that much of one's political awareness was gained at the old boy's knee. He had the awesome habit of farting in public. Who put that in. I well remember my first, as it were, entry into the political arena. He carted me along to the garage wherein he was at the time employed, for in those days comma you must remember comma the species known as Busconductor was yet to become extinct. Little did the old chap realise this at the time but nevertheless he did achieve a minor notoriety, fame, call it what you will. I well recollect his settling me down on a bothy table — if you'll forgive the expression — and vanishing downstairs. Merciful heavens.

Heh wee man, what did you think of it today? at the garage. Was it a load of rubbish?

Paul looked up.

Dont take it too seriously. The buses is a rotten job. That's how I jacked it. Terrible. Mummy'll be back soon; you hungry?

Yes.

Heh listen, how come you say yes instead of aye all the time? Naw son, seriously.

Paul glanced at him, and then back to the television. A child is a dwarfish entity. Heh! fancy a game of snap?

Yes.

Paul's laugh has also got that gurgling sound. It is a much better laugh than Hines'. But maybe he will develop something more akin to Hines' in the years to come. Hines' laugh is not a good one. In fact it sounds terrible, really bad — awkward almost. This isnt to say it is unnatural. It just seems not to spring from a source of well-being. Now when Sandra laughs it makes a special sound — it could have a disinterested bystander wanting to rush up and throw his arms round her immediately. That is the difference between his laugh and hers. And Paul has hers, it is an expression of happiness. Yes, he gurgled, the dear old boy had the most peculiar of laughs; it seemed to spring from a source of something or other, one never quite had a fucking clue as to the what.

ooo

They rushed to the front door and grabbed her as soon as she entered, both cheering; and Sandra laughing. Let me get my coat off!

No time, cried Hines, kissing her a loud smack on the lips. Then he pushed the door shut and lifted the boy as she took off her coat They waited for her to put it on a hanger inside the wardrobe, before returning to the kitchen.

God it's so warm, she said, walking straight to the fire and heating her legs.

Yous woming! How come yous dont wear breeks when the weather demands it?

She stuck out her tongue.

That's the trouble with nowadays, this fashion carry on . . .

He had forgotten to boil the potatoes; they were lying unpeeled on the bottom of the sink. Everything else was ready. He began to whistle as he turned on the tap; he washed them and peeled them very quickly, then chopped them into very small sections. Hot water remained in the kettle; he set it to reboil. Heh Sandra . . . He grinned. Fancy the pictures?

That's a smashing idea. She had a shoe off and was heating the sole of her foot. He strode over and they embraced: the foot she had been heating she settled on his instep.

You're looking great, he whispered.

She held him more tightly and he raised her up about 6 inches from the floor. Then Paul was talking and he was tugging at her skirt at the same time. Hines let her onto the floor and walked to the oven. The people were on strike at daddy's garage. Lifting the lid off the cabbage pot he forked at the cabbage and then he lifted the lid off the skillet and forked at the stewing sausages, which came apart they were so tender. The water approached boiling point inside the kettle; he poured it into the pot of potatoes which he set to cook on a gasring.

She was looking at him. Paul had been continuing to yap and had now stopped.

Aw aye, he said, naw it's just eh . . . He shrugged: I jacked it. Heh Paul, get the table set.

Really?

Aye.

After a moment she said, Did anything happen?

Eh aye, quite a lot. There wasnt a strike; there was nearly one. A load of bla bla. I had to go in and see auld McGilvaray about a line. There was one waiting for me when I went in this morning; Head Office.

O Rab.

Ach I knew there would be, things were piling up, and Thursday's always the day for it.

What happened?

Nothing — they were going to sack me. Heh you wee man come on, set that bloody table! Hines chuckled and walked to her, laid his hands on her shoulders. It's okay.

She sighed. She added, Sorry; it's just something to take in.

I know.

What're you going to do?

He moved to get his tin; he prepared a cigarette. He grinned: Stop smoking, that's what I'm going to do!

She didnt smile.

Naw, the thing is, I'm no quite sure what the score is. I chucked it on the spot, there and then; so . . . he shrugged, I'm no sure if I'm

216

supposed to work a week's notice or what. He smiled, I dont think they'd let me!

O Rab what did you do? was it bad?

Christ sake Sandra.

No I just mean, if it was bad, for references maybe.

References!

Well if you just walked out.

You dont get references off the buses.

No but if you're going to start for a new firm, they'll want to contact them.

Hh. He exhaled smoke and returned to the oven.

Well they will.

Christ sake Sandra. He lifted a lid from a pot and replaced it. Paul was on tiptoes, reaching into the kitchen-cabinet for cups. Hines passed them out to him.

You always do things so suddenly.

I'm sorry, I thought you'd be glad.

It's not that.

Well what you acting like this for? christ. I thought that was what we were talking about this morning. I mean when we were talking this morning Sandra, that's what we were talking about, me leaving the buses.

She nodded.

You're a worrier woman you're a worrier!

Somebody's got to.

. . .

Sorry. She shook her head. He had gone over to her; and he clasped both her hands. Again she shook her head. See this mummy of yours! he said to Paul; amazing, she's amazing. One of these days you'll understand that.

Sandra's eyelids had closed and he kissed her forehead. D'you mind if we just stay in though . . .

Aye. Aye, he said, I do mind. This is supposed to be something good — a celebration.

She nodded.

You're supposed to be glad.

I know . . . She smiled, I should be; shouldnt I.

Eh aye, aye, you should be. He made a daft sort of gesture, as if he was about to burst into song or something. Sausage and mash and

217

the juicy cabbage, he cried: Served from a trio of vessels.

I'd still prefer it though, if we stayed home.

Aye . . . He nodded, Of course. Just a daft idea.

It wasnt daft.

Naw but, he sniffed and glanced about, picked up his cigarette from an ashtray and got another light for it from a gasring. Sandra was moving to sit down on her armchair, before doing so she bent to kiss Paul on the forehead; he had been kneeling on the floor near the television set, amusing himself with the pack of cards. Hines checked the potatoes with a fork. He stayed by the sink until they were ready. Sandra seemed to be watching television. It was a peculiar situation.

There is a situation fairly similar — if not the same — whereby one is waiting, one is standing, waiting, considering a variety of items. Then for some reason the chest is struggling to heave. The shoulders have become as though wilted, as though a spring has finally collapsed, having one aware of the weight of one's head.

Emotionally drained perhaps. One can be emotionally drained, such that the chest struggles to heave. You steep your feet in warm water.

Sandra can sit there and he has no idea what she is thinking, absolutely none. That is a peculiar thing. They have known each other for more than 5 years and lived together only slightly less. He doesnt know what she thinks. He is no longer sure she thinks well of him. She used to think well of him. Now she doesnt seem to. Yesterday she left him for good. Now that really is a strange thing. Because she loves him.

Because she loves him she came back. She went away because she doesnt think so highly of him as she used to but returned because she still loves him.

It is probably a matter of time till she leaves again.

Eh . . . he turned to her. The other night there, did you really go to the pub with your Office pals?

She nodded. Her face was saying please be careful about what you say next.

Naw, he said, it just eh — yesterday, had you decided in advance? I mean the night before . . .

How d'you mean? Her face, showing he shouldnt be saying anything at all now.

What I cant figure out is how you would leave the way you did, taking Paul and that I mean . . . christ sake Sandra. He shook his head. You never planned it did you?

No. She nodded, signifying Paul and how he would be listening to what was being said and who was to know if he wasnt following every last word.

Hines shook his head. This week's been the worst week of my fucking life. Sorry. He grinned, I mean they're all fucking rubbish but this yin's the fucking rubbishest. He stopped grinning and turned to face the sink for a few moments. The chest struggles to heave. An interesting point: the weight of one's head; to lay one's head on a weighing machine such that the neck is not involved, so that you can get an exact reading. He took the lid off the potato pot and forked at the spuds — although he didnt have to. Because the water was almost totally clear. And totally clear water means unboiled spuds.

He smiled at her but her face . . . her face was so terrible, it was so fucking sad, so sad it was so fucking sad, really sad. He shifted to stare at the venetian blind, through the gaps, to the gable end at the far left corner, the gapsite with the street lights through the absent tenement line; you get the cunts running away, they go tripping down the stairs and searching for new pastures, their weans bringing up the rear, that look on the wee faces: what's going on here! nobody's telling us what's going on but there must be something otherwise — otherwise what? otherwise how come we're getting pulled down the fucking stair out into the fucking cold.

We're off to see the world.

Hullo there Uncle Vic, that's me arrived. Here I am, and the whole stretch etc., anywhere I fucking like, cause that's me arrived, here I am, and if I just walk back out the door there's that entire fucking vista, the whole thing, Australia.

In a picture they saw on television a wee while ago there was this amazing bit where the husband was standing, a dejected figure, out on a balcony; the door opens silently and in comes his wife, dressed in her going-to-bed clothes: Darling . . . come to bed. What a load of shite that was; that was really a load of fucking shite. You get auld Boabbie at the window, he sits looking, he looks to the hills when it is or isnt misty, when he can see through the highrise. Heh mammy! does he still sit at the window!

That's a nice question. Kind. A very kind question to put before one's mother. That's the kind of question Hines puts. He puts that

219

question. How come he puts that question.

He opens his mouth.

Such a time has rarely been experienced. What you do is slow down. You pause, and you wait; there is no twitching allowed; you must stand there; quietly; not moving; not one iota; while the murky waters of the sultry Seine; the moody waters of the sultry Seine, you see the dancing girls, wee Toulouse with the sketch pad, the slow walk down by the river, wheeling the pram, the wean gurgling away while the young couple stroll, not having to chat, knowing each other so well and so content there, just strolling, with the wean in the pram and the rest of the day, still to come. O jesus. What you do is shut the blinds, you shut the blinds.

Sandra was gone from her chair, out of the kitchen.

Emptying the water from the pot Hines began to dish out the food. Paul got himself onto his chair at the table. Hines winked at him as he placed a plate of food in front of him, then he went ben the front room.

She was sitting on the settee. Away you go, she said.

Closing the door he went to sit beside her and he put his arm round her shoulders, keeping it there when she tensed.

Sometimes I hate you Rab. She brought a tissue from the sleeve of her jersey and wiped her nose. You say things . . . she blew her nose, shaking her head.

I say things that arent good.

You say things that are bloody . . . She halted, shaking her head again.

I didnt mean it; what I said.

O God.

Honest.

If you really feel that way then you should go, you should just bloody go.

Where to? He grinned. There's nowhere I want to go. I want to stay here, in this bloody dump. I want to stay here.

Why do I have to bloody cry. She sniffed then blew her nose.

You have to cry because — I dont know.

She sighed and looked at him.

The grub's on the plate.

I wont be able to swallow for a bloody hour.

He chuckled.

Rab . . .

He glanced at her.

What're we going to do?

That's what I was wanting to ask you. He smiled; he shook his head. I dont know, christ, I dont know.

Should I see about going full-time?

No yet — no unless you want to.

I dont really want to.

Dont then, there's no need.

But what if you cant get a job?

He shrugged. After a moment he said, I'll be getting broo money; it'll no be that bad.

She didnt reply.

Christ Sandra, the wages I've been lifting . . . be better off.

Maybe I should see about it then, about going full-time.

If you like.

O God.

Naw I mean honest, honest Sandra, if you want to go full-time then go full-time. I'm just saying I dont think it'll be necessary; honest, that's all, that's all I mean.

O God . . . she shook her head then sighed.

It's this land of the regal brits! its neither here nor there. He sat round to face her, grinning. I've been trying to tell you that for years!

She smiled.

Naw, he said, honest — honest Sandra you want to have seen it; terrible, no kidding ye, terrible, really bad, really bad — that's how I jacked it; poor auld Sammy, the shop steward, bad; fucking McGilvaray, the way he belittled him, terrible; jesus christ. One thing's for sure, he wouldnt've done it with Willie. Willie'll make a good shop steward. They'll probably make him an inspector! They dont bother making Sammy an inspector — he's no a danger you see; they only make union men inspectors if they're dangerous. Poor auld fucking Sammy. And he's no a bad shop steward either; that's the thing. Hines grinned. He doesnt like me. Well he doesnt dislike me. What I mean is I dont scare him. I think Willie does; I think Willie scares him — probably because he's after his job. Naw . . . Hh; I dont know, I dont fucking know . . .

He was sitting forwards, facing into the electric fire; he leaned his elbows on his knees.

What actually happened Rab?

What actually happened. Hh; nothing. Nothing at all. A load of rubbish. He smiled, I blew it. Strike or not strike and I plumped for the latter. Peculiar, most peculiar. Perplexing in fact, very perplexing; a very perplexing kettle of coconuts. He snorted then smiled; he shifted, to look at her. D'you know what I wonder? I wonder if a cunt like McGilvaray's more scared of somebody like Willie. Naw I mean — christ, he's got more fucking reason!

In what way?

Well . . . he shook his head. Naw, just . . . He shook his head again; and he stared back at the fire. He got up and walked over to plug it in, then switched it on. There was a crackling, tinny sound as the electric bar began to heat. He sat back down and put his arm round her; she leaned her head on his chest. Naw, he said, I know it's daft I mean

The door had opened very suddenly. Paul; he paused in the doorway, and then he walked to his cot and peered into it.

I'm glad you've left, whispered Sandra.

So am I. The trouble is the driving: I really wanted that bloody licence.

Och!

Aye I know but . . .

You can get it somewhere else.

Where? there isnt anywhere else — no unless it's an ordinary fucking driving school and they cost a fortune.

But would it make that much of a difference for getting a job?

Eh . . . Hh; probably no, but at least you could go places. He snorted then chuckled.

She slapped him on the chest: I saw your present today.

What was it?

I'm not telling you.

D'you wear it or play with it?

A bit of both.

A bit of both! Sounds like one of your American fucking doughnuts!

They laughed briefly. Paul came across; he leaned on Sandra's thighs and said, I ate everything up.

Mine as well I hope! She laughed again and pulled him up onto her lap.

Heh wait a minute! Bloody cheek — slaving over a hot bloody oven all day and this is the thanks I get! He jumped to his feet and marched to the windows crying, That's it now, that is really it, the last straw, the last fucking straw and no mistake; spend half your life cooking meals and look what happens, bloody mountains out of molehills! No wonder the country's in the state it is!

He marched back to the settee; and he knelt down on the floor in front of them. Listen, he said; how d'you fancy Australia? land of the long hot summer. Seriously, d'you fancy it? I could write to that brother of mine . . . Naw, I'm being serious.

Well for a start, you've not got his address.

My Uncle then. Hines shrugged. I'm being serious Sandra.

You're being serious . . . She was looking at him. And when he nodded she also nodded. Maybe.

Maybe . . . he scratched his head. Maybe . . . He stood up. That's good; maybe. Maybe'll do.

223

5

There were showers in the washroom but they only supplied cold water. Hot water was supplied by tap at each of the sinks which were all situated on the floor. When he had rinsed the soap off himself he told Paul to wait there, and to make sure he washed properly. He crossed to the rear wall and switched on a shower, gradually moving from the outside of the spray to directly beneath the jet, but only for an instant before dashing out and through onto the bank of the pool, to dive straight in; he swam the crawl to the deep-end, the breast-stroke on the return. Only five other men were in the pool, swimming its length at different speeds, back and forth and back and forth. Hines returned to the deep-end still doing the breaststroke. And touching back into the shallow-end he called Paul from the washroom, and told him to let the dirty water out of his sink.

The water reached to the top of the four steps at the corner of the shallow-end. Hines had walked to there. When Paul arrived he told him to walk down the steps. The boy stooped to fix his hands onto the bank, facing away from the pool towards the washroom; his left foot came to rest on the top step then withdrew as the water lapped onto it. It's cold, he said.

It's not cold at all, come on, give me your hand.

Paul knelt on the edge of the bank with his right knee; his left was over the edge, his foot a couple of inches above the water. He kept his hold on the bank with both hands and lowered his foot onto the step.

That's fine, now just put down your other foot and then you can go to the next step.

Paul did this; he had to twist round, facing away from the washroom, towards the dressing-cubicles, moving his hands out farther from the edge. As the water lapped Hines pushed with it a

225

little, so that it went above the boy's feet and for a moment he rose onto his toes, but then relaxed again, both feet on the step.

Fine now Paul; I want you just to step down onto the next yin. You can give me your hand.

He was peering down under his body, trying to see his feet maybe, or the steps, but his vision was obscured by the edge of the bank.

Naw son you'll have to come closer in.

Dont touch me daddy.

Hines had moved forwards; he stopped. Dont worry. I'm standing back.

Paul was advancing backwards, and shifting sideways a bit; he saw his feet on the step; he raised the left and dipped it off the step, keeping it submerged about a third of the way down to the second.

Fine; fine — just keep it there till you're ready.

He shifted the position of his hands a little and his left foot continued down until his toes touched the step; he was looking at his foot.

That's it, fine.

Paul had settled his foot now and was putting some of his weight onto it. It was an awkward position he had got into, his body side on, left leg twisted while his right bent, and he swivelled, to lean his left elbow on the bank, his other hand moving to the edge, raising his shoulder, easing his right foot up and along.

That's good son that's good.

And he moved his body now, stepping down onto the second step. The water lapped to his knees, he still faced the dressing-cubicles. Hines stepped to the bank to see his face. You're doing good, he said, but d'you no remember when I took you the last time? You were just a wee boy but christ, aye, you were good — I think you just came right in. I'm sure you did. D'you remember?

Paul nodded slightly.

I'm sure you just jumped in, and I caught you — d'you remember?

I just want to walk down daddy.

Aw I know, I know. Heh . . . Hines grinned: Watch this. You watching? He waited until the boy had turned enough to see, then he stepped back and sank down onto his knees, the water coming to beyond his shoulders. He laughed and ducked his head under, and out, and stood upright, wiping his eyes and shaking his head.

Paul nodded.

226

Ya wee mug ye! Okay . . . he smiled. Ready for the next step?

He nodded, glancing round and down; and he glanced at the washroom, at the dressing-cubicles and round to see the opposite end of the pool. The attendant was chatting to a man on the bank there and their voices carried; both were smoking.

Okay son, now you've done two steps and there's only another yin to go and then you've got the last.

He had been looking down at his feet; now he glanced to the bar and made to reach it, he gripped it with his left hand, his right turning, keeping a hold on the bank and he was stepping down with his left foot while his right hand came along the edge of the bank in a stuttering movement then off and grabbing for the bar, and as he gripped it his body swung round, his right shoulder bumping against the corner of the tiled wall, he gasped, the water reaching up his back, almost as far as his neck, and his feet walked up the wall; he fixed them against it, his body arching so that the water only reached his waist.

Smashing, that's smashing Paul, well done.

He laughed; it became a loud shudder, then a shiver.

You didnt even do the steps, you just done the bar straight away, that's really great.

A man trotted out from the washroom onto the bank and plunged right into the pool causing a huge splash. Paul was clinging to the bar and leaning into the corner, facing out to the dressing-cubicles. Watch this, said Hines, tapping him on the shoulder. And he climbed out and stood on the bank about a yard from him. Right, he said, count to three; then I'll dive. You've got to count but, right? Right, on you go.

He didnt say anything.

Right Paul now, one two three!

One two three.

Four, cried Hines and he dived. He dived to the bottom and twisted, swimming back to the corner underwater, to come out beside him. He laughed and wiped the water from his eyes, shaking his head.

Dont! Paul glared, jerking away from the splashing, almost cracking his head on the edge of the bank.

Now that's silly, that is silly, you nearly banged your head there.

It's cold.

It is not cold. Well it is right enough, but just a wee bit, compared to that last time, that last time we were here it was colder. Heh is your feet touching the bottom?

No.

No, christ, that's good. Heh, listen . . .

Paul had started shivering loudly and rocking up and down to avoid the lapping of the water.

Fine, that's fine, just keep moving about and you'll soon get warm, that's the way; okay now, I'll just take your hand . . . Okay? ready?

He was staring out into the washroom; an attendant had come along, carrying a pail, whistling as he walked in the direction of a door marked Private. Hines make to take the boy's hand but he kept his grip on the bar. Okay son, just let it go now . . . He tugged gently.

I dont want to daddy.

Naw it's okay but I'll take you, dont worry, I'll no let you go — heh! you dont think I'm going to let you drown do you! eh? is that what you think! Hines laughed; he applied a bit more pressure to withdraw his hand from the bar. Okay, you ready?

Paul said nothing.

Heh now come on, remember that last time! you jumped right in and I caught you and I was holding you right out christ — you were nearly swimming.

He nodded, maintaining his grip on the bar.

Come on son.

I dont want to daddy.

Ah you'll be fine. And he covered both the boy's hands with his own and took them from the bar, lifting him away from the bank and out some ten yards, holding him waist high to the surface. He told him not to kick so much then held him at arms' length by the hands, and began dipping him down and up a little at a time until eventually the boy wasnt gasping so much. He moved backwards, the momentum carrying Paul close to horizontally; they continued the breadth of the shallow-end and returned, then back and forth.

ooo

228

Sandra had been shopping; she was by the entrance turnstile when they came out, and Hines took some of her bags as they walked to the cafe. She was cheery, speaking about various things. She had redeemed his suit. In the cafe they ate bridies and beans accompanied with tea and a glass of orangeade for Paul. She asked if he was still going to the *Vale* after dropping him off at the nursery but he shook his head, there was no point.

Quite a crowd queued at the bus-stop. Complaints about the time they had been waiting; apparently no buses had passed for half an hour. He brought his tin out to roll a smoke but it was too windy and he returned it into his jerkin pocket. The first bus to arrive continued on beyond the stop, it halted at the traffic lights; the doors opened and three people got down onto the pavement. Those at the bus-stop were indignant. Sandra had grinned and turned away.

Another bus appeared, and behind it another could be seen. More complaints.

Before stepping aboard she gave him the remainder of the shopping bags. They waved to her as the bus moved off from the kerb. The traffic lights were showing green; the bus continued across the junction, round the bend in the road. Hines passed a couple of the lighter bags to the boy while they walked to the nursery. The Supervisor was standing in the corridor when they came to the cloakroom and Hines smiled to her, whispered cheerio to Paul. He rolled a cigarette in the doorway. A group of toddlers and three women approached from the street; he exchanged hellos with them while gathering the shopping bags and working their handles onto his wrists so that his hands were free.

Instead of going home immediately he crossed the road and went into the nearest pub and ordering a pint he walked to a table at the wall and dumped the bags on the floor there. Back at the bar the man serving nodded to him and commented on the weather. Farther along a man named Michie was trying to attract his attention and when Hines acknowledged him with a nod he asked if it was his day-off. Hines smiled and said it was. He borrowed the *Daily Record* from the barman and took it back to the table; he read it until finishing his pint. A man was coming in as he was going out and held the door for him to pass.

Across the road a woman who lived up the next close asked how Sandra was keeping, she hadnt seen her for ages; she was in a hurry but gave him a cheery goodbye.

Upstairs he dumped the bags on the bed, switched on the television and the gasfire, made a cup of coffee. The house was tidy. Eventually he dozed. Before leaving to collect Paul he drank another coffee.

ooo

At 5.30 he laid out the food. The whiting werent dressed. There was a packet of dressing in the kitchen-cabinet. He washed the potatoes and peeled them, washed them again and dried them. He put the chip-pan on to heat the fat then chipped the potatoes, occasionally whistling. When the last chip was in the pan he put on the shallow-frying pan to heat, put in the fish to cook on a slow gas. He wiped the pull-down section of the kitchen-cabinet, filled the kettle from the tap and set it to boil. Everything was ready by the time her key could be heard in the front door lock.

He had set the table. While Sandra and Paul settled themselves onto their chairs he laid the used utensils in the basin in the sink and added washing-up liquid, he mixed in water from the tap, hot water from the kettle. When he sat down eventually a round cream sponge was lying in the centre of the table. Sandra smiled. Friday night.

Paul's method of eating fish is not a good one. Hines' grandfather passed on a better one to himself, his brother and his sister. The portions of fish are forked into the mouth: bones are ejected via the tongue. Hines' father used to scoff at this method. He preferred not eating fish. He wasted so much time rooting out bones with his knife and fork that it always went cold. Sandra didnt scoff but she preferred taking the bones out beforehand. Paul was following her. Hines had washed his plate and cutlery as well as other utensils before they had finished eating. Laying her cup of tea beside her plate on the table he carried his own to his armchair and sat down. He rolled a cigarette, gazing at the back page of the *Evening Times* she had brought home. After a time Sandra said, Why dont you go to the *Vale* Rab? find out what happened.

Ach . . . he shrugged. Then he sniffed. Actually I *was* thinking of going out; but I thought I would see the auld man.

Is that a good idea?

I'll be on my best behaviour.

Sandra continued clearing the table. It might be good if we all went — the three of us; it's a while since we've seen them.

He nodded.

We dont have to. It's just an idea.

Hines shook his head: He'll no be drinking in the Drum tonight; he'll be down in Partick, seeing his auld mates.

I thought he'd stopped it?

Nah, you know the way he goes, he takes spells. He'll be back there for two or three months. And then he'll get sick of it again, and stay local.

Sandra nodded. Still, she went on, I could go with Paul — I'm sure your mum could do with the company. We could see you later; you and your dad could just come back on the bus together.

Aw aye.

You dont fancy it?

Naw it's no that; it just seems a lot of bother.

Mm.

D'you fancy it yourself?

Not really. I just thought . . . She had poured him a second cup of tea. While handing it to him she smiled, I only suggested it because I thought it was a good idea. It's not important, it's just we havent seen them for a while. And I know the way you and him end up after a drink.

Healthy discussions!

Ha ha. As she sat down she added, I thought you would've been going to the *Vale* if you'd been going anywhere.

Ah well aye, to be honest, I was thinking I might head along there if the auld man wasnt to be found. He reached for the tobacco tin. Paul was laughing at something on television. A comedy programme. How was work by the way?

Sandra drew him a look.

Naw, I'm genuinely interested.

Well if you must know we were busy. By the way, Jean was asking

231

if you were coming to the Christmas-do this year.

Was she?

Yes.

Hh.

Sandra smiled. Then she said, Seriously Rab, I'd like you to come.

Aw christ.

You dont have to.

Naw, it's no that Sandra I just eh . . . he made a face.

Paul laughed again. The three of them watched the programme for a period. Hines brought over his piece of sponge cake and ate it. He lifted the cigarette he had rolled from the top of his tin, and struck a match. When he exhaled he said, I'm going in for my shift the morrow morning. I've been thinking about it, it'd be daft no working the week's notice.

Sandra was looking at him.

Naw, I was just eh — I think it'd be daft. The cash and that I mean I'll be barred off the broo for 6 weeks and they'll send me up the S.S. And the money you're making, they'll just deduct it; so that'll be us, getting the absolute minimum. With Christmas coming up and the rest of it, he shook his head, we'll need the dough; that extra week'll make the difference. No think so?

She nodded.

It's a late week starting Sunday. He grinned. So I'll no be sleeping in. And no signing-off sick, I promise! Naw Sandra, it'll mean a full week's wages; plus with the Sunday and then next Saturday being a backshift, an additional 8 hours money. It'll help tide us over.

After a moment she said, It's your decision Rab.

Aw aye I know. He nodded. I know it is; naw, I just think it'd be daft not to.

Do you think they'll let you?

What d'you mean?

I thought you just walked out.

Aye . . . he leaned to flick ash into the ashtray.

Paul got up from the floor, he left the kitchen. The lavatory door opening and the click of the light switch.

Sandra was gazing at the television.

Hines coughed slightly, inhaled on the cigarette. His face screwed up as he exhaled. I'm trying to remember what exactly I said, when I was in with McGilvaray — I mean I said I was resigning but I dont

232

think I said anything more than that. I didnt actually say I was chucking it on the spot, I just eh . . . he sniffed and sat back on the armchair. He reached for his tea; it was lukewarm and he drank it all.

Paul came in. He knelt on his spot on the floor.

Then Sandra was looking at Hines, her eyebrows rose a moment and she smiled, then she looked back at the television.

About twenty minutes later he was shaved and wearing his suit, had a shirt on beneath his jersey. He walked downstairs, paused at the front of the close. Rain was falling steadily but not too heavily. He buttoned his jacket, upturning the lapels and collar, stepped out to the right, keeping tight into the wall of the tenement. Round the corner he began trotting, on beyond the stop for buses to the garage. It was a blue bus he boarded, he was going to Drumchapel.

Apart from the clusters of boys and girls hanging around in doorways the shopping centre was deserted. During the bus journey the rain had become heavier, then sleet. Outside the pub he unbuttoned his jacket and shook himself, using the sleeve to dry his face and forehead.

A blast of hot air when he entered, from a fan above the door. There was a space at the head of the bar directly beneath a colour television set which was attached to the wall: an old man had his elbow on the counter; he clutched a half-pint glass of beer, staring up at it; and he had to shift his position for Hines, his head twisting sideways so he could continue viewing.

Quite a few barmen served and soon he had a pint; he moved out from the space and stood as though he too was watching television. Later he bought another pint and walked towards the far end of the pub where a large group gathered about a darts board. At one of the tables near to here Frank was sitting but at another table sat a man and woman he recognised, they lived up the hill and were acquainted with his parents. He went over to chat with them, he stayed for several minutes.

At the other table Frank introduced him to the company. He did know some of the faces and it turned out a couple had been to school with Andy while somebody else was wanting to know where Barbara was staying these days. Then Frank began speaking, talking about the old days, the carry-ons they used to get up to in the classroom along with Griff and Milligan and the rest, those long walks they used to go during the summer holidays — that time somebody stole his maw's frying pan and they cooked eggs but they stuck to the bottom cause there wasnt any lard.

Hines was included in the next round of drinks. Now and again somebody would have his name called from the darts area and would leave to chalk the score before playing the next winner. The conversation had become general; a discussion about how the rest of the night was to be spent, with some in favour of travelling into town to go to the dancing or something while others were wanting to stay put and maybe get a carry-out to go and play cards in somebody's house. Hines was asked what he was doing and he said he was going straight home, he had an early start in the morning. He finished the pint and refused the offer of another. He had to wait half an hour for a blue bus.

Through the close and up the stairs he paused on the first landing, he smoked a cigarette.

Sandra was reading. He walked to the sink and filled a kettle of water from the tap and put it to boil. He was saying how his old man hadnt been in any of the usual places so he had just ended up going into the *Vale*; he met Barry McBride and a couple of others and they told him nothing had happened yesterday; but they hadnt spoken personally to the shop steward so maybe something was happening and they just hadnt heard.

He went ben the front room to change clothes. Paul was asleep. Back in the kitchen he waited for the kettle of water to boil then made a pot of tea.

A foreign film was beginning. Sandra had switched on the television for it. He passed her a cup of tea and sat down with his own.

ooo

234

Farquar wasnt an angry driver but and that's the difference. Angry drivers are fucking hopeless man I'm no kidding ye — I mind I was on with a cunt and he smashed into a car on purpose, went smack right into the middle of it and the poor bastard inside came flying straight out the door and got flung yards away; the car turned a fucking circle, two circles. There were genuine reasons why the cunt should've been so angry but none for crashing — excuses I mean; no fucking excuses. And he was hell of a lucky the poor auld fucking injured party never died — although, right enough, he wouldnt've been done for dangerous driving let alone manslaughter or whatever the fuck. But he knew I knew he done it on purpose. And he never even fucking bothered man, just acted as if nothing had happened bar a bad accident of a crash. And being a smart conductor as usual I was right out there capturing witnesses before the smoke had fucking settled. An accessory after the fact Willie, an accessory after the fact. Just as well I dont believe in guilty bastarn consciences. That poor bastard too, lying in the middle of the road, all twisted to fuck, legs and elbows everywhere. He was in the wrong. Because of where he had been when aforementioned incident occurred, to wit, with his car fucking bonnet poking out the side street, trying to bully people into letting him out onto the main drag. A right fucking imbecile! But still, no reason for crashing into him. No kidding ye man it never pays to get angry on a bus. Once that starts you're bang in trouble; you've got to take it calmly, calmly calmly calmly.

Is that right?

Aye it's fucking right, ask anybody.

I'm no asking anybody I'm asking you ya orange bastard ye.

No point asking me, I'm no involved, I just give out the descriptions; that's the conductor's job, get the witnesses and say what is the what.

Keech.

Is it fuck keech. And I'll tell you an even better one. My first week in the job and I'm on with a cunt who shall remain anonymous for the simple reason he's still in the garage. We gets to fucking Argyll Street — 3 o'clock on a Saturday afternoon and the place is mobbed man really mobbed; we stops at Jamaica Street traffic lights. I'd been late to get on the bus and it was so fucking busy I'd no even had a chance to see who was driving never mind the state he was in so anyway, the bus, stopped, for fucking ages, and all the punters're

235

beginning to fidget and look about, but I'm so fucking new at the game I dont know anything's up — I'm rushing round getting the fares in quick, having a wee kind of inner competition to see if I can clear the top deck before the lights change or something. I didnt even notice they'd been at green and back to red and back to fucking green again, till I starts hearing all the beep beeps, and then I looks out the window, and all the traffic, rows and rows, all jamming up, all beeping their horns and fucking

I know who it was.

What?

Who you're talking about, I know who it is.

Naw you dont.

Reilly snorted.

You dont.

Aye I fucking do.

I must've told you then.

How?

Cause you wouldnt fucking know unless, that's how.

Reilly shrugged and then he smiled. Okay, what happened?

Hh.

Naw, tell me.

What d'you mean tell me! if you already know what's the fucking point.

Reilly shrugged.

Hines swivelled on the seat and raised his boots onto the back of the seat in front; he closed his eyelids.

I'll tell you one, said Reilly.

Drivers or conductors?

The latter.

The latter! hh. Am I involved?

Naw.

I dont want to fucking hear it then. Does it concern irate punters at Bridgeton Cross? a certain Old Firm game on New Year's Day? because if so, if so . . .

If so what?

If so fuck all ya fenian bastard ye; I dont want to hear it.

Aye well you're going to fucking hear it cause this bus isnt moving for another ten minutes.

Ten minutes! Ten minutes! what d'you mean ten minutes ya cunt ye it was ten minutes a half a fucking hour ago!

Rubbish.

It's no rubbish.

Aye it is: rubbish, rubbish rubbish rubbish.

Aw give us peace for christ sake Reilly.

I'm giving you fuck all peace.

Come on, get the bus moving.

Too early.

It's no too early at all man I mean the . . . Hines sniffed, and after a moment he sat up, brought out his tin and prised off the lid. When he was tapping the tobacco down the length of the cigarette paper Reilly took out a packet of tipped cigarettes and extracted one. He waited for Hines to finish rolling his before striking a light. Then Hines said, How was the game on Saturday?

Murder; no opposition — we could've put out the fucking reserves . . . He yawned and got up from the seat; he sat down again.

Hines shifted his position, he wiped the condensation from the back window and looked out.